I0764355

The Progeny of Angels

HAFNIUM, GOD OF FIRE

Book 1

Barbara Dean

Published in the United Kingdom in 2013
by Newpole Books

ISBN Hardback 978-0-9572470-6-2
ISBN Paperback 978-0-9572470-3-1

Produced by
The Choir Press, Gloucester

Contents

The beginning . . .

As the Earth falters under the assault of mankind's ever-increasing intellect, an evolved form of life from another universe plans a return to Earth. Their mission is to safeguard the Earth and the surrounding galaxy from the destructive forces of mankind as they reach a new level of advancement that will propel them forward and beyond the Earth to other-worlds.

The Holocene race inhabits a solitary planet within Universe Nine, the central universe to all universes, which otherwise is a place of nothingness, a void. They are a race of travellers passing through the eight universes that surround their own, observing and, at times, intervening in the affairs of the worlds within. They exist as pure mutable crystal energy and have a catlike appearance, with long tails, faces without chins, and long, flowing hair like crystalline shards of ice. Seen and unseen, they cast their silhouettes at will.

Chapter 1

The Twelve Holocene Elders

The twelve elders were gathered in the council chamber, an open-roofed forum of pristine whiteness standing out against the shadow of a darkened sky. The elders gazed downward into a circular breach in the forum floor, the Sphere of Knowing – a void of zero energy that passed through the black holes of space and allowed access to all universes beyond Universe Nine. They sat passively observing the planet Earth, in Universe Four, as a scene of devastation opened up before them.

Local farm workers and their families were trying to rescue cattle and sheep from their waterlogged farmland on the east coast of Britain. The mournful baying of the stricken animals was drowned out by the sound of the approaching water, which roared like thunder towards them. Within minutes it was over; the farm buildings had disappeared, along with the animals and their keepers, as the ocean swept in to reclaim the land. The consequence of global warming on planet Earth was taking its toll.

Lia, high consul to the Holocene people, gazed into the sphere. 'What is happening to the planet Earth is grave indeed,' she remarked dispassionately, the condition of physical emotion now in the distant past for her race.

The elders nodded their agreement. Lia raised her hand towards the sphere and the scene of devastation disappeared.

Lia continued, 'It is time to return to Earth before mankind upsets the balance of creation beyond their part in the forthcoming challenge. Mankind is in need of guidance. We must slow their progress down in order to prepare those who will survive the coming holocaust on planet Earth.'

Counsellor Glashadou stood up to address the forum.

Lia glanced briefly at his silhouette of pure energy and, acknowledging him, invited him to speak.

Glashadou began, 'Those on Earth who are to be saved from the coming devastation are on the move. The migration of the 'lightworkers' has begun. When those who are to survive have been separated from the body of mankind, and the migration is complete, they will be known as 'the one tribe of man', the Otom.'

Lia nodded, her silhouette fluctuating impassively. '... Those who have overcome the Neanderthal darkness of their ancestors and evolved with responsible consciousness,' she added, her memories of physical life beginning to awaken.

Glashadou listened to her words and thoughts; his memory of a physical life was also vague, but he knew instinctively it was not a life to which he wished to return. Glashadou continued, 'Yes, Lia. We of the Holocene race initiated mankind's journey to enlightenment. It was our decision to merge with them and awaken them to a spiritual evolution. We engaged ourselves in the Earthly experiment and cannot further the journey of our race until we have turned mankind away from annihilation. We must finish that which we initiated.'

'Yes,' she replied, 'the Earth challenge has failed in so many ways, and we are in part responsible for that failure.' Lia's image flickered, signalling her change of energy.

Glashadou moved nearer to her, as if to put meaning to his words. 'You, like all of us, see no purpose for mankind while they persist in their barbaric warring. However, our race merged with mankind in order that their intellect and spiritual nature would evolve. Our race is linked with mankind, and we must encourage them to become as we are ... to evolve. It will happen. Mankind will survive the horror that awaits them and evolve beyond the material desires that the Holocene intellect has allowed them to accomplish.'

Lia smiled in agreement and their images merged in a bond of friendship.

Councillor Raphiel was next to speak. 'The decision has been made by Hafnium, creator of Universe Four, that for mankind's next challenge we will again join forces with them. That time has come.'

The council remained silent for a moment. All were concerned about the forthcoming challenges.

Lia closed her eyes, her energy flickering like a breeze upon the landscape, as memories of life as a female Earthling came flooding back: the struggle, the pain, and joy of the human experience. 'We have reached the Ninth Universe and are ready to move on. It is a journey our race looks forward to, one that will take us to the source from which all creation began. That journey cannot take place until those of our people who are to return to a physical life upon Earth have completed the task set before them. We must return in order to safeguard the Earth and the newly emerging 'one tribe of man'.'

'That is so, Lia.' Raphiel's silhouette strengthened with her words of encouragement. 'This will be our last challenge before we ascend to the source of creation beyond the Ninth Universe. We must again live among mankind and become part of his destiny, with the knowledge that all physical life, which has been created from stardust, will again become star energy – as we have. The sun already grows bright before it dims on mankind in Universe Four. It will only be a moment for us, but for mankind it will be a long journey.' Raphiel stood down.

Lia visualised the solar star in Universe Four, with her nine orbiting planets that were watched over by the master of challenges, Chiron. It was a planet that was little known to the Earth people, yet one that observed every decision made by mankind on a moment-to-moment basis. With her thoughts still on the planet Earth and the challenge created there, Lia thanked Raphiel for his words.

Ormus now stood before the council and Lia felt the energy of her consort grow strong within the forum as he greeted the council of elders.

'Greetings,' Ormus said wryly, 'from one who will again become a man of the planet Earth. It is indeed a challenge and one that I look forward to. We have a duty to guide mankind through his next challenge. Those of our race who already live among the Earth people are awaiting our arrival. Let us hope that our journey is successful.' Ormus stood down.

Glashadou spoke again, this time of the difficulties that the chosen ones were experiencing upon Earth. They had found their way alone at the beginning, but the gatherings had started, and they were being drawn together as one force. Glashadou smiled warmly, '. . . a force born of the Holocene star.' He spoke his final words with the love he held for his race glowing with his energy.

Lia and Ormus now stood together in the place of high consul, they being the 'choice absolute'. The council of elders remained silent as the one voice of Lia and Ormus began to resonate throughout the Holocene world, all matters discussed by the council of elders becoming the immediate knowledge of the telekinetic Holocene people.

'The forum is the place of decision for the Holocene people. We have agreed with what is asked of us by Hafnium, the God of Fire, and creator of Universe Four. We are to guide mankind's progress in the coming one hundred years change upon Earth. The decision has been made to move those of mankind who are now the lightworkers to safety. Before the devastation of the atomic holocaust, they will migrate to the world below the Earth's oceans, where the Mer people and their King, Zrsiofour, will enfold and guide them.' Lia and Ormus paused for a moment as the atmosphere about them began to change.

Daylight had followed night rapidly, as four solar orbs chased five moons around the gargantuan planet of Holocene. The forum was now a blazing sphere of icy whiteness, a phenomenon that Holocenes showed great reverence to at the break of day. The atmosphere began to cool, as the light of the solar orbs bathed the planet in light. The elders closed their thoughts to the Earth's inhabitants as they bathed in the icy atmosphere that was to be enjoyed after the mere chill of the night. When the solar orbs had risen to a high point, the elders returned to the matter at hand.

Lia and Ormus continued, 'Following the migration, mankind will return to the Earth's surface after forty-five years has passed and remain there until the ultimate war on Earth has been fought, after which they will prepare to leave Earth for Mars. During those remaining fifty-five years, while they prepare to migrate to Mars, a transformation will occur amongst the one tribe of man, the Otom; a transformation that will allow them access to the new world, Mars, and beyond Universe Four to Universe Six. Those of our people chosen to guide these migrations have been and are being born among mankind. Those of the council to join them will be Raphiel, Glashadou, Lia, and I, Ormus, along with many more of the Holocene people.' Ormus and Lia then stepped down.

The council of elders placed their hands across their chests, their thumbs linked and fingers spread, giving the sign of the Holocene race. 'The council and the people are agreed,' they answered.

Within the sphere a silhouette of a dove appeared – the sign of Holocene peace.

Ormus and Lia's energy flowed towards each member of the council, embracing them to become one, as they continued to speak to their people. 'It is good that the spirit nation of Saturn will be joining forces with our race for the journey to Earth. We will have a stronger chance of survival in physical form with a Saturnian parent joined with an Earthly mother. It is considered unwise for our race to be nurtured by human parents during our period of infancy: Earth is a dangerous place and we could become immersed in the horrors of humanity and struggle for survival before we are able to help.'

'Indeed,' replied the elders, who remained, 'those who journey to Earth will be safe under the guidance of a Saturnian parent. All is ready. Our love will be with you to protect you through whatever you may encounter.'

'That is so,' Ormus answered softly. 'I am ready for the journey to planet Earth. It is such a beautiful planet with its sunsets of golden pink flame. If only one did not know of the darkness within.'

The Sphere of Knowing began to pulse as the void of antimatter surged upward. Ormus took his place above the sphere, his crystalline silhouette fading gradually, as he was drawn downward into the void to journey back to a physical life in Universe Four.

Ormus turned to Lia. 'I will take my leave of you now,' he said, 'for I have an old Saturnian friend to find, in order that I may weave your childhood into the Earth's past before you join me.' Ormus descended further into the core and then disappeared into the vortex of energy that would again bring flesh to his being, as he travelled trillions of light years back into the past.

The challenge ordained for mankind was open upon the universal chequerboard, and those from the 'other-worlds' would watch the game begin. The remaining elders sat observing the void, their energy flowing back and forth in perfect symmetry. They watched as Ormus grew into adulthood and then on some fifteen hundred years, while experiencing all he needed to know.

Lia waited a moment before entering the sphere – a brief time in her world, which would pass as hundreds of Earth years.

Chapter 2

Lia and Ette Dubar

Lia felt her world fall away as she entered the Sphere of Knowing. Before her the 'casket of dreams' held her genetic code, which lay inert, waiting for the spirit of life to spark another cycle of existence. A human female upon the wintry Earth felt the moment of conception; her womb now incubating the one named Lia and another, an Earth child named Ette, twins as unalike as one could imagine. These fashioned, the spirit moved on to create a multitudinous reality for them to experience during their lifespan under the supervision of a Saturnian father, who was to be widowed at the birth of his twin daughters.

Lia lay upon the soft warm bed, her thoughts idling on the passage she had just read. The author had written, 'Our time in the world of dreams is vital to our health and well-being and the decisions we make in our lifetime. It is in our dreams that we live out our natural and deepest emotions – emotions that are stultified and falsely moulded within the framework of our early years, thus creating the person we are conditioned to be. In our dreams we are the person our spirit-soul urges us to be.'

Lia stretched sleepily, 'What dreams will this night bring to me?'

Lia and her twin sister, Ette, having recently celebrated their twenty-first birthday, were visiting London with their father. The Hotel Renoir, where they were staying, was a hotel they both knew well. The girls had spent many weekends as guests of the proprietor, Ralph Major, a close friend and associate of their father, René Dubar.

Earlier that evening Lia and Ette had walked along the busy south bank as the October sun disappeared below the busy skyline. Ette was leading the way, chatting and laughing and enjoying the freedom from the family business. Lia listened to Ette babbling on as usual; both sisters happy to be out in the open air.

Ette was tall and slim, with waist-length red curls and skin of a paleness that emphasised her large golden eyes. She was dressed to be noticed in a long-sleeved blouse of green silk, covered by a short sleeveless jacket of dark green velvet, below which a swirl of orange and brown petticoats covered a pale cream linen skirt. On her feet she wore dark orange sandals embroidered with sequins and carried a large, scruffy bag to match. Lia had laughed at the fanciful outfit and Ralph's son, Edward, who was always happy to be in Lia's company, had laughed with her. Lia smiled at the memory and pulling her long slender body into a sitting position, she closed her eyes and began to brush her long dark curls; she always felt wonderfully content at Renoir's.

Lia and Ette lived and worked in the family business in Cheadle Manor Village, a picturesque village near the east coast of England. Hotel Dubar was a small hotel well known for its simple, yet superb, French cuisine and good wines, and Lia loved working there, even though it was hard work and left little time for other pursuits. Ette was not so keen and regarded other pursuits of more importance. In fact, Ette had gained her freedom through motherhood, and so the majority of work allocated to Ette had shifted to Lia. Lia didn't mind; she loved the village, and there were always people passing the hotel's open door – the problem was they no longer came to eat. Recently, the business had ceased to be so busy, although it still thrived. The cattle disease and the subsequent quarantine that had existed for months had bankrupted many of the farmers in the region, destroying much of the wealth of the local community, and the continuing lack of visitors to the area had made the situation worse.

Lia's father was being pressured by the bank to repay a small loan commitment, which only added to his frustration. Lia wondered how many people felt the same in the turmoil of the present economic situation. The bank had been so encouraging, offering her father a mortgage to extend his conference room for wedding parties. It had been Lia's idea in truth – her passion, and now she felt awful about it. The bank had assured her father the investment was the way forward. 'Trust us,' they had said, 'we will support you …' A lack of banking knowledge can be fatal when you are borrowing money, Lia now realised, which to her continuing annoyance, she had learned the lesson too late. Her father had allowed her to make the decision and within a year, lending rates had doubled and the property market had crashed. René Dubar was struggling with the repayments, and the bank was about to call 'time'. As her father had told her, 'This episode will be a valuable lesson to you in the future.' She had felt so guilty, and yet so angry, at her tender age of twenty-one – it did not seem fair.

Lia thought of her childhood, when things were simple, when if she was upset or angry she would show her feelings with tears and tantrums. She sometimes wished she and Ette could be those children now. Lia thought of Ette, who wasn't at all interested in running the hotel, whereas she was and most times she had a good head for business, and though she had started with an unfortunate set of circumstances that would have deterred many from trying again, she was determined to make good for her father's sake.

With these resolute thoughts for the future, she pulled the covers around her and lay still until her eyes began to blur and she drifted into sleep, complete calm descending upon her as she disappeared into the world of dreams …

Chapter 3

The World of Dreams

The Holocene elders observed Lia's passing through one dimension of physical life to emerge in a world where dreams thrived within their own reality. It was time for Lia to meet Ormus.

In her dream state, Lia could hear and see the thoughts and dreams of the world as it slept. The consciousness of mankind floated through her head, and it was wonderful – lover's dreams, mother's shopping lists, people's anger released from the mental leash, thoughts of hoped-for holidays, children's birthday wishes – on and on they flowed in an endless stream of coloured energy. And oddly, *she understood every meaning of the magnificent colour and sound language.*

As swiftly as she had been immersed in the song of mankind, the image moved on to another place in the dreamtime. Lia now stood on the summit of a mountain and Ormus stood before her. Lia remembered nothing of the man facing her or even that she was also part of the Holocene race. Ormus was now an elderly man with bright blue twinkling eyes, longer-than-average grey hair and standard height and build. He appeared physically old but had a youthfulness that shadowed his aged body, and his countenance had an air of importance about it. She observed the shift from young to old for a while, until his form settled to become the man of years.

'Who are you,' she asked, 'and where are we?'

'My name is Ormus, and we are standing on the celestial mountain which arcs the planet Earth.'

'What is a celestial arc or mountain, and who is that sitting on the large rock?' Lia asked, in her usual fashion of one question followed immediately by another. She pointed to a quite portly, elderly man with a studious look that was accentuated by the spectacles balanced on the tip of his nose.

'That sombre creature is Raphiel ...' Ormus replied, pausing before he answered the first part of Lia's question. 'And where do you think one would find a celestial arc?'

'Around the Earth's outer atmosphere, obviously,' Lia answered, while at the same time thinking that the one called Raphiel looked very much like an older version of Ralph Major, her father's friend and proprietor of the Hotel Renoir.

'Then, why did you ask the question?' Ormus asked.

Lia was about to reply when Raphiel spoke to her.

'Welcome, welcome to the world of dreams,' he said, introducing himself. 'It's curious, you know,' he said, addressing Lia directly, 'humans spend their life dissecting each other's intelligence,' he paused for a moment to absorb the beauty surrounding him, 'the assumption being that the cleverest become the most powerful, and the dullest suffer for it – and in some ways this is correct. The creator of this universe will forgive anything except the unwillingness to continually absorb knowledge, to learn by your triumphs and mistakes, whatever your station in life.' Raphiel stared out at the galaxy. '... Where was I? Oh yes, in addition, if it is of any interest to you, rabbits, whales, dolphins, and all cats are the most intelligent species upon the planet, because they apply the primary thought process better than any other Earthly creature – except for the 'wise ones', of course, who are alien life forms to the Earth.' Raphiel continued to address anyone in the dreamtime who wished to listen, 'Mankind, who is able to build the most amazing monuments upon the Earth, is still way down the list with regard to intelligence, he being clever but not instinctively bright! The fact is, most humans are considered the bringers of disaster by all other Earth species, and the reasoning behind this is that they do not listen to common sense. However, we are here to help them, not to judge them.' Raphiel paused, which gave Ormus a chance to speak.

'Well, I quite like them,' Ormus said. 'In fact, I think they are wonderful, and the choice of menu you find at their tables, well, I find most agreeable. I had a friend once who would winter with me and who ate nothing but fast food – don't you just love the name! He did, of course, die at the tender age of forty years; he grew so large he went off bang in fact – can you imagine that, the fast-food death?'

'Be quiet, Ormus,' Raphiel thundered. 'The creator of this universe has a hard stick to beat us with, which he will use if he feels it necessary.'

Ormus smiled brightly, having no remorse for his lack of compassion. 'Don't mislead Lia, Raphiel. The only one that beats us is ourselves. Hafnium has no part in it.'

'Well, compassion goes a long way towards a good character,' Raphiel answered, knowing that his retort to Ormus had given the wrong impression.

'And so does good humour, Raphiel.'

'Yes, Ormus, but not at another's expense.'

Ormus's story had reminded Lia of her friends at school, with their thrice-daily consumption of crisps and Coke and her father's response to their bad eating habits. 'Crisps and Coke for breakfast – they will suffer for it later.'

Lia and Ette had gone through their school days known as the 'garlic kids', a misery that their father waved aside with the contempt that the French show for English cuisine and its lack of the prime ingredient for any Frenchman, *le* garlic.

Raphiel, whose expression had changed from sombre to angry, and finally to snappy, retorted, 'Have you finished speaking, Ormus? We are having a serious talk here.'

'To a human, death is serious,' replied Ormus. His blue eyes twinkled, and his face crinkled with merriment. 'Sorry, Raphiel, just rendering some light-heartedness to the situation,' he added, aware that things would get serious enough as time went by. He looked at Lia and winked, while at the same time thinking, *she, dear lady, has a tendency towards the serious side of life. Oh well! That's one of the reasons why she was chosen for the task.*

Lia, elated and amused by the banter going on between the two strangers in her dream, gave a bright smile back. Surprised by her reaction, Ormus thought, *Now, that's a smile! A break in the clouds at last – she appears to have found her sense of humour.* Ormus shifted his attention aloft, knowing Lia's gaze would follow. Looking up, she realised that the sky appeared unlike anything she was used to seeing. Lia continued to gaze upward as a rainbow formed above her, then another, and another, until the sky was filled with colour. She began to shout excitedly, 'I have never seen anything like this before! It's like being inside a multi-coloured ball. I'm standing inside a sphere of rainbows!' she ended incredulously.

'The rainbows are always there,' Ormus replied, 'The difference being that now your sense of sight is released from its limitations, and you can see the beauty of the world's healing dome in its true reality. The sky is never just blue, and the world is not going through just one season; they are all there at all times, because nothing can die. Everything is eternal and, therefore, spring hides behind winter, as do summer and autumn. Do you see, my dear, everything that ever was, always is, and will be forever?'

Lia, being unsure of this, did not answer.

Raphiel spoke again, 'Lia, we have brought you here to show you how things really are and how far all species have ventured from reality, especially the humans. They no longer see what actually *is*. The life spirit is fading from the physical Earth world, and its species no longer live together in harmony, because mankind has stifled the intuitiveness of his spirit, taking other species with him. Once upon a time *all* life forms would have been aware of the rainbows. The generations to come are in danger of fading further into darkness until all Earth species cease to exist. This is the fifth time that the Earth's life forms have been in the position of near extinction, and now the celestial Initiators are coming once again to help. Extinction has been the fate of many species on Earth, although, in reality most have evolved into other species. So it is with humans, but if they continue evolving as they are doing, they will become extinct. The celestial Initiators want to help the human race evolve towards the sixth universe because they are their nearest cousins. Can you believe that?' Raphiel sat pondering on his last words. 'Chalk and cheese, I say . . .'

'But how can I help, and who are the Initiators?' Lia asked, intrigued by Raphiel's comments and bemused to think that she had been chosen. Lia stood beside her companions, the excitement welling up inside her. The thought of a true purpose to her life made her feel important and confirmed her belief that there was a part for everyone to play in life, a purpose that showed, however small or grand, all things being equal, they were all equally important *Where did that come from?* Lia wondered.

Ormus replied, 'That is what we are going to discuss now. The celestial Initiators are the ascended of the fifth-world race that now inhabit the world below the Earth's oceans, the Mers. They were a race of humans that were ready to move on to the sixth universe. They were powerful beyond anything man has achieved since their time, but at the same time, most of their race had become iniquitous. Money and powerful weaponry ruled their world, until fortune turned against them, as is happening on Earth at this time. Their 'time' was erased from this world and sent below the Earth's oceans, from which the pure race of the Mer has risen under the guidance of a wise one, the Holocene, Zrsiofour. Mankind has searched across the world's oceans for evidence of this time in Earth's history, but they have never found it.

'You mean Atlantis?' Lia asked.

'Yes, Atlantis,' Ormus answered. The Initiators are the celestial keepers of all knowledge. They are the spirit/angels of the Mer race that once was man, as are the stars the spirit/angels of present mankind.'

Raphiel continued to answer her first question. 'To help, we must first discuss the problem and then form a plan, which we hope will give us the solution. However, Lia, before this can happen, your way of processing your thoughts must change. Let us find somewhere comfortable to sit down, and then we can tune your mind to the task at hand. I think it's always a good idea to start at the beginning, don't you?'

Ormus had already found the perfect place and was sitting on a ledge looking out towards the Earth far below him; he sat within the silence, breathing in the luminous stillness. Lia and Raphiel went and sat down beside him, the three now facing towards the west as the sun began to sink over the celestial horizon.

Raphiel began to speak as a giant hologram appeared to enclose the space around them. It would be morning before he finished his story, and the sun would be rising in the east.

Set against the radiance of the setting sun was the story of mankind's beginning and later times as he merged with the alien Holocene race. A memory triggered in the back of her mind, a conversation from the past, something . . .? Then it was gone.

Raphiel's words drifted towards her. *'Remember, you are special to us and we are known to you . . . '* his words died away.

Lia continued to watch the story within the hologram, as down the ages mankind continued to evolve, on and on until the time of the twentieth century. Suddenly, everything began to move at a much faster pace; planes filled the sky and cars choked the roads. It was the industrial revolution, a past that, in truth, she had taken very little interest in. The scene changed to show the Earth beginning to choke and falter from mankind's pillaging of her rich resources, which had left colossal damage to her surface. Devastating wars, far more deadly than mankind had ever known, began to manifest everywhere upon the Earth. Sickness came in all disguises, and food intolerances began to poison the human race. Sadly, other species began to disappear. Earthquakes dissolved whole cities, swallowing all surrounding life. The Earth was angry and dislodging her abusers as world scientists were no longer able to find cures to save mankind. Now was the time for the celestial Initiator's intervention. Man had become to himself a god and, in doing so, he had tipped the balance of nature upon Earth. At this point, Raphiel repeated Lia's question.

'And what are you to do, my dear? Well . . . you are to help the world's nations by going among them and putting a spoke in their wheel of material greed. Wherever you go, there will be changes that will manifest, regardless of your will, and by your very presence you will create endings and beginnings. Mankind needs a wake-up call that will be listened to, but, alas, for many it is already too late!'

'The situations I am watching now, I watch most days on TV and think little about it.' Lia felt disgusted with herself; it had all seemed unreal somehow, because it was not in her own backyard. Lia looked at Raphiel, realising what he had said. She continued, 'But I am just one person – what could I do? I have nothing to offer ...' her words trailed away; she was stunned by the future that might be thrust upon her.

'You are as we are, Lia, of the Holocene race, and, when you awaken from this dream, you will know you are special but will not remember why – not until the time of your transformation.' Raphiel stood up and stretched.

'Transformation?' Lia responded.

'Not for yet a while,' Ormus echoed softly, knowing the avenue down which her questioning would take them.

The hologram had disappeared, dawn was breaking, and the first rays of the sun showered the eastern horizon with a golden orange hue. Down below, the birds were singing their wake-up calls; the world was beginning to stir. Lia wondered if she was dreaming; this felt real and so exciting. She realised that she no longer felt any fear of the plan. *Where is this courage and confidence coming from?* Lia felt she could be part of this, without any doubt, as though it was what she had been waiting for.

Raphiel spoke again, 'Lia, I will leave you in Ormus's care for a while in order that he can prepare you for the challenges ahead.'

Lia offered a thank-you, although she was not sure why – was the expression of gratitude just the habit of a lifetime? She began to ponder on the misuse of language and the slow disappearance of its true sense.

Raphiel, on hearing her thoughts, commented, 'The younger generations now use a hyped-up slang that often has little in common with the language of the ancients, and there is a real danger that the true meaning of mankind's languages will be forgotten. The same could be said of the old crafts that are fast disappearing; as the interest in them wanes, they will be forgotten forever. A time is coming when all knowledge, be it written or electronically recorded, will be wiped from the face of the Earth.'

At this point Ormus arose from the ledge. He could see that Raphiel's words had frightened his new apprentice. 'Come, Lia, there is work to do, but first we must have breakfast!' He walked towards her and lifted his cape over her shoulders. Before she had time to say goodbye to Raphiel, she and Ormus were flying over the ledge high above the Earth. Slowly, Raphiel became a speck in the distance until Lia could see him no more. Before her she saw the world, its colours of blues and greens changing in front of her, as she and Ormus sped forward on their journey. Ormus listened to Lia's thoughts: Never had she dreamed the world could look so wonderful! The word *Holocene* entered Lia's mind as a sense of joy flowed through her and all fear was left behind.

The Earthly blues and greens began to take on a misty hue of grey. They were descending into Cornwall on a dull, rainy August day, warm but uninviting for the tourists that normally flocked there in the summer season. Ormus thought idly of when Lia would transform to the awareness of a Holocene. She would see then just how far mankind had separated from their spiritual nature and their compassion for their own and other species upon Earth. Lia's Saturnian father had done his work well. René had protected her from the harshness of the human race by his discipline and commitment to single parenthood. Ormus felt in high spirits. Lia was by his side again.

Chapter 4

The Halls of Learning

Ormus sighed with relief at the downcast weather. At least he was coming home to some peace and quiet, and after breakfast he would take Lia through her first test without being disturbed by crowds of holidaymakers. Ormus descended into the cove at Tintagel.

When they had landed, Ormus shouted above the noise of the wind sweeping in from the ocean, 'We're here at last!' Then, beaming with pleasure, he said, 'Welcome to my home!'

Lia felt the gusts of wind blowing up from the sea; they whipped the sand into her face and made her eyes smart. *What's there to grin about?* Lia thought. *Surely his home is not on this beach.* Lia's thoughts drifted to her cosy bedroom beyond the dreamtime, and she felt a longing to return there.

'Come along, Lia, let's get into shelter,' said Ormus, leading her towards a cavernous hollow within the rock face.

As they reached the entrance to the cave, Lia realised the high tide was sweeping rapidly inward and, looking towards the cliff path, she could see that the water had reached the steps, almost blocking the only way off the beach.

Ormus read her thoughts. 'Don't worry, Lia, you are quite safe with me.'

For some unknown reason, this started a feeling of unease in the pit of her stomach. Lia did not like deep water and believed the oceanic world to be unpredictably dangerous and, so far, this experience looked to be no exception to the rule.

'Come! Come!' shouted Ormus against the din of the waves breaking near the cave entrance. Lia followed cautiously.

'Now, my dear,' he shouted, 'follow my steps and you will be fine.'

Ormus walked into the cave entrance, with Lia following behind him. The sea was moving nearer and nearer as the waves rolled over the beach to slap against the rock face near the cave. Ormus continued moving deeper into the darkened hollow, climbing over the rock pools to avoid the deep water they contained. Lia, by now, was in a fever of panic, stepping quickly to stay close to Ormus, while he told her to observe the pathway between the rock pools.

Ormus stopped suddenly. 'Lia, stay here,' he commanded softly, 'while I climb down into this opening and, if the pathway is clear, we will go this way to my abode.'

Unnoticed by Lia, Ormus chuckled as he descended into the gap and out of sight. Lia was left alone to the full force of her burgeoning fear. Looking forward from her position, she realised that there was an opening to the cave from the other side of the cove and that the sea was entering from that point. At that moment, a huge wave roared into the cave and spread water almost too where she stood. That was as much as Lia could take, and she was unable to resist the urge to flee. Lia screamed out Ormus's name, but there was no answer. She called once more, and then, like a filly in the Grand National, she was off. In her panic she forgot the carefully mapped route that Ormus had shown her on the way in. She ran, falling into the deep whirls of salty water just waiting for her. Scrabbling and sobbing, she made her way to the edge of the cave and, as she ran out through the cave entrance a giant wave came rolling in to meet her. Lia felt the smack of salty water hit her face as it sprayed up around her, dragging her down, leaving her breathless and choking as she stood there not knowing what to do next. Suddenly Ormus was by her side, his cloak coming around her shoulders as she was lifted aloft until they were sitting on the cliff-tops above the cove.

'Sorry, my dear, but I decided to run you through your first lesson in obeying instructions, and all before breakfast!' Ormus mused, trying to hide the world-weariness from his face. Then, turning to face her, he said sternly, 'Remember this incident, Lia, and when I give you a command, you will do well to carry it out to the letter. Otherwise, my dear, I cannot be responsible for the consequences and your safety.'

Lia felt embarrassed for her misdemeanour; being an inwardly sensitive person, she was easily placed in a situation of regret. Lia made a promise to herself that from that day forward she would do as instructed while journeying with Ormus and that she would listen and obey – however frightening the experience.

Ormus smiled as he listened to her thoughts, for he knew how soon those words would be forgotten.

Lia spoke only to break the silence that she alone felt uncomfortable with.

'Where has Raphiel gone; is he not going to join us?'

'Master Raphiel has gone to the University of the Third Eye; it is one of the many halls of learning within Universe Four.'

Oddly, Lia understood. 'I think I have been there,' she replied.

Ormus answered, 'Yes, you have, Lia, many times in your dreams and other existences.'

'I remember now,' Lia answered. 'I was there with a group of people and the masters. Someone asked. "Which university are you with?" and I replied, "I don't know," and I remember feeling very uncomfortable with my answer. Immediately, I became aware of a new master, who came to speak with me. He told me that I was a student at the University of Change. Then I woke up.'

'That is correct, my dear. Your preparation for the challenges has been in the making for quite some time. You have always questioned the reason for your existence and, therefore, you have sought the truth within the meaning of life. The knowledge you search for will be found within the challenges that you will soon face.'

The word *challenges* passed through Lia's thoughts: *What challenges, and how will I transform to become a Holocene?* Lia continued with their conversation, wanting to ask many questions but holding back. 'When I was growing up, I always imagined, from a very young age that is, that the only real thing about any creature, including us humans, was our eyes. My feelings were that the rest of our bodies were made of a rubbery substance and that looking into the eyes of another person, animal, anything ... gave you a feeling of the spirit within.' She paused momentarily, thinking deeply about what she had said, and then she continued, 'I felt that the eyes revealed the spirit in all things of an animal nature.' Suddenly Lia felt separate and alone.

'I understand what you are trying to say, my dear,' said Ormus, 'and we have all felt the loneliness you feel at this moment.'

'Yes, it comes and goes all the time,' Lia replied simply, making little of the extreme isolation that would often engulf her for no reason that she knew of.

Both became silent. They had come to an understanding that would bond them as friends and soul mates who instinctively understood each other.

'Ormus, why do you live here?' asked Lia.

'Because, my dear, many thousands of years ago, when I first came to Earth, I was given the post of 'keeper', to watch over the great leaders as they passed through their Earthly life spans. I was to protect the Holocene intellect existing within mankind and to be the 'keeper' of their souls. And this was my place of mysticism – Cornwall – which was my abode and has remained so.'

'What do you mean, "Holocene intellect existing within man"?' Lia asked.

'Well,' said Ormus, choosing his words carefully, 'mankind does not simply turn up here for a term of years. He has a purpose to fulfil, as you have chosen *your* purpose, my dear.'

Lia wanted to interrupt, to ask him what purpose she had supposedly chosen, but she refrained from doing so.

'At the beginning, man was only matter and was without a soul; now he has a soul born of the Holocene intellect, which has a purpose to fulfil.' Ormus observed Lia, his soul mate, in her true likeness – so unlike the girl that stood before him, unsure, unknowing of her true wisdom. 'The purpose for my return to Earth differs from yours only in that I came fifteen hundred Earth years before you in order to reacquaint myself with the Earth man: to live as one of mankind, while retaining my Holocene powers and the knowledge of the universes. I have the ability to change all physical energy into other forms, including myself, which is called 'shift-shaping', and I am called a 'gifted one'. I have returned here many times to ease the journeys of those in a position of leadership, and I can tell you, Lia, Earth's history has been going from bad to worse as each era passes. Now we and others like us are incarnate on Earth to turn the tide of mankind's looming extinction and it will be a tenuous fight that will span one hundred years.'

Lia was spellbound by his words, her frightening experience within the cave now forgotten. Ormus held his hands aloft and uttered something in a language she did not understand; immediately a bright fire sprang up in front of her. Warming and colourful, the heat from the fire began to dry out her wet clothes. A bowl of steaming chocolate, her favourite drink, appeared beside her and in her lap a plate of hot food that looked and smelled delicious.

'There now, Lia; I know you want to ask many questions, but it is time to eat.'

'Thank you, Ormus,' Lia said appreciatively, picking up the hot chocolate. Lia closed her eyes and sipped. *Heavenly*, she thought, *just heavenly . . .*

Chapter 5

Hotel Renoir: Lia Meets Glas

Lia woke from her dream, her hands still cupped as if holding the steaming hot chocolate.

'What are you saying, Lia?' Ette had been sitting in the connecting bedroom listening to Lia talking in her sleep. Ette smiled down at her sister. She had been up for some time and was now holding out a cup of tea to her. 'You were talking. What were you saying?'

'I don't know, Ette,' Lia replied sleepily, 'What do you think I was saying?'

'Nothing sensible,' proffered Ette, smiling again. Her sister's presence was somehow comforting to her. It was lovely to spend time together; her life now was always busy with her fiancé and new infant.

Lia sat up in bed as a flash of her dream came back to her. What was the word she wanted to remember, so crystal clear in her mind and then gone in a flash?

'We must hurry if we want breakfast; the dining room will be closed in half an hour,' Ette shouted the words behind her as she hurried through to the bathroom. 'Come on, Lia, move yourself, now.'

'I'm coming.' *Oh, what was that word . . .?*'

'Come on, Lia; hurry, please, I want my breakfast . . .'

After the girls had finished their breakfast, Lia left Ette on the balcony and went to sit in the garden. The morning mist had disappeared like magic as the first rays of the sun burned away the rain-clouds. She lay back in the garden chair staring up at the blue sky. Today there appeared more colour; it was as if she were looking through the prisms of a crystal and seeing the colours of the rainbow in the clearness of quartz. Parts of her dream were returning, and Lia questioned whether she was awake. The dream had been so real, and she wondered if she should tell Ette about it. At that point, she heard Ette calling her and, looking towards the dining room balcony, she saw her sister descending the steps. By her side were two gentlemen whom Lia recognised immediately. They were Ormus and Raphiel, the two men in her dream. Ette came towards her, her attention completely absorbed in her companions as she chatted furiously with them, while Edward walked quietly behind.

'Lia,' her sister enthused, 'I was worried about you. You have been missing for some time.' Ette gave her a big smile.

Lia smiled back. Ette loved an audience; it was when she was at her most adorable. 'I have not been gone that long,' she replied.

'Long enough for me to make some new friends,' Ette replied back with emphasis. 'They are old friends of father's would you believe?'

Ormus read Lia's uneasy thoughts and introduced himself and Raphiel.

Lia answered quickly. 'But we have already met, haven't we?' she said raising her eyebrows. Lia moved to where Edward stood and slipped her arm through his for reassurance, her remark having gone unnoticed. 'I want to talk to you later, Edward.'

'You sound very serious, Lia – is everything all right,' he asked, amused at the mystery in her voice.

Lia felt safe again; she had always had precognitive visions, particularly when dreaming, and she knew that this meeting was a sign of things to come, but whether good or bad she had not worked out as yet. Her thoughts were interrupted by Ormus's greeting to a newcomer, whose name was Glas. Glas, ignoring the others, walked towards Lia and, with a knowing wink, held his hand out. Glas appeared to be a bright young man, with vibrant energy and possibly a quick temper to match, his bright blue eyes showing instantly his sense of humour and quick-wittedness. Lia, for some reason, took exception to him and extended her hand rather coolly as they exchanged introductions.

Glas turned to Ormus, asking, 'Well, how far have you got – have you explained anything? Is there any chance of breakfast?'

'One thing at a time, Glas,' Ormus said quietly.

Edward cut in, 'Perhaps I can help with the breakfast,' and turning back towards the steps, he said, 'I will bring you a tray to the garden.'

Glas thanked Edward and sat at the table to wait for his breakfast. Ette ushered Ormus and Raphiel to sit with him, all four chatting loudly, much to the annoyance of Lia who had come into the garden to get some peace and quiet.

Ette was asking them about their stay in London and how far they had travelled. 'And why have you travelled from Cornwall, one of my favourite holiday spots?' she asked boldly, as if the information were rightly hers to know, and giving a generous hint that might lead to an invitation for a short vacation.

'My dear Ette, we have gathered together for a special reason, and we will soon be on a pathway that will separate you and Lia for some time,' Ormus said mysteriously.

For a moment Ette was rendered speechless.

Lia's ears pricked up at Ormus's statement. 'And where are we going, if we are to go our separate ways?' she asked as fragments of her dream cut through her thoughts and then disappeared as quickly.

'Well, first, we must go to Cornwall, where all will be explained to you.'

'That sounds like fun,' said Ette, who, having recovered, was beginning to get flustered with excitement, although she hadn't a clue what they were talking about.

'Don't be silly, Ette, we do not know these people; I am certainly not taking any journey with them, and neither are you,' she answered curtly.

Glas butted in 'The invitation was extended to you alone, Lia.'

Lia glared back at him.

Edward was now crossing the lawn towards them, and walking

with him was Lia and Ette's father, René. Both girls jumped up to greet him as he held out his arms to them. Ormus and Raphiel shook his hand warmly, while introducing Glas, who by now had taken the tray from Edward and was devouring his breakfast hungrily.

Lia, having been surprised by the appearance of her father, was now feeling rather ill-mannered. She was still puzzling over the likeness of Raphiel to Ralph Major and sat back silently in her chair, while Ette chatted to her companions as if she would never stop.

René sat down beside Lia to ask her to take on a task for him. He wanted her to go with Ormus and his companion, Glas, to Cornwall. 'It is important; otherwise I would not ask it of you,' he said in broken English. 'I wish you to look at a small cottage in between Tintagel and Boscastle; it sounds an ideal place for my retirement, and I would like your opinion.'

Lia became concerned. 'But you have a home in France, Father. Why—' Before Lia could finish what she wanted to say, Ette interrupted them.

'What about me?' she countered, disappointed that her father had not included her. 'And what about retirement, Father? Are you going to sell the hotel?'

'Later, Ette; I will explain when we go home tomorrow. Today you must stay here and keep Raphiel company.'

'Very well,' she answered, disappointed at not being invited along.

Edward, who had only heard the last of the conversation, asked, 'And how long will Lia be gone?'

'She will be back with us late this evening,' René replied, helping his daughter from her chair to encourage her to depart with Ormus and Glas.

Ette, already over her disappointment, was making plans to take Raphiel on the town to do some shopping. 'And then we can have lunch in one of the floating restaurants on the river,' she said, waving goodbye to Lia as she walked towards the steps arm in arm with Raphiel.

Edward walked with Lia, 'Try to have a pleasant day. Whatever your father has planned for you, I'm sure it will be worth the journey. Tonight we will all have a late dinner together, and you can tell us about your mystery trip.' Edward smiled reassuringly.

'Edward, what I wanted to tell you was that they were in my dream last night, those two ...' she said, waving her hand in Ormus's and Glas's direction.

Suddenly Ormus was by her side. 'Come along, Lia; we must be on our way,' he said leaving her remaining words unspoken.

The three left Edward to watch them go.

Chapter 6

The Twelve Initiators

As soon as the three companions entered the car, Lia began her heated questioning: Who were they, and why had they been in her dream, and what was their association with her father, René?

'I know I'm a master of patience, but even I find your questions, which are fired like missiles, a trifle irritating!' Ormus answered evenly, his aversion to forceful women who were not able to argue a point delicately being well hidden.

Lia calmed down at his statement, and embarrassment showed in her suddenly rosy complexion.

'Don't be angry,' Ormus said quietly, reading her thoughts. 'There is nothing to worry about. All is well, and you are not in any danger,' he ended cheerily.

Lia's thoughts were spiralling downward like an out-of-control skier on a sheer mountain slope.

'Stop!' commanded Ormus quietly. 'You are leaving your senses behind. Do you think your father would ever put you in danger? Think back to his friends and his deep interest in the worlds beyond this and your own interest in his work – which, as it happens, was the reason you were born. We have been waiting for yours and many others' coming of age in order to set in motion a sequence of challenges that will guarantee mankind a future.' Ormus's words died away, and he closed his eyes. 'Now be quiet and let me rest.'

Lia sat back next to Glas. 'I must remember when I'm next in a panic not to show my anger,' she said guiltily, having been surprised by Ormus's directness. 'I must not shout but be direct, keep my cool, and make it plain what I will and won't accept.' Lia sat up straight with renewed confidence, her dark waist-length curls flowing out around her.

Glas began to laugh at Lia's formal declaration, as was his way, laughing his way through life and never making an enemy. 'Humans are so needy, Lia, they need to know they will continue to exist as they are; otherwise, they feel threatened, just as you do now.' He started to laugh again.

From the back of the car, a hushed voice said, 'Be quiet, Glas, and concentrate on your driving.'

'Sorry, Ormus.' Glas continued to laugh for a time, but Lia took no offence at his genial put-down. Ormus's choice had been spot on; Glas was just the person to help smooth Lia's stormy pathway on the journey ahead.

When Ormus woke from his rest, he began to explain Glas's part in the task before them and much more with regard to René, her father. Lia and Ette's mother had died at their birth and their father had brought them up on his own. During their childhood they had spent a great deal of time at their father's home in France and therefore had enjoyed the customs of both the English and French ways of life. It was while they were in France, at their father's vineyard, Château Dubar, that they enjoyed the company of his somewhat eccentric friends, their common pastime being astronomy. At certain times of the month, they would gather around the giant telescope in the planetarium, which was obscured at the back of the large country house, to watch the cosmos until the break of dawn.

Lia immersed herself in the passing greenness of the countryside as they journeyed towards Cornwall, while hanging on to every word that Ormus spoke. Like the piecing together of a jigsaw puzzle, Ormus put meaning to the many times in her childhood that she had trusted her father's actions without understanding why. Ormus explained that her father was a Saturnian master, a protector of those from the outer worlds that were on Earth to help mankind.

The car slowed as they entered Tintagel, a small village that sat above the craggy cliffs of north Cornwall. It seemed like an adventure to Lia, whereas to Ormus and Glas it was business as usual. Ormus beamed, his blue eyes twinkling within his craggy old face. Lia giggled at this, her laughter infectious enough to make Glas roar with laughter as well.

'Let's take up the challenge. Let's go out there and do it!' Lia said feeling excited. The thought of becoming empowered sounded like fun, and she was impatient to get started.

Ormus smiled wryly at her naivety. At last Lia was beginning to feel at ease with her new friends and even the task in hand.

Glas spoke to Ormus. 'We must be away, as they will be waiting for us.'

Ormus nodded.

Lia asked, 'But where are we going now? We have only just arrived in Tintagel, and Ormus, I haven't seen your home yet.'

'Later, my dear, later; plenty of time for that. We must travel a while longer to meet the twelve Initiators, and maybe – if we are 'unlucky' – the thirteenth. They will not wait for us if we are late, and Glas is wise to hurry us, as usual – always the wise adviser you see and the reason why he was chosen. You will always be in the right place at the right time while Glas is your companion.'

An arm came around Lia's shoulders and, once again, she was flying high over the landscape. Below her, the sea sparkled in the light of the sun's rays and the cliff-tops looked amazing in their display of greenery. Little specks of life moved below her, both folk and animal, all moving back and forth, going about the business of enjoying themselves.

How insignificant we are as individuals, Lia thought, *but when we band together, how strong, powerful and resourceful we become.*

Ormus shouted above the force of the wind, 'We are strong because we are *one*; it is only when we forget this to be the truth that we become weak and falter. Unity is also the strength of the followers of Aspheseuos, who stay together because they cannot survive alone. When a human is equipped to experience life, he will often go off alone to gather his wisdom, whereas the 'dark ones' always stay grouped together to persuade those of the light to stray from their intended goals. I have visited some awesome places where sacred energy sites have been taken by the dark powers. Loud inharmonious music can be heard all through the night, and humans high on drugs and alcohol, run amok. They are terrible places, so deep in the powers of darkness that they will cease to exist as we know them, as all expended energy ceases to exist and is transformed into another form. These sacred sites have become shelters for the evil ones, and they have empowered many of the children of man. This twenty-first century evil is spreading rapidly, along with many new diseases.' Ormus was relieved that the conversation had opened up. It was important that she understood exactly what she must face. 'You see, Lia, the sacred energy sites are the great power sites of the ancients, and mankind has grossly misused them by allowing an imbalance of evil to flourish. It is difficult to protect these sites now, because many of them are below sprawling cities and the only obvious sites are the churches, monasteries, and cathedrals that were built on these places of ancient worship.'

Lia listened knowingly, for although she had lived a sheltered life, she had a wide knowledge of the evil of mankind; her father had made certain of that. Her father and his friends had educated many into their knowledge during their lifetimes, each one teaching the importance of universal law upon Earth and how important it was to protect the sacred sites, the landmarks that connect mankind to the cosmos. René Dubar and his acquaintances of astronomy knew the hundreds of sacred sites by recall and had taught Lia the same. Mankind lived a parallel existence to all existing species within the universe, and it was the sacred sites that linked them together. Ormus was confirming her father's teachings.

Not needing to ask further questions, she changed the subject. *Ormus, who are the twelve Initiators?* Without realising, Lia was beginning to use her telepathic skills; she had put the question to Ormus from her thoughts. He, in turn, began to relay the answer without the use of his voice, which, to his relief, was far easier than having to compete with the north wind that was whipping the sea below them. *We know them as the ancient souls of the Mer race and commanders of Hafnium, the grand master and creator of Universe Four.*

Again, Lia did not pose any questions, and Ormus knew there would be none. Lia's father had trained her well in the knowledge of the universe's creator, Hafnium. Ormus pointed down towards the approaching cliff top and they began their descent. Lia could see before her a theatre hewn in the side of the cliff face, and she began to feel uneasiness in the pit of her stomach. Ormus felt her apprehension.

'Everything is going to be just fine, Lia, just fine.'

Below them Lia observed the tiered rows of seats that were carved deep into the cliff face, semicircular rows that looked down upon a theatre stage. The stage was a large, naturally weathered platform hewn from the jagged cliff face with the ocean beyond as its backdrop. The theatre stage stood empty as Lia, Ormus, and Glas alighted. They stood motionless, waiting. Lia's stomach churned with apprehension. The sky turned dark, as a hologram appeared within the curvature of the cliff face. Within a three-dimensional beam of light, a white temple became visible. Between the high front circular pillars, Lia could see a vast marble floor stretching endlessly backward, its continuity fluid. It disappeared through an arc of light deep within the cliff face. Upon the vast marble space stood a long white table, at which twelve beings robed in white were sitting. Lia felt the breath sucked from her body. These were the twelve Initiators, whom she had seen many times when staying in the house of her father's ancestors – she had seen them in her dreams and recognised instinctively their likeness to the twelve astronomers that came together with her father at Château Dubar.

Chapter 7

Hafnium, God of Fire

The three companions sat beneath the hologram, the scene above them one of unworldly beauty such as Lia had never witnessed. Around the marble pillars hung vines heavy with ripe fruit, the purple hue merging with the abundant green foliage. A light, magnificent in its intensity, bore down upon the celestial scene as shadowy, undulating billows of silver, gold, and blue rolled across the heaven.

Ormus and Glas did not look up; this was the opposing mirror of Earth, as life is to death, and mankind had long since deviated from any likeness to heaven. Lia gazed naively upon the apparition and wondered where this world of perfection was.

The collective voice of the Initiators echoed above them, 'Welcome, we can begin.' They turned towards the light manifesting from deep within the cliff face. 'The vibration of light you see before you is the key to accessing the past, present, and future of this and other galaxies – a curtain lifted upon the moment, which is really all there is.' As the Initiators spoke, the light began to change and images of the Earth's current devastation were expressed in various rays of yellow, each ray representing a location upon the Earth. Forty-five years on, the shadowy figures of millions of men, women, and children were still passing through the valley of death. Their spirits could be seen floating between Earth and the psychic plane, where they would remain until they were ready to let go their attachment to the physical world and journey on to one of the higher levels created by Hafnium, architect of Universe Four.

The Initiators continued; their voice was measured and strong like the sound that emanates from the ocean: 'The journey of these souls will take many light years, for they are the ones that hang onto the physical world, even though they are physically dead. The psychic plain surrounding Earth is where mankind endangers his soul, his mental and etheric energy remaining suspended in the illusion that he is still a physical being.' Again, the Initiators directed their vibration towards the light and the hologram became immersed in an emerald hue. Shadowy, elemental colours were encircling the sphere of heaven, signifying the vibrations of love in all Earthly aspects; some were so intense they were restrictive and demanding and some so weak they were harsh and unforgiving. Lia felt the good vibrations flow through her body, such as the love of a good mother or a great leader, both helping mankind to progress in the right direction. The changing hues of green began to fade, to be replaced by a rainbow, and then, as before on the mountain, rainbow followed rainbow to envelop the sky.

Such a wonderful sight, thought Lia.

Indeed, reflected Ormus.

They watched spellbound as each rainbow became a three-dimensional picture revealing mankind's spiritual development through his various stages of evolution, up to the present time. The Initiators explained why they were to intervene: 'Mankind, though his actions appear civilised and intelligent, has, in fact, reverted to the barbaric and demonic behaviour of his past; he is out of control . . . '

As Lia listened, she became aware of another voice above the collective of the Initiators.

'. . . and his spirit, my being, is suffering.'

Something told her that the 'voice' was the source from which all life within the universe was created. She listened in wonderment as the voice continued to speak alone, explaining that *all* life in Universe Four must balance, that *all* mental thought surrounding the physical world, Earth, must eventually manifest as matter, be it positive or negative, and that a concerted effort must now be made to turn mankind's destructive thought around to positive vision.

'I, Hafnium, creator of all life within Universe Four, say unto you that *all* must come to know that where there is a build-up of destructive forces upon the Earth, where there is misuse of energy transferred into any material resource, then redress must be administered to correct the balance!'

'That means we are all responsible, connected in spirit. We are all part of the "one", and the one must balance,' said Ormus quietly to Lia, realising that her concentration was distracted by the meaning of *all*, as a word in a book that is not understood and confuses further meaning.

'Absolutely,' Glas uttered disdainfully, as one does when being held responsible for another's ills.

Ormus shot Glas a warning look, as a soft echo of Glas's one word rebounded across the theatre. Ormus suddenly felt concerned.

They continued to listen to the master.

'When energy within our galaxy becomes unbalanced, and the giving and taking nature of *all* is not harmonious, then the powers of light are awakened to balance these negative forces. *I* created man in my genius, but he has caused division within my universe.' Hafnium became silent for a moment.

Lia's short lifetime swept before her, emphasising any wrongdoing that had taken place within her darker moments, and she began to feel remorse until she was made aware of the giving nature that balanced her character.

Remember that all facets of our emotions are a representation of love, both good and bad, Lia. Ormus conveyed his thoughts to her and then continued to listen to the voice of Hafnium.

'Finally, what is to be done? It is this: The unnatural subjugation of so many by so few must end. The whole concept of giving the soul a physical vehicle, the body, is for the soul to learn the lesson of independence, not dependency. There will always be those who use the dark powers to control others, those whose desire body urges them to confine other souls and take more than is wise. The resulting misappropriation of energy upsets the law of balance, leaving a shortfall for others, those who are also experiencing the journey of physical matter. Hence, we have an imbalance between those of mankind stricken by the desire for material glut and those who are denied their rightful quota and are stricken by poverty and disease. There has been no tangible soul growth in centuries for mankind. His spirit is misplaced, and his faith in the divine has vanished into the depths of his despair. Mankind is so far behind other life forms in my universe that he is in danger of being consumed by the darkness of oblivion. If change does not come, mankind will be forgotten.'

Lia listened with the uncomfortable feeling that it was she who was being addressed.

The voice continued tenderly, 'Have no fear; there is hope, for darkness can never completely overcome light – for light can always reach into darkness, which peculiarly, is how this situation came to exist.' Hafnium heaved a sigh; his responsibility for all within his universe was becoming heavy. 'Curiosity killed the cat! It is an anecdote of mankind, is it not? Never a truer word was spoken, for when mankind first went seeking experience, many became the followers of Aspheseuos, the thirteenth Initiator, and now they are addicted to the sweet nectar of his evilness and have passed into darkness. When those souls decide to find the light again, then the darkness will lose its power over them, and light will reign but for a short time once more – the perpetual shift between light and darkness being the vital balance of my creation.' Hafnium's mood changed suddenly and he began to chuckle, a gentle thunder that made its presence heard upon the etheric. 'Besides,' 'he' continued, 'what would I do if I did not have my brother's knight to challenge my knight?' Hafnium felt good about the pleasure his creation had given him. 'Aspheseuos's darkness feeds my creation, as does the love of the souls of light, and both make up my being in whole. Aspheseuos helps me shake off my boredom and remain balanced. He is my brother, whom I love for what he is . . . and what he does.'

Is Aspheseuos the devil? Lia wondered.

You are to make up your own mind about that, mused Ormus.

The sky turned black, and a giant crack of thunder split the silence.

Oh hell, now the fun is starting!

Apprehension engulfed Lia as she picked up Glas's thoughts. From the lower end of the table to the high end there glowed a brilliant spectrum of light, which Lia knew was the energy of Hafnium. The twelve Initiators were now enveloped in the Creator's purity, which shielded them from the darker energy of Aspheseuos. Hafnium's mantel of divinity was keeping their soul energy hidden, in case Aspheseuos decided upon some trickery. Among the twelve Initiators there now sat a thirteenth, the dark angel, Aspheseuos.

Chapter 8

Aspheseuos

'Greetings brother, how welcoming you are!' Aspheseuos gave a defiant laugh. 'Why do your Initiators hide from me – surely their faith is unquestionable?' Again, he laughed defiantly.

'Greetings,' answered Hafnium. 'Do not be dismayed by this display of apparent rudeness. I was just being thoughtful. I would not wish to flaw you with the power of their light, for we have games to play and all opponents must start on equal terms – that is only fair.'

'Oh, 'nice one'. That will put him in a good humour!' Glas, forgetting where he was, had spoken the words aloud. A pair of burning red eyes turned towards him.

'Bad move, Glas.' As Ormus spoke, both their statements began to spin in the air above them, the words echoing repeatedly.

Lia screamed inwardly at the sight of the cloaked beast. The creature's red eyes continued to bore down upon them.

Lia whispered, 'I thought you said he was an asset to have around, Ormus?'

'Glas is, most of the time, my dear,' Ormus replied.

Now the words the three had spoken were swirling and rebounding above them; the sound became deafening.

Suddenly the voice of Hafnium cut in: 'Enough!' The echoing ceased.

'Aspheseuos,' said Hafnium, 'this is as good a time as any for you to meet my champions in the challenge for mankind's continued existence. These good souls are to go among the lightworkers who have forgotten me and give them a wake-up call. I am really looking forward to the challenge, my brother. You have had a lengthy run of luck lately, the stakes are high, and it is always a pleasure to challenge you.'

Lia wondered who the lightworkers were as she studied Aspheseuos's slothful appearance. His bull-like head was surrounded by short coarse hair that curled around his forehead and ears, and just above the centre of his forehead protruded one bulbous black mole to make perfection of his ugliness. Lia realised that her apprehension had gone. How could she fear such a creature?

The chaos and disorder present on Earth had been created in his image, which was Hafnium's plan. Aspheseuos created fear, and those of mankind who were inherently good turned away from logic when faced with fear. *What a perfect balance to the creativity of Hafnium.*

Lia wanted to know why Hafnium had continued to allow the existence of this ominous creature, if removing him was all that was needed to right things upon the Earth. And who were the light-workers that had forgotten Hafnium?

Hafnium answered, 'There would be no soul growth for mankind without him. He alone is not the cause of the wickedness upon Earth. Aspheseuos provides an opposing pathway for the light-workers, enlightened man, to pursue – and pursue him they do, while they forget me. I, as opposed to Aspheseuos, do not speak of eternal hell, which exists only in the minds of men, but of a timeless oblivion where the soul regenerates and emerges transformed. That is why I can never be overcome by Aspheseuos's stagnant energy, because I am the power that creates new form by erasing stagnant souls at will.'

The light of Hafnium moved towards and around his brother, Aspheseuos. Within the light, Lia saw the ugliness dissolve to reveal a most beautiful angel.

'You see now why I love my brother, as I love you and all life, because he is my creation.'

Lia listened while pondering on her judgemental thoughts of Aspheseuos moments ago.

'Do not feel remorse,' said Hafnium. 'The reasons for your judgement were humanly acceptable, and your perception of right and wrong will keep you safe upon the pathway ahead, especially in times of danger. After all, I don't want a challenger knocked out in the first round, do I?'

Aspheseuos laughed, only this time it was like a myriad of crystal prisms, as he bathed in the light of his brother's love; slowly his laughter melted away.

Hafnium instructed them, 'Come forward and sit at the table.'

The three companions moved forward to sit where Aspheseuos had been.

'Today, Lia, you have been invited to join the many that are working upon Earth to bring light back into the dark places. The darkness is not the work of my brother; he only reflects evil for mankind to desire, as I reflect the opposing eternal spirit to live. I have created the mirror of opposition. Evil manifests from the desire body that I gave mankind when first encoding him, and the desire body's purpose is to turn man's reasoning upside down, to make him think and create. It was when first I decided to separate my completeness and become a kaleidoscope of many fragments, to allow those fragments to manifest into matter and exist in many forms that would evolve naturally within the universe . . .,' Hafnium paused hesitantly, '. . . in order to discover what I am capable of on my journey back to completeness.' Hafnium sighed; sometimes he felt so alone, so isolated, and his next statement was to console this feeling, a feeling he had passed on to all races, all species of his manifestation. 'We are not alone,' he said to comfort himself. 'There are parallel creations, universes, where my kind, my 'family' are doing the same as I. I was born to create, and all decisions as to how my universe evolves are mine, and so I fashioned my sister to create opposition.'

Do you mean that creature is a female?

Ormus answered: *Both natures, Lia.*

Hafnium ignored the thought and continued, 'As my fragmented consciousness burst out into the darkness, I decided to create what mankind now mimics on Earth, the so-named Public

Limited Company, wherein decisions would be made by more than one. I created a multitudinous ever-contemplating energy to oppose Aspheseuos and his followers. Now, however, I have reason to challenge mankind's freedom to choose independently. Mankind needs collective guidance. He has become dangerous to his own survival.' *I have become dangerous to my survival.*

The light of the Initiators dimmed a little and then grew strong again. Ormus saw this as a point of concern. Were they concerned for Hafnium? A flash of another universe pierced his memory, Universe Nine, where the ninth creator was beyond such games of folly. Then the memory was gone.

'Change has to come for the Earth lady, Gaia, and the time she has left will allow for the synchronicity of all that I have brought into being.' As if to ease the concerns about him, he concluded, 'I am content with the challenges that will manifest from my decisions.' No more would he allow them to know of his inner thoughts.

The three listened intently to Hafnium as he continued.

'Today you will feast with me, the feast of commitment,' he paused as within his light the form of an angel appeared. 'This is my son, the only one I have imagined into being. From his prototype came man, woman, beast, bird, and insect – all creation. You are all *one*, and therefore there *is* only one. *All* and *I* collectively are the entire *one*. Absorb this knowledge to sustain you. Absorb this power to know yourself. For when you acknowledge this, you bond yourself to the whole.'

The three knelt before the angel who came forward to offer fruit and wine from the celestial vine.

Lia made her commitment to the creator of Universe Four to remember always that she was part of Hafnium, the 'collective spirit', and to help those who had forgotten his existence. The hologram and all that it had contained disappeared, and for Lia, the greyness of the cliff face towering above her made her wonder if it had ever happened.

Lia, Glas, and Ormus stood alone upon the empty theatre stage.

'Why is the vine fruit chosen for ceremony?' asked Lia, never having thought about it before.

Ormus answered, 'Because wine is like the blood that nourishes our body, as the flesh of the fruit nourishes our body; we are one with the vine.'

Lia thought of her father's friends and associates. 'Ormus, who is my father,' she asked?

'Your father is a Saturnian lord of karma, of destiny, and he has come to help mankind and protect the Holocene people who are here for the same purpose. That is all I will tell you at this time,' Ormus said resolutely. 'Come, we must return home. As he spoke, he placed his cloak around Lia's shoulders. Lia felt the surge of cold air as she was lifted from the ground. Swiftly they gathered height above the theatre stage, with Glas following them, his body buffeted by the back draught of Ormus's cloak.

'Steady on, Ormus, you're a bit old in the tooth for speed levitation.'

'Pull yourself together and stop twittering,' Ormus shouted irritably, suddenly feeling his years. *You* would *bring us back to Earth with a remark like that,* thought Ormus. *There is no longer any respect or consideration between generations, and it is a dangerous demise.* Ormus could hear Glas' laughter as he followed behind. Lia wondered if the older generations realised what a mess they had made of the world and why so many young people now lacked respect for them. Ormus, listening to her thoughts, knew she was right.

That evening, back at home for dinner, Lia lied about her day in Cornwall and her visit to the cottage she never saw. Ormus had described the picturesque cottage high up on the Cornish cliffs, telling her what she was to say to Ette and Edward. Lia had felt uncomfortable with the situation, as Ette bombarded her with questions and Edward remained suspiciously quiet, which made her feel guiltier. But René and Ormus had insisted she must not tell the truth.

Chapter 9

Ormus's Home

The following morning Ette was to return with her father to Cheadle Manor, where he entertained his business associates and she took charge of her infant son. René loved to have Ette around at these times; she was a natural ambassador, if not businesswoman, and his associates greatly admired her ability to host business deals to the satisfaction of both parties. It was a good team effort and one that always attained the best deal for René's French wines.

Lia waited until her father and Ette had left, and then she slipped away from the hotel, telling Edward that she would be spending the day shopping. When Edward asked Lia where he could meet her later, she told him somewhat evasively that she was not sure, which made him feel even more concerned about what was going on. He knew his father's friend, René, was having financial difficulties with his hotel, and he wondered if this had weakened his finances in France. Edward went back to his book-keeping. 'Life goes on,' he muttered, trying to dismiss his anxiety.

Lia waited at the bottom of Oxford Street, where she had arranged to meet Ormus and Glas. When the car pulled up beside her, she jumped in and they pulled away into the heavy traffic. Lia was about to ask lots of questions, when she remembered the day before and where her outburst had led her. Her anxiety dissipated. 'Where are we going today?' she asked, quietly.

Ormus smiled, 'To my home, my dear.'

They abandoned the vehicle in the nearest underground car park a short walk away from Hyde Park. Passing through the gates, they headed for a secluded area of the park where, using Ormus's 'usual mode of transport', they lifted high above the city and headed for the coast. On the journey, Ormus's thoughts conveyed to Lia much of the place that had been his refuge for hundreds of years. Before long, the seagulls' calls below them signalled their approach to Tintagel. Home was a cottage upon the cliff-tops, but beneath the Cornish cliff face was Ormus's most-frequented home, a cave that only a few knew of. At high tide the walkways connecting the caves were flooded, and, once you were in, there was no way out until the next low tide.

Ormus told Lia, 'This is not a problem for me, as I am able to travel without form,' which he termed loosely as *being out*.

Lia's thoughts returned to Raphiel's remark about *being out*. She would ask Ormus when they alighted what it meant. Ormus, on hearing her thoughts, answered.

'Do you remember your dream in which Raphiel told you that when the appropriate time came it would be explained to you, the meaning of *being out*?'

'Yes,' Lia replied.

'Well the time is very near when you will have your answer; in fact in the next day or so,' Ormus said without more explanation.

Having reached their destination, they landed in the village car park overlooking the cliff face. The three companions turned their attention to the seagulls that were squawking their greeting to Ormus and then soaring towards the clear blue horizon.

'Goodbye, my friends,' replied Ormus, mimicking the squawks. 'Goodbye and thank you for your greeting.' He turned his attention to Lia and continued their conversation. 'Well, my dear, this is my home!' he said proudly as he set out towards the fields at the edge of the village, with Lia and Glas following …

Lia gazed at the large cavernous opening before her. The dreary hike down the sloping cliff path to ocean level was now forgotten, as thoughts of her first cave experience came flooding back. Her shoes began to sink into the soft warm sand, willing her not to move.

Ormus sensed her fear and continued lightly, 'It would be

extremely inconvenient for me to be walled up in the caves at high tide. Just think of the places and folk that I have to visit; it would be no good at all. As you know, my dear, I have the power to "pop out" whenever there is the need. All I have to do is think it, and it is done and I am where I need to be.'

Lia remained silent, her stomach churning.

Ormus continued crisply, ignoring her panicked thoughts, 'For you, Lia, there will now begin a period of training, starting with meditative thought. And when you are able to meditate, to free your mind of all thought, you will gain mastery over the most marvellous form of travel, being out.'

'Nothing to it!' remarked Glas, 'It's as easy as making pie.'

'And when have you ever made a pie, Glas?' Ormus said quietly. 'Take no notice of him, Lia,' Ormus said softly. 'It will not be easy to bring your concentration to the required stage of development. Not at all easy, and it will not happen quickly; for many it can never be achieved. I tell you this because when you fail at the beginning, which you will do . . . do not be disappointed, and keep your mind resolute upon your goal.'

Lia, now eased by Ormus's words, moved towards the cave. Glas was now far ahead and did not hear the remaining conversation between them. They could hear his voice in the distance echoing back from the damp cave walls.

'Come along you two!' he shouted back, 'The tide's coming in, and my feet are getting wet.'

The three companions eased their way downward into a succession of dimly lit caves, now and again slipping on the wet seaweed clinging to the sides of the rocky path. After a while, Glas turned to the right of the pathway, and they came out upon a rock-strewn beach.

Lia stood motionless for a while as she took in the colour of the beach, which was mostly amethyst with surface rocks that were a multitude of pale colours. 'Where are we, Ormus?' she asked after commenting on the unusual rainbow colours of the rocks that were strewn across the shoreline.

'They are beautiful, aren't they?' Ormus replied. 'They are crystals from the Mer world, and each colour has a name and individual healing property.'

Lia asked her next question. 'How far down have we come, if there is a beach here when the beaches on the coastline are flooded by the tide?'

'When we entered the first cave below the water line, we crossed the threshold to the void. What you see here is not unnatural. We have entered the world of Mer. If you look beyond the shoreline, you will see the mountains of Mer rising above sea level.'

Turning to follow his gaze, Lia looked up to see a dazzling skyline, below which sheer walls of coloured rock crystal rose up majestically towards the horizon. Lia realised it was not a skyline, but a roof of lime-green crystal, so far above her that she had not realised what she was looking at.

Ormus continued, 'It is the same below the oceans as above, a world of forests, mountains, valleys, and vast desert plains enclosed beneath a skyline of natural crystal light that gives life to everything that exists here.'

Lia was tempted to gather some of the crystals from the beach.

Ormus read her thoughts, and, turning to look in the direction in which Glas was rapidly disappearing, he said to Lia, 'Come now. We must not loiter here. The beach is one of many doorways between your world and Mer which holds the secret of the void. The void, or zero energy, is the space in which travel takes place between all worlds and universes. As I have said, the doorway is the beach itself, which, if any of the crystal fragments are removed, will cease to exist. The one who has taken the crystals will become their likeness and remain as part of the inaccessible beach for infinity.'

While Ormus had been speaking, his attention had been distracted by the length of distance between them and Glas. By the time he looked back at Lia, it was too late; his words had fallen on deaf ears, and Lia was vaporising in front of him. Lia was holding a crystal that she had selected from the beach. From the moment she touched it, a burst of light from the crystal had penetrated Lia's body and was drawing her towards the cliff face.

Ormus shouted a warning, 'Drop the crystal, Lia. Drop the

crystal!' He ran towards her ever-disappearing image as she was drawn towards the crystalline rock face.

At Ormus's command, Lia dropped the crystal, which now lay hidden among the thousands of crystals within a few paces of her. She had felt the substance of her body begin to melt away the moment she had picked up the crystal; her hands had started to go numb, with the rest of her body following rapidly. As she was being drawn towards the cliff face, only the dragging sensation within her head remained. Lia felt terrified; her body was completely numb.

Ormus had been calling Glas. He needed help to avoid the disaster that was upon them. On hearing Ormus's calls of desperation, Glas had turned around and was rapidly retracing his steps along the beach. In a very short time, he was standing next to Ormus, heaving with the exertion of running. Immediately he realised the gravity of the situation.

Ormus shouted in alarm. 'We must find the crystal and replace it – hurry Glas!'

Ormus was now franticly retracing his steps, looking for the crystal that Lia had dropped as she was drawn towards the cliff face.

Glas stood still and thought for a moment. *Don't ask Ormus the colour of crystals; he is too absorbed in finding it.* Glas called to Lia, 'What colour, Lia? What colour crystal did you pick up?'

Lia could barely think now. Her mind was becoming as numb as her body. Many broken thoughts drifted hazily through her mind. *I am being turned into crystal* ... Shards of icy solidness began to replace her ever-increasing state of oblivion. *Soon she would part of the rock face for ever.*

Glas asked again: 'The colour, Lia. Please think. What was the colour?'

Lia slowly retraced her last moments on the beach as her hand had reached down to pick up a most extraordinary crystal of sapphire blue. The moment Glas heard the words *sapphire blue* he began to search for Lia's crystal. Both Ormus and he knew that the crystal would have absorbed her physical matter and, on close inspection, would reveal her life energy within. They must find the crystal; her life depended upon it, although the step beyond that was unknown to them. Ormus was now beside himself with grief. Lia, having been returned to him, was about to be taken away again. Desperately, he searched for the crystal he had seen her holding. Emotion was a thing he had not involved himself in for a long time; at this moment it was in full flight.

Glas tried to ignore Ormus's emotional energy that was escaping onto the beach. It served only to distract them from their purpose at this time. *Pull yourself together, you old fool.* As Glas' thoughts drifted into the atmosphere, Ormus heard them. It was like a bucket of cold ice; immediately Ormus started to think clearly again, but Glas had called for help.

The Mer angels answered Glas. 'The secret lies in looking for the tear in the void caused by the taking of the crystal. Find the tear, and the crystal will come to you.'

Glas and Ormus began to search for the tear by retracing Lia's journey towards the cliff face. And there it was: a tiny tear in the fabric of the Mer world from which Glas and Ormus could see the universe beyond. Ormus knelt before the tear and placed his hand over it. From further down the beach, the sound of crystals moving together became more distinctive as Lia's crystal emerged, then rose into the air and circled above them. Finally, it drifted down into Ormus's outstretched hand. With the crystal safely back in place, Lia's body emerged from the cliff face and began to solidify. As soon as Lia was back to normal, Ormus continued on the pathway they had begun. He had tried to warn her but too late, and if she disobeyed again, she would no longer be considered worthy for the task. Both she and Ormus would remain on the beach forever.

Lia was breathless as she reached Ormus who had walked on without a word. Lia's thoughts were still scrambled from her experience in the rock face and her limbs felt unbearably heavy, but something told her to keep up. She felt Ormus's anger towards her and wished, oh wished, she had listened to him.

Glas walked at a slower pace behind them. He knew that Ormus was furious with him for having left them behind.

Ormus began to climb. His body felt old without the power of his magic, which had temporarily diminished while he searched among the crystals, making his ascent much slower. Lia climbed behind him, her large eyes wide open and anxiety etched upon her face. As they neared the top, he reached down to help her and then perched himself on the rock next to her. From where they sat, the world of Mer looked incredibly beautiful and majestic, and, if it hadn't been for the anxiety she felt at Ormus's coldness, she would have thought she was in heaven.

Ormus was enraged at her thoughtlessness and remained silent.

At that moment Glas appeared.

Suddenly Ormus said sternly, 'I cannot help you any more. It is not within my power to do so. From this moment on, if you do not heed my warnings and commands, you will perish … that is the rule of Hafnium. Absolute discipline is expected of his disciples.' Ormus spoke the last words softly and was silent for a while. Then he said, 'If we had been unable to find the tear in the beach and replace the crystal, you would have remained locked in the cliff face for eternity, and the gateway would have remained closed forever to those who needed it. You did not heed my calls on the beach and so put us both in danger. Come, we must press on.' Ormus remained silent for the rest of the journey, and both Glas and Lia knew better than to utter a sound.

When the three companions reached Ormus's cave, night had fallen. Ormus ushered Lia to a couch and produced some warm food, a hot drink, and a glowing fire for her comfort. After that he bade her goodnight and disappeared further into the cave, to ponder on the events of the day and how next to move forward. He felt most concerned. Lia needed so much guidance – did he have the time to teach her all that she needed to know?

Glas had been left to his own devices. Ormus was angry that he had scuttled on ahead, leaving Lia and himself behind. The misadventure had all been planned as another test for Lia, and she had failed again. As for Glas, Ormus had expected his support and felt let down. Glas could be so irritating … Ormus sighed and settled himself in his favourite place; he lay down and stretched out upon the couch of horsehair. Ormus thought of his favourite tipple, which appeared before him; he poured himself a glass of sherry and drank it down. 'Mm, the best tipple in the world.' Ormus poured himself another, producing some good cheese and bread to go with it. *Yes*, he thought, *the simplest things are the best.* He downed the second sherry and poured another. 'I will sleep well tonight.' Barely had Ormus spoken before he was asleep, the cheese and the third sherry untouched. As he rested peacefully, he heard Hafnium's voice.

'You have done well today, Ormus, my loyal Holocene friend. Lia will listen to you from now on, for she has been truly frightened by her experience and is ready to follow the ways of the ancients. Well done! And good luck with the challenge ahead.'

Ormus's body began to mend, the healing of deep sleep transforming his tiredness and replenishing his mystical powers. Today's events had taken a great deal of his energy; there would be no 'going out' to those needing help in the dreamtime tonight. Ormus needed to rest.

Chapter 10

Lia's Awakening

It was three o'clock in the morning and Edward sat alone in the dining room looking out towards the garden. Unable to sleep, his mind continued to churn over his worried thoughts. When Lia had not returned that evening, Edward had rung René, asking for an explanation to her whereabouts. He knew instinctively that all had been planned and Lia had not gone missing. René had promised him an explanation in the morning when he and Ette returned to London.

Over dinner that evening, René had taken the opportunity to tell Ette of Lia's departure and that she would not be at Renoir's when they returned. In the morning, they would leave early for London, and he would tell Edward of Lia's whereabouts.

René had skilfully manoeuvred through the difficult conversation with his daughter, being accustomed to living with subterfuge. His mortal life had been one of a parallel existence between hotelier and wine merchant and the higher calling of protecting Saturnian and Holocene souls incarnate upon Earth. He would not tell Ette and Edward the whole truth. *How could he?* The truth would seem incredible to them. For now, he would rely heavily on their respect for his judgement, and all explanations would be given on a need-to-know basis. René's thoughts idled on his first-born twin, Lia, and he realised sadly he was saying goodbye. *When next we meet, the Earthly child that I have raised will have changed forever.*

*

Glas and Lia sat waiting for Ormus to emerge from his sleep. They had been awake for hours, both anxious to know how Ormus would be after leaving them without a word the night before. Would he still be in a bad mood? Glas hoped not, for thunder and lightning would be the order of the day if so.

Lia said, 'I wished I had not come with you. Father and Ette would have returned to the Renoir by now, and I would be in the breakfast room with Ette looking to enjoy the day.' Lia's words tumbled out irately.

'Don't be silly, Lia,' Glas said, not wanting to remind her that Ette was not in the breakfast room but still fast asleep in her bed at the Hotel Dubar. Glas knew that if he told her that, he would be obliged to follow the statement with an explanation of time, or the non-existence of it in the binary domain which they had entered last night. Right now, Glas was not in the mood for explanations. Let Ormus have that pleasure!

The binary domain was a timeless zone that existed between the Earth's surface and the world of the Mers. Its existence allowed communication and travel by non-physical beings between the Earth's underworlds. The binary domain was a microcosmic replica of the macrocosmic spaces, black holes, or void encountered within and between Universe Four and other universes.

'You know you would rather be here,' Glas continued cheerfully.

'I would not!' Lia countered, feeling a large bout of obstinacy coming on, 'and don't tell me what I'd rather be!'

Glas wanted to tease Lia further for her childish outburst but was interrupted by the sound of Ormus's footsteps. Ormus strode past them towards a cooking stove that was materialising in the corner of the cave and, without a word other than his magical mutterings; he produced a glowing fire within. Upon the stove's black iron top there appeared a large steaming kettle, followed by the pots and pans needed to produce a full-cooked breakfast. The smell of bacon and eggs began to fill the air. Immediately, the damp, poorly lit cave began to alter in appearance and mood. Gone were the smells of seaweed and damp rock as warmth began to spread throughout the cave, shedding a lighter atmosphere all around. Ormus stood quietly with his eyes closed, focusing on his magic. Next to appear were four chairs and a table covered in a bright red checked cloth, upon which a most scrumptious continental breakfast began to materialise: platters of delicate almond and apricot pastries, dripping with sweet icing sugar, and warm croissants with the aroma of melted butter still wafting from them.

Lia had thrown off her mood and was eyeing up the cheeses and ham that were waiting to fill warm, crusty rolls just begging to be eaten. Glas loved fruit and began to salivate, as upon the table a large basket appeared filled with every early summer fruit that the Earth gave forth. The smell of ripe summer berries mingled temptingly with the aroma of melting butter. Finally, fruit juices and a fresh brew of tea appeared.

Glas and Lia looked at each other, waiting for Ormus to tell them to sit down and tuck in.

'Hmm,' Ormus cleared his throat to address them, 'before we eat, there is something that must be discussed.' It was the first time he had spoken to them that morning.

Lia and Glas let out groans of disappointment.

Ormus responded, 'Anything worth having is worth waiting for, don't you agree?'

There followed a stony silence.

Ormus drew a hand over the breakfast table, and the contents and aroma magically disappeared. He sat down at the table and beckoned them to join him.

'Now,' said Ormus, 'the reason for this handsome spread,' and he pointed to the empty breakfast table, 'is to introduce you, Lia, to a lady for whom I have a lot of respect and who is to be a companion to us for a while. I thought that you might get acquainted over breakfast . . . dinner . . . and supper!'

Glas knew exactly what Ormus meant, but Lia looked mystified.

Lia could still smell the buttery croissants, which had appeared very real to her, and she thought to ask, 'Where are we? What is this place called?'

Ormus smiled at Lia for the first time since the incident on the beach. 'It doesn't matter what name it is given, only that you understand that here time and matter do not exist. From here, we can journey into the past or the future; everything here is illusionary. We have entered the binary domain, which exists between the surface of the Earth and the underworlds below it.'

Lia remained silent, suddenly tired of the new world. She wanted to go home. *I don't want to play these games,* she thought, her body language conveying the same message.

Glas, being accustomed to the binary world and the disappointment that it could produce when one awakened from a dream to realise it was not real in the physical world, did not comment.

Ormus broke into her thoughts sharply. 'This somewhat cruel temptation is a good lesson for the changes you are about to encounter. It will be necessary for you to mingle in circles where those about you will not have good intent in mind, and the company of the good lady you are about to meet will be essential to your well-being within the world of illusion. You are about to be reborn, Lia, to become aware of your Holocene ancestry. When the transformation is complete, you will need guidance while you learn wisdom with these powers, the powers of the Holocene race from the Ninth Universe. At the moment, that which is consciously acceptable to you as an Earthling from Universe Four has no comparison with the intellect of a Holocene from Universe Nine, or indeed, the countless other-worldly natures you will encounter. Although,' he countered softly, 'there are many worldly races whose behaviour is of a similar lowliness to that of an Earthling. Present company accepted of course, Lia, my dear.'

Lia realised she was being made fun of and felt her cheeks go red as she thought of her moody outbursts being her worst character flaw.

'That's witty, Ormus.' Glas started to laugh.

'Yes, Glas, I'm a very funny fellow.' Ormus's eyes remained stern and Glas stopped laughing.

'Sorry,' Glas said sincerely. 'My apologies for yesterday, it was most inappropriate leaving you both to find your way alone.' Glas waited for a change in Ormus's eyes and, sure enough, he saw that his apology had healed the rift.

The air cleared when Glas apologised. Ormus felt that an understanding between the three was now in place and they would continue their journey with an acceptance of the fact that the three were one in word and deed, and would be able to rely upon each other from then on. Ormus held his arms aloft and began to chant a lullaby: Lia's body started to disappear in a shroud of crystalline energy.

Where Lia had stood, a Mer angel began to form with an infant cradled in her arms. The Mer angel's energy filled the cave with a spectrum of blue and silver light that when striking the walls of the cave, was as lightning to the Earth. The mortal infant was placed upon the cave floor to begin its growth through childhood to adulthood, while the genetic information of the Holocene was created in the memory of Lia's human genes. With the transformation completed, Lia's knowledge of the two races was merged as one. It was now up to her to actualise that knowledge, and in order to do so, she must believe the unbelievable information that would enter her mind as her telekinetic psyche began to emerge as logical mental thought.

The Mer angel hovered above Lia while she lay suspended in a chrysalis death. Ormus motioned to Glas, who, anticipating Ormus's gesture, stretched his long legs and slowly got to his feet. Having gone through the process himself, he was now expected to support Lia in hers.

A gathering of Mer angels had entered the cave to witness the rebirth. All those present focused their attention upon the female beginning to emerge from her chrysalis state. Lia's physical appearance would be unchanged, but her personality would be transformed. The Mer angels whispered their approval, and the cave became alive with the sound of the sea's swirling energy. Lia's awakened consciousness was to bring a rare spiritual awareness to her physical life upon Earth.

Within the gossamer cocoon a human figure began to stir. Lia felt as though a piece of food was lodged in her throat as, unable to breathe, she sat bolt upright and began to cough violently. Ormus's voice told her that it was her first drawing of breath, which calmed her. The eyes of the reawakened female, Lia, opened to survey the binary world of which she now knew everything. Lia's eyes, light golden in colour, bright and knowing, would in time read other's minds and souls flawlessly; nothing would be hidden from her consciousness. Slowly she untangled the shroud of white from her body and stood up to look about her. Lia's rebirth was now complete.

Ormus looked with approval upon the transformation; Lia was not physically changed, although her new personality seemed to have altered her outward appearance. The Lia that now stood before him was a woman who appeared to be in command of her life. Ormus's good friend René had been right when he remarked, "I am about to lose my Earthly daughter, Lia". The Lia they had known was gone, and the celestial qualities of the Holocene female that Ormus knew well had imperceptibly replaced her.

Lia turned to gaze at the Mer angels who were beckoning her to a small rock pool.

'Come and look,' they called to her. 'Observe your transformation.'

The words floated through her mind as slowly she stood up and moved towards them. The sound of their watery voices echoed against the cave walls as they separated to allow her a pathway. Lia stared at her reflection in the water and a familiar figure stared back: a tall female, slender and beautiful, with long dark hair that curled about her waistline. But her enlightened mind told her that the old Lia was gone.

'How do you feel, Lia?' Glas asked.

Lia looked towards him and smiled, 'I feel fine, thank you, Glas.' She felt that her mind had somehow expanded, as though she knew of everything about her.

'There is so much more for you to know, Lia.' Ormus said, reading her thoughts.

Turning to Ormus, she asked, 'May we eat now? I'm famished.'

For reasons that Lia did not understand, she offered her hands to Ormus, who took them in his own and kissed them gently.

'But of course, Lia,' said Ormus wholeheartedly. 'I apologise to you and Glas for making you wait so long.'

Lia took a long look at Ormus; she sensed a knowing but could not grasp why. Ormus conveyed nothing in his eyes that she might read; her untapped wisdom was now the equal of his. Ormus lowered his gaze. They had agreed before they departed their world that she would not know him in this.

'This is the part of human nature I don't like!' Glas announced moodily, suddenly feeling quite left out.

'And that is?' said Ormus, his eyebrows rising slightly.

'All this etiquette rubbish.' Glas realised he was already missing the flustered human qualities that appeared to have died with Lia's transformation.

'Straight and true, that's all you need to be, straight and true,' Glas ended defiantly. He was feeling uncomfortable with what he called 'tearoom chitchat'.

'Oh, I don't know,' said Lia, teasing Glas with a smile. 'I could get used to it.'

Ormus smiled at the web she was spinning. Whether he could be close to Lia or not, he was enjoying this moment of poignant humanness.

'Well, Lia, let's hope you remember when next you're in a huff . . . !' Glas was unable to finish his statement, as he was now in a huff himself and not sure whether he was going to like the new Lia.

The Mer angels whispered softly to her, 'Remember, Lia, be aware of the lack of civility and compassion that is now acceptable within the human race and the hurt which you may thoughtlessly convey. Glas is experiencing the loss of his friend Lia. There is a goal that you are not aware of yet, and we advise you to treat your new countenance with appropriate caution. You must become approachable to *all* you encounter; otherwise, those who you want to reach, to listen, will not hear you. The challenges will fail if you appear separate from those you are to counsel. You must be like a chameleon, merging comfortably with those who seek your help.' The Mer angels became silent, knowing that the old Lia would emerge again and be in need of Glas' help and advice.

Lia pondered on the Mer angel's warning and thanked them.

They in turn, wished her well and bade her a safe journey

throughout the challenges to come. They told her that they would be watching over her at all times. 'When you need our help, you must ask; otherwise, we are powerless to intervene.'

'What shall I ask?' Lia enquired.

The Mer angels replied. 'Remember this chant; it appears childlike, but that is its power: "Ocean waves empower my soul, to help me reach my treasured goal." As soon as you speak these words, whatever the danger, we will come to help you.'

'Thank you again. I will remember.' Lia repeated the rhyme until she was sure she would remember it.

Ormus waited as Lia absorbed the 'spell of need', and when he felt sure she was able to evoke it, he called to her, 'Lia, breakfast awaits and the tea is brewed. Come and enjoy your first meal as a human with Holocene powers.' Ormus paused and then smiling, he added, 'Oh, and there is someone else joining us for breakfast, the someone I'd like you to meet.'

No sooner were the words off Ormus's tongue than the acknowledgement was accepted, and his good friend Strawberry Cavil materialised in front of them.

Chapter 11

Strawberry Cavil

Lia studied the lady of years for a moment while Ormus introduced them. Strawberry Cavil appeared to be a wise lady, with a sweet and lively nature that displayed a colourful personality. Strawberry's dark grey eyes sparkled with laughter from within a rounded face with a ruddy complexion; her short bobbed hair, which had been coloured dark green, was fashioned atop her head like the leaves upon a strawberry. This lady loved life, and it showed in her short round jolly countenance. Lia noticed a semi-transparent tail flickering busily around the human form, and Strawberry's head appeared to exude most of the energy that she empowered, which Lia likened to the rotating propellers of a travelling helicopter – Strawberry's feet had yet to touch the floor. Lia watched, fascinated, as the tail continued to swish back and forth. This lady was a Holocene who was not going to hide the fact.

'Lia,' Ormus's voice cut into her thoughts, 'I would like you to meet Strawberry Cavil.'

Before Lia could answer, the lady started speaking.

'Hello, my dear. It's lovely to meet you at last. Ormus has told me so much about you, and I am going to be your companion on the forthcoming challenge ... in order to help you through the tricky bits, so to speak.'

Lia opened her mouth to respond, but the lady continued without waiting for her to comment. Lia realised she would have to get used to this. Strawberry Cavil was born of the star Aries, and Aries people, as Lia was to find out, do not hang around for answers; they are too busy being out there in the front of things. Lia began to feel at ease with Strawberry; she sensed that she was a companion to be trusted and that when Lia had anything important to say, Strawberry Cavil would listen.

Strawberry was silent for a moment while she placed herself at the table and prepared to tuck into the spread before her with her napkin secured neatly upon her lap.

Ormus said to his guests, 'Shall we begin?'

When they had finished their breakfast, the three companions remained seated while Strawberry Cavil continued to eat and chatter. They were fascinated by her ability to talk and eat simultaneously – and with such expertise. Strawberry continued to eat in such a delicate manner that the gradual disappearance of the remaining food went completely unnoticed by all, including Strawberry herself. Finally the table was bare, save the crockery, and the arrangements for where they would take Lia and who she would meet had been carefully organised.

Strawberry turned to Lia who sat quietly by her side. 'Your first challenge will be at the Chequers Ball, which I'm sure you will find thrilling. But I will tell you more about that later.' Strawberry waved a hand in the air as if to thrust her statement into the background.

Instinctively, Ormus, Glas, and Strawberry knew it was growing dark in the world above. Beyond the binary world, time had slipped by and morning had turned into night. Breakfast had become dinner to become supper, and Lia now understood Ormus's curious remark of earlier.

Strawberry stood up, 'We must leave for my home at once. Where I hope, Lia, you will be very comfortable as my guest.'

It was no sooner said than done. Strawberry stood up and raised her ambiguous tail above her head to draw a small circle in the air. As she did so, a hole appeared in the ceiling of the cave, which widened as she rotated her tail in an outward spiral. At length, a hole big enough for her to pass through appeared in the upper boundary of the binary world, and they looked up to see a full moon casting its brilliance down upon them.

Lia felt Ormus's cloak come around her shoulders, as he lifted her up through the hole in the roof of the cave and out into the night sky above. As they lifted above the Earth, Lia became aware of the dazzling night stars resembling a mass of fairies dancing around their mother, the moon. In the Cornish bay below them, Lia could hear the dolphins connecting with one another as they called out a soft and sleepy goodnight to their friends.

Goodnight, thought Lia happily.

Goodnight, Lia, they replied.

The four companions continued moving rapidly inland until the calls could no longer be heard. Strawberry and her entourage continued to fly at speed towards her home in London.

Strawberry loved London, a busy city that was full of people hurrying nowhere, to do nothing of great importance, other than to make money and then to hoard it or to spend it on things of little importance. In the eyes of the world, this was a thriving place where mankind lived an orderly, but restless existence.

The four companions set down outside Strawberry's home, an old Victorian building in Matlow Street. The elegant residence was a picture of neatness with six stone steps leading up to the front door of the house, and on the front porch hung some very impressive flower baskets. The elegant white-framed windows were draped with fine lace curtains, a sharp contrast to the black boundary railings that separated the house from the pavement. At pavement level, the railing curved upward to the entrance and downward to the basement door. The basement led to the kitchen and breakfast room, where Lia could see a light behind the lace curtains. Inside the room, a table had been laid ready for breakfast with a red-and-white-checked tablecloth, blue patterned china crockery, and a vase of yellow sunflowers that added a final touch of warmth to the bright array of colours.

The four companions ascended the steps to the front porch.

Strawberry pushed the familiar brass bell. 'Home at last!'

Inside, a *ding-dong, ding-dong* resounded in the hall. The flowers on the porch, whose petals were closed against the night, rustled their mantles of many colours. They began talking softly.

Lia, aware that the flowers were talking, wondered if it could be so.

Most certainly, Ormus responded. *Remember, believe the unbelievable.*

The whispers of the flowers floated around them like a breeze among the treetops: *All life on Earth is aware of the coming changes, and we are all part of the change. Good luck – our thoughts are with you, Lia.*

Lia realised she was being told that the Earth's plant life was in the way of things, to take a severe blow, but it seemed not to matter to them and they were wishing her good luck instead of worrying for their own kind.

'Thank you, and good luck to you,' Lia whispered back.

Strawberry cut in, 'Lia, you will find that those you are destined to meet here in London have a common weakness. They are as blind as a bat and as deaf as a gate post when it comes to serving mankind – other than for them-selves. So now is the time to hide your trusting nature beneath a protective cover, for you will need it.' With that, Strawberry banged loudly upon the door, while thinking; *I hope some traits of human conflict have remained merged within her dual personality. Holocene intellect is a divine attainment, but an Earthling's insensitivity can be very rewarding at times.* Strawberry would not have worried about future events had she heard the Mer angel's warning to Lia. She stood tapping her foot impatiently, while the maid could be heard running to open the door.

'Hello ma'am; we were expecting you a lot earlier and were getting worried.'

'Stop fussing, Lily, and where is Joseph?'

'Just coming, Madame!' The two servants stood before them in their uniforms of black with white trim.

'Go in, go in!' bustled Strawberry. 'Let's get the door shut!'

Lia whispered another quick thank-you to the flowers before being whisked through the door by the force of the three bodies behind her. With the door shut, Strawberry, now soft and non-commanding, beckoned Lily and Joseph to her and gave them a big hug.

'Hello, my darlings; how are you?' Strawberry turned to the three guests standing in the hallway and said, 'I want you to meet my cousins Lily and Joseph, whom I love dearly,' Strawberry beamed excitedly. 'They are going to help us with the challenge ahead and will stick by me through thick and thin.'

Lily and Joseph came forward and greeted them warmly, 'Welcome, welcome to cousin Strawberry's home.'

Chapter 12

Lia's Coming Out

'A ball gown, don't you think, for Lia?' Strawberry made the statement as she and Ormus sat having an early cup of tea in the breakfast room. Lily and Joseph were up and about their duties. Glas and Lia were still sleeping soundly upstairs.

'I think that will be most appropriate, my dear,' said Ormus. 'And I am sure she will be thrilled by a shopping trip with you rather than me. I will create a suitable contrivance of chiffon and lace for you to purchase.'

'Ormus, you have always had such a lovely way with words; I can almost see the dress you have chosen for her and so appropriate for her face and figure.' Strawberry visualised an ivory-coloured chiffon dress, the perfect colour for Lia, with a matching lace bodice. 'I will take her shopping as soon as breakfast is over.'

'Perfect. Perfect,' Ormus uttered the words as if to himself, as he got up from his chair and went to the door. Turning, he spoke again. 'I must make arrangements for our invitations to the Chequers Ball.'

'Of course,' replied Strawberry, raising a hand in a gesture of farewell and then relaxing back in her chair to enjoy her tea.

Lia heard the front door bang shut and, jumping from her bed, she ran to the window just in time to see Ormus hail a taxi and jump into it. Lia could not hear his command to the driver and felt a jolt in her stomach. Was he going to leave her here with Strawberry and Glas? Lia went back to her bed and climbed in, pulling the white linen cover over her body. Everything felt wrong!

Where was her father, and why had he asked her to accept this journey? Lia wanted to know more about where she was going and the reason for it. Suddenly her body no longer felt familiar to her touch, and a long tail seemed to appear and then disappear. Lia's heart began to thump as her body became ice cold, and then it happened. She began to lift from under the covers. Slowly she pushed the covers aside and without them to anchor her she lifted some more until she hovered below the ceiling. Lia's thoughts turned to Ette and she began to cry. To her amazement, large tear-drops rained down upon the white bed linen like splintered pieces of an ice cube; her large eyes opened wide with horror at this unbelievable experience – her tear-drops had frozen in transit.

I want to go home! Lia's cry came from deep within. *I want to be myself again!*

A knock came at the door and, without waiting for a reply, Glas made his entrance to find Lia hovering below the ceiling wide-eyed with embarrassment. Lia was both angry and relieved at the intrusion.

'Don't you wait for an invitation before entering a lady's room?' she yelled at him, her embarrassment now more to the fore than her ice-cold body and frozen tear drops.

Glas responded with a bemused look, as he hurried around the room looking in the cupboards and under the bed. When he had finished, he remarked in surprise, '*I beg your pardon!* Is there a lady occupying this room? Seems more like a Holocene spirit to me – with, might I add, a most ungracious attitude'

Lia started to tell him just what she thought, at which moment Glas superimposed his Holocene form upon his human body, his handsome face now sporting a rather fine catlike transformation. Glas wiggled his ears. Lia watched for a moment and then began to laugh, so much so that she began to cry again, but this time with laughter.

'I heard you crying, Lia, and I felt you ought to know that you can go home whenever you choose by repeating the words given to you by the Mer angels and wishing to be only human again. Do you want to try?'

'Oh yes,' said Lia.

'Then come down to the mirror; come on.'

Lia, thinking of the floor, hurtled down towards the mirror.

'Steady on, old girl, the human body has not got the buoyancy that a Holocene form has. Only athletes should attempt the free fall you have just performed.' Glas made a mental note to speak to Strawberry about Lia's lack of control with her precarious aerodynamics before they continued on. Otherwise, with the additional powers bestowed upon her, she would become the talk of the neighbourhood, especially with stunts like the one she had just performed. Glas laughed at the memory.

Lia was now busy peering in the mirror at her two images and trying to recall the words of the Mer angel's chant. "Ocean waves empower my soul, to help me reach my treasured goal," Lia said the words aloud. 'Ocean waves empower my soul, to help me reach my treasured goal.'

Lia thought of herself as only human and waited while the Holocene form disappeared, leaving the one reflection of her. Lia smiled; she felt herself again. 'You know, Glas, this experience must be akin to being very, very ill, when you no longer recognise the body you are living in as your own. It's as though someone or something unrecognised has taken control, and you are powerless to do anything about it.' Lia paused, pondering her words deeply, the tears welling in her eyes. 'How sad I feel today.' Lia began to cry again.

Lia, you have a choice, and the time has come to make it! Ormus's voice cut into her thoughts.

'Ormus, where are you?' Lia spoke the words aloud, surprised by the voice in her head.

'I am very near and always will be; have no fear of that. You will always be able to search me out if you really need me. Right now, I am busy preparing the ground for our visit to the Chequers Ball. Details of which, as Strawberry has told you, will be revealed in due course. Make your decision now, my dear, either to return to Ette and a singularly human life or to continue the adventure of duality in that beautiful human form that you have been given, and with the knowledge of your Holocene ancestry. Which is it to be?'

Lia stared into the mirror; she could see a clear image of Ormus and the Lia she knew. A silhouette of Lia the Holocene hovered behind them. On hearing Ormus's voice, she regained her courage and whispered, 'I will carry on with the challenge.' The Holocene female vanished within the human form of Lia.

'Do you think I am beautiful, Glas?' Lia asked, suddenly feeling happier and a bit cheeky.

Glas shuffled uncomfortably. 'Well, I wouldn't go so far as to say that, but you do have lovely ears for a human. Just look – they are slightly pointed,' he said, directing her gaze back to the mirror.

Lia, startled by his comment, looked closely at her ears in the mirror. 'They are not, Glas.' Lia puffed with pride, 'And if they are, I'd say they were something to be proud of!'

'Breakfast is ready!' The breakfast gong rang as Strawberry shouted up to them. 'Come along you two sleepyheads; it's time to be up and about.'

Lia sprang out of her pyjamas and into her jogging suit, *time for a bath after breakfast.* She swept out of the room in two bounds with Glas calling after her, his hands still over his eyes to spare her modesty.

'What have I just said to you?' His words, although spoken loudly, were unheard by Lia, who was already at the door of the breakfast room. Glas shook his head as he left Lia's bedroom. 'What are we going to do with you? I hold my breath in trepidation.' Glas smiled happily; the old Lia had returned.

'Not for too long, I hope,' the voice from the mirror replied candidly. Ormus was chuckling as the taxi pulled up in front of the Halls of Chequers. 'Timing's just right,' he said to the driver as the vision of the mirror and his companions faded from Ormus's watchful eye.

'Pardon?' said the driver.

'Nothing, just an old man's ramblings,' Ormus replied. Paying the driver, he jumped from the taxi and mounted the stone steps leading to the Grand Halls of Chequers. Ormus felt, as he ascended, that the enormous granite lions standing at the bottom and top of the entrance steps were watching him; the granite statues looked almost alive in the early morning light. Up the steps he sprang like Peter Pan, watched from below by the astonished driver with unbelieving eyes. *Oddly athletic for an old-timer.* Ormus laughed at the driver's thoughts as he continued swiftly to the top of the twenty stone steps. As he reached the top step, the door opened and Ormus disappeared inside.

Chapter 13

The Halls of Chequers: The Masters of the Four Directions

Ormus stood in the Inner Sanctum of the Outer Hall. He knew he must wait until he was invited to pass through the doors that opened onto the circular staircase and led up to the Inner Hall. Ormus, not wanting to waste a moment's precious time, continued to practice his art of imagery. After all, practise is what keeps you in perfect shape. Ormus's thoughts became playful: *shape and size, ones and twos, threes and fours, all keys that access doors.*

There were many great masters who had stood within the Halls of Chequers but none that understood the key to numeral perfection as did Ormus. Mathematical symmetry was the key to the universe, and few surpassed Ormus in the ability to create items of matter from this knowledge. Ormus began to create the wardrobe that Lia would need during her stay with Strawberry Cavil . . .

While Strawberry, Lia, and Glas sat having their breakfast, things were becoming very lively upstairs in Lia's bedroom. Furniture, doors, and drawers were opening and closing, as Ormus relocated items of female clothing from a well-known department store in London to Lia's bedroom. Ormus had chosen a favourite store of the wealthy to acquire Lia's wardrobe, where the elite and trendy went for their fashion accessories and most other items, as well. In fact, if you hankered after an elephant and were able to house one, it was the store to ring. On this particular morning, anyone curious enough to look upward while going about their business would have seen all manner of female attire floating skyward from an open window on the top floor of the department store. Delicate items of ladies' underwear, skirts, blouses, shoes, and bags – a complete wardrobe of female attire – floated towards the river and eventually disappeared through an open bedroom window of the Cavil residence in Matlow Street.

With Ormus's shopping list completed, he paid for the items taken, transferring fifty-pound notes into the appropriate tills. He waited to see that the purchases had registered as paid. *Heaven forbid that Strawberry might be accused of stealing,* he thought before turning his attention to the next item on his list. Ormus created the ivory chiffon and lace ball gown that he and Strawberry had spoken of the night before and transferred it to where he wanted it to be displayed. Moments later, the dress stood in all its perfection in the front window of the department store, for all who passed to admire – and stop to admire it they did.

With the transactions completed, Ormus opened his eyes to see Mercer, Master of the Doors, waiting patiently. Ormus acknowledged his presence respectfully, for none entered Chequers without his consent. Mercer had not interrupted Ormus, for he knew that this master never wasted time when he could be doing great works.

'Good day, Mercer.'

'Good day, Ormus. Follow me.'

Ormus followed Mercer as he mounted the stairs to the Inner Hall. Mercer wanted to add that it was good to see him again, but he thought it unwise; he was aware it was a sensitive area for Ormus.

At that moment, a thousand voices rang out, 'Welcome back!' The Masters of the Four Directions were applauding Ormus's return.

Ormus mounted the last step and strode through the large oak-panelled doors in front of him. Before him all masters and craftsman of the fourth universe rested in one form or another upon the walls and ceiling of the Inner Hall – but never on the floor of blue and silver chequers, the universal sacred space, where the challenges of Universe Four were played out.

There had been so many opposed to Ormus's eviction from Earth, the sentence given to Ormus from the masters of the Four Directions in favour of the thirteenth Initiator, Aspheseuos.

Ormus's troubled mind travelled back to his expulsion. The first Holocene mission had been to initiate the integration of their spiritual intelligence with the creature named man, and displace his human need to shed blood. While the former had been accomplished, mankind's need for bloodshed remained. They had failed to bring about a complete transformation in man; Ormus had been recalled to Holocene, and Aspheseuos had remained the victor. Now Ormus was challenging him again, and it was the masters of the North Wall Kingdom, the absolute wisdom of the four directions, that he must first ask help of to challenge Aspheseuos on behalf of mankind's future existence . . .

Ormus had read Mercer's thoughts, as if reading the daily paper full of sentimental rubbish, and he forgot them just as quickly. Ormus had little time for thoughts of sympathy, unless they were followed with positive action. His thoughts rested upon the years that had been wasted as mankind had utilised his altered intelligence while continuing the barbarism that his human genes were capable of. Quickly Ormus dismissed the memory, knowing that a seed of bitterness grows strong roots very quickly.

'It's grand to be back,' Ormus said light-heartedly, 'and thank you for your welcome. Lead the way, Mercer; my anticipation for 'feeling' the Inner Hall again is making me impatient.'

The first to speak were the masters of the East Wall Kingdom, all speaking together with the quickness and innocent babbling of youth. 'Welcome, welcome, Ormus. It is so exciting to have the most honoured of masters back in our midst. We are looking forward to being with you and learning from your wisdom.'

'Thank you,' Ormus answered sincerely, for he had no grievance with the youthful souls of the East. Like the wise fool, they were beginning a journey that would take them through all seasons and to all corners of the universe in order to learn and gain their wisdom. This wisdom would only be completed when they reached the North Wall Kingdom, the place of knowledge and establishment . . . unless, of course, they became the followers of Aspheseuos. Then, sadly, they would become established in the Halls of Darkness for a period of time that would seem like eternity, as Ormus well knew.

The masters of the South Wall Kingdom spoke next, their voices quick, satirical, and, at times, arrogant. 'Why, Ormus, old friend, how the devil are you?' They chuckled mockingly, and Ormus's temper started to rise. With great discipline, he regained his composure, and his voice rang out with calm sincerity.

'Thank you, my friends of the South Wall; I can feel you have brought your warmth here tonight,' Ormus swallowed hard while trying to keep his thoughts in check. One unguarded moment for them to access his thoughts and they would have won the first round of the games, which all in attendance knew was the initial welcoming challenge. Ormus wiped all thoughts of their egotistical treachery from his mind, knowing that they of fire and war had been only too pleased with the sentence imposed upon him. His period of absence had left them free to impose their warring, irrational, and stubborn attitudes upon the naïve innocence of the young masters of the East, the infant souls of the universe.

The masters of the West cut in with the guttural sounds of an old witch. 'Ormus, we hear you have brought a challenger with you who will, it is told, heal this world of mankind's destructiveness.' The sniggering voices of the West Wall were joined by heated laughter from the voices of the South. A voice croaked above the deafening noise, 'When will we meet such a noble human, Ormus?'

Ormus controlled his thoughts with the discipline of one who is holding onto a cliff edge with his fingernails . . . he drew a deep breath, drawing courage from the silence of the East and North Wall Kingdoms. For him, their silence showed their support and strength. Feeling calmed, Ormus replied, 'At the Chequers Ball, my friends. I hope you will be able to contain your excitement until then.' Ormus turned to the North Wall and spoke of the reason he had come. 'My Lords, I ask your permission to bring, as my guest, one named Lia Dubar, and to ask your protection for her in the challenges ahead.'

'Your wish is granted, Ormus,' answered the masters of the North Wall Kingdom, 'but before we close the challenge, which you have passed with honours, might we add, we wish to make this statement.'

There was a pause filled with anticipation. The masters of the East Wall listened with held breath. The South and West Wall waited, hoping for an anticipatory ticking off for Ormus, and they were not disappointed.

The voices of the North Wall continued, 'Ormus, you have returned to us in order to take up another challenge for Hafnium. The challenge will, at best, leave you acutely drained of your Holocene powers; at worst, it will take you away from your beloved ninth universe and your own kind if you fail again. However, perhaps that is what your soul reaches out for. You alone know the secrets of your soul.' The North Wall became silent, giving Ormus time to reflect on what had been said. 'We commend your bravery and persistence, Ormus, and will make this promise to you: that, whatever the outcome, we will look after the one who you call Lia Dubar and return her to her destined pathway when her Earthly life is over. But should you fail this time, you will not be able to return, and the Holocene race will be severed from you. We have warned you, Ormus. Good luck with the challenges.'

Ormus felt the emotions of both fear and love well up inside him, feelings he had thought he would never feel again.

'Thank you, my Lords.' The statement was barely audible, as he bowed first to the North and then to the West Wall, followed by the South, and then the East. Ormus turned towards the doors and swept through them. He had come to pick up the challenge and was leaving triumphant. Mercer stood by the front door and bowed as Ormus made his exit. Ormus remained silent as he passed by him and out into the morning light.

The cabby who had delivered Ormus to the Hall of Chequers was returning to the same spot just as Ormus descended the steps. Ormus hailed him and jumped into the taxi, instructing the cabby to return him from whence he had come. The cabby looked at the old man in his rear-view mirror.

'Do you know, sir,' he said, 'I can't remember a thing since I left you. What I've been doing . . . only the Lord knows.'

'Don't worry, my friend, it happens to me all the time,' Ormus replied lightly, wishing the cabby's confused state away as they continued on their journey.

The cabby was now whistling happily, 'Show me the way to go home . . .'

Ormus sat back in the seat; he felt drained suddenly, and very old. 'Perhaps I do want to disappear from it all,' he muttered softly to himself. 'Why do I always take up these challenges?'

Ormus heard a myriad of twinkling voices about him.

'Because you love the source from which all life manifests, and we love you, Ormus.'

Ormus sighed and whispered, 'Thank you', allowing the Mer angels to do their work as he drifted in their ocean of healing energy.

Chapter 14

The Shopping Trip: Lia's Ball Gown

With breakfast finished, Lia lay soaking in her bath. Strawberry had made her excuses and shut herself away in her study to make the final arrangements for the Chequers Ball. There were little things that Ormus would never be bothered with, such as flowers and the finishing touches to an elegant appearance that only a woman appreciates. Strawberry opened the study door and called out to Lia, 'I cannot hear the bath water running away. I should be able to hear it now. Come along, my dear, we have a morning's shopping to take care of.' Strawberry waited, listening for the sound of water running down the waste pipe; satisfied, she closed the door and continued with her phone calls.

Lia, now dried and perfumed, opened the wardrobe door to choose from the beautiful garments within. From the reflection in the door mirror, she could see delicate lingerie in an open drawer of the dressing table behind her. Lia drew a bright yellow dress from the wardrobe and, turning towards the dressing table, she walked over and reached in. Lia held the pale lemon silk garments to her face. The sensation was so soft and silky . . . beautiful, and the perfume was very exotic. The perfume was the same fragrance as the toiletries she had found in the bathroom and, slipping the undergarments onto her long, sleek form, she sighed happily. 'I could get used to this with a bit of encouragement,' Lia giggled and slipped the yellow dress over her head. Then she slipped her feet into the yellow sandals that lay on the wardrobe floor and looked in the mirror again, this time at her reflection. Lia felt the heavy feeling return to her stomach; she whispered, 'I miss you Ette.' Lia banged the wardrobe door shut and left the room.

'Hey – where's the fire, daffodil?'

'Very funny, Glas, but not as funny as that hat you are wearing.'

They were interrupted by the appearance of Strawberry at the bottom of the stairwell. 'How lovely you look, Lia. That colour is breathtaking against your dark curls.' With Glas she bantered lightly, 'And your red hat is very cheerful; it suits your energetic personality.'

Lia called out as she ran down the stairs, 'I agree with you, Strawberry; it's certainly very cheerful.'

The front door opened and out into the morning air they swept, Lia buoyant on the lively energy that both Glas and Strawberry exuded. The flowers rustled their good mornings as the three hurried by them. Once out on the street, Strawberry hailed a taxi. Immediately one pulled up alongside them, and out stepped Ormus.

'Good morning,' Ormus greeted them, and then, turning to Lia, he said, 'My dear, you look lovely.'

'Thank you,' Lia replied, smiling brightly. *I like him more and more,* she thought.

'Off you go then, and don't buy the town,' Ormus chided.

'Now, now, Ormus,' said Glas. 'Don't go giving her ideas.'

Ormus ushered them into the waiting taxi and as they waved their goodbyes, the taxi pulled away and headed for the town.

Ormus's pale complexion and tired stature had not gone unnoticed by Strawberry, who now sat quietly pondering the future events, unaware that Lia was speaking to her. Suddenly she came to. 'Pardon, my dear, what were you saying?'

Lia answered, 'I was wondering how you came by the name of Strawberry; it isn't a name normally given to a child, is it?'

'Quite right, Lia, I was given the name because of a birthmark that lies below the breastbone on the left side of my rib cage. It is shaped like a strawberry and is as big as the palm of my hand. Marks of this nature, as you may know, are sometimes called strawberry marks, and so Strawberry became my nickname. My real name is Odelia Margarita; however, I am quite happy with Strawberry.'

Glas spoke for the first time since entering the taxi. He loved London – it was his home, and he was a frequent visitor to the Cavil residence. Born on the north side of the Thames in a not-so-affluent part of town, he loved roving in and around the city, never tiring of the elegant shops, the brightly polished cars, and the general appearance of the well-maintained rows of elegant houses.

'Lia Dubar,' he said. 'That seems to be a name with a fortunate history. What is the history of the Dubar family, Lia?'

Lia gave Glas a long look, pausing before she spoke. She knew of Glas' poor background and his subtle jealousy of people with money or old family traditions. She also knew that jealousy was an emotion that invited people to achieve for themselves, a hidden gift that helped many to accomplish much.

'The Dubar family come from the southern region of France,' she answered. 'They have lived and traded there for many centuries as wine producers. Château Dubar is the name of the vineyard.'

'Go on; I'm all ears.' Glas pushed his hat to the back of his head, the gesture making him look even more overconfident than usual.

Lia felt uncomfortable, but, with a smile of encouragement from Strawberry, she continued, 'Our mother died when Ette and I were born and father raised us on his own.'

'With help from a nanny and other live-in servants, I'm sure?' Immediately Glas felt ashamed for being so cruel but felt too proud to admit it. His upbringing had been one of total poverty. Glas' father had reared him after his mother had died when he was six, his father being a disciplinarian with a liking for alcohol. Glas' childhood had been difficult and certainly not comfortable. It was only after he met Ormus that he had become aware of his real identity and the reason why he was experiencing an Earthly life.

Strawberry, shocked at his comment, looked harshly at the young man opposite her.

Glas took warning from the look in her eyes.

'Father is an astronomer who has many friends that share his interest in the universe beyond Earth. Ormus has told me that he is of great importance to the changes that are coming, but beyond that I know little of his work outside of his being a wine merchant and hotelier.' Lia felt uncomfortable and no longer prepared to accept Glas' questioning. She had been deeply hurt by his remarks and had remained quiet about her father's secondary occupation, which she knew a great deal about. Her feelings of closeness to Glas had suddenly diminished.

Glas felt the separation acutely and realised he was not so much a Holocene but very much a human with a huge chip upon his shoulders. 'Well, that's some story, Lia,' Glas said, finishing with an apology that was totally sincere.

The taxi drew up outside the department store. The driver sat staring into his rear-view mirror at his passengers. *Perhaps I need a holiday. Since I picked up that old guy this morning, I haven't been feeling too well.*

Strawberry poked her head through the open window, making the cabby jump. He had noticed the silhouette of a long tail above her head as she sat behind him. Trembling, he took the money from her outstretched hand.

'Thank you,' he stammered.

'Could you pick us up here for our return journey?' enquired Strawberry.

'No,' said the cabby. 'I don't feel well. I'm going home for a lie-down.'

'Oh, you poor man,' said Strawberry. 'I wish you well.' Strawberry turned to join Glas and Lia, who were eagerly awaiting their visit to the shops, the coolness between them now gone. Turning back towards the cabby, they said, 'Goodbye and thank you.'

The cabby barely heard them as he pulled away into the path of an oncoming bus. The bus driver beeped his horn while muttering sarcastically under his breath, 'Have a nice day!'

In front of them stood a very impressive shop; Lia glanced up at the ornate fascia rising in front of them, one, two, three, four storeys high, with gracefully decorated display windows that sparkled from the constant cleaning and polishing. Lia's eyes focused on the crowded revolving door with shoppers hurrying in and out. How like life, she thought. What goes in must come out; what goes up must come down – a continual motion in one form or another. She wondered what changes today would bring and if there would be more transformations. Lia felt Strawberry's arm slide into hers and gently guide her towards a large display window.

'Look, Lia, isn't it beautiful?'

Lia followed Strawberry's gaze until her eyes settled upon the chiffon and lace evening gown in the window. She murmured, 'Oh, it's beautiful, Strawberry.' Lia took in the elegance of the bare-shouldered dress and floating chiffon wrap, with matching cream silk slippers, and a hand purse decorated with real pearls that matched the necklace around the model's neck.

'Let's go in and have a closer look,' said Strawberry, guiding Lia towards the revolving door.

Glas followed the ladies, happy to observe the shoppers going about their business and to smile at the beautiful young ladies that caught his eye. Eventually, with all the distractions around him, Glas was left behind. When Lia and Strawberry reached the gown department, Glas was nowhere to be seen.

Lia suddenly became quiet and concerned by this. Strawberry asked, 'Is everything all right, my dear? You do not seem very happy.'

Lia, surprised at this remark, rallied quickly, not wanting to offend Strawberry. 'No, I'm fine, really – thank you so much for bringing me. I can't thank you enough.' Lia meant what she said and would not have missed it for the world, although her least appreciated pastime was shopping, unless for something necessary or to browse through the odd and interesting. Living in the country and doing the day-to-day running of the business for her father, she normally would not have the time for window-shopping. Right now, the swarm of people bustling and bumping past her was making her smile disappear further and further into her face.

'Do you have much shopping to do, Strawberry?' Lia asked.

'No, my dear, I am only here to shop for you at Ormus's request.'

'Oh!' a startled Lia made no other comment but followed Strawberry until they reached the counter in the gown department.

A young smartly dressed woman approached and asked them if she could be of assistance. Strawberry asked to see the chiffon and lace gown in the window, without giving the size required, as she knew it had been made for Lia and would therefore fit. The young woman did not ask the size either, or for which lady the gown was intended, but simply called the window dresser to dismantle the gown from the display. This done, the shop assistant led Lia to the changing rooms and helped her into the gown.

Lia shivered pleasurably as the coolness of the chiffon flowed down over her head and body. She ran her hand over the snug-fitting lace bodice, her fingers feeling the sensation of crisp lace in contrast to the delicate chiffon. The assistant buttoned the tiny pearls that ran from below her shoulder blades to the base of her spine. Next, the shoulder wrap, so delicate and sheer, decorated with tiny matching pearls, was placed around her shoulders. The assistant knelt to help Lia with the silk slippers and then stood up to place the pearl necklace around her neck. The assistant then stood back and smiled approvingly.

'That, Madame, was made for you.'

'I agree,' said Strawberry with a sigh, remembering a time when she could have done the garment as much justice, 'Stand up straight, Lia, and put your shoulders back,' commanded Strawberry, 'and smile!'

Lia complied, not because she was told to, but because she felt so beautiful. *I was right,* thought Lia. *There was another transformation on the way.* Lia saw Ormus in the mirror behind her, and this time he was there in the flesh.

Ormus had followed them to the department store after a quick breakfast and a change of clothes. He was now looking very smart in a dark navy suit and with his hair cut to an acceptable length. Judging by his appearance, most passers-by would think him a gentleman of means. Ormus turned to the shop assistant and thanked her for her polite and efficient service, after which he asked her to pack the dress with the matching accessories and send them round to the Cavil residence. He then offered her his card to charge the items to his account. The assistant, although she was always treated with courtesy by local shoppers, almost curtseyed to Ormus, whose gentle manner made her feel like a very special person.

Having thanked the assistant, Ormus turned to Strawberry. 'I will go and find our young friend, Glas, while Lia is being helped out of her gown. We will meet in the jewellery department, if that is suitable to you, Strawberry?'

'Of course, Ormus. We will be along shortly.'

Glas had been meandering in the confectionery department, which was one of his favourite places. He liked nothing better than to smell the delicious aroma of fresh chocolates and percolated coffee. At each of the three entrances to the confectionery department there was a small refreshment area where these items were served all day, and that is where Ormus found Glas, about to order. Glas had offered to buy Ormus a coffee and a dish of handmade chocolates, but he had politely refused. Ormus told Glas they would return for coffee later; in the meantime, they would join the ladies in the jewellery department, and so they headed in that direction.

Strawberry and Lia, having arrived some five minutes before Ormus and Glas, were peering into the glass cabinets filled with all sorts of valuable trinkets. After greeting them, Ormus ushered them in the direction of the ring counter.

Lia followed behind with Glas, teasing him gently because Ormus had told her where he would find him. 'I know where you have been, sampling the chocolates. Did you buy any to share? I bet not.'

Lia giggled and Glas took on an act of defensiveness.

'The reason I have not bought any to share is that we are all going for coffee and chocolates after this purchase, whatever that is. Besides, I would have thought you have been spoilt enough for one morning.'

They laughed together, both now thoroughly enjoying the shopping trip.

Ormus paused at the first counter and then moved on to the second. He seemed to be satisfied that the second cabinet housed the required item.

He beckoned Lia forward. 'My dear, look at the tray in the top left-hand corner. Do you see the ring that is shaped like a pair of dove wings with a pearl in the centre?'

Lia peered in at the ring. The band was decorated with small diamonds with a pearl at the centre point.

'Yes, I can see it. It's beautiful.'

'Then, if you like it, you shall have it.'

'Oh, thank you. Yes, I do like it very much,' Lia stumbled with her words, embarrassed and delighted by the attention she was receiving.

'Then it is yours, my dear,' Ormus replied.

'Thank you,' Lia said while thinking that the Chequers Ball must be quite an occasion.

Ormus paid the assistant and put the ring in the inside pocket of his jacket. Then, turning to Lia, he said, 'While you and Strawberry look around, I will take Glas to the gentlemen's outfitters to collect his evening attire. He must be as well presented as you, Lia, as he will be escorting you on the night of the Chequers Ball. When we have completed our purchase, we will meet you and Strawberry in the confectionery department for refreshments.'

With all agreed, the two couples went off in opposite directions.

Back in the taxi after the shopping trip, they sat back gratefully as the vehicle moved slowly along in the busy evening traffic. Lia watched as people scurried back and forth, jumping into taxis and onto buses. She watched with a detached inquisitiveness, her eyes viewing the world but her mind wandering through the events of the day. It had all been so lovely, and she could still taste the mixture of fresh coffee and chocolate in her mouth. Glas, to redeem himself, had purchased two boxes of chocolates, one for Strawberry and for one her. Lia held the chocolates in her lap; she felt safe and secure sitting next to her three new friends, who felt more like family to her now. In her hand she clasped a tiny box, a gift she had managed to purchase while momentarily alone; it was a gift for Ormus . . .

Chapter 15

The Chequers Ball

It was two days following the shopping trip and the day of the Chequers Ball. In the morning, Strawberry visited the hair and beauty salon alone. Lia's natural beauty was flawless, and, apart from some assistance to dress on the night, there was nothing else to be done. Strawberry had worked tirelessly with Lia, preparing her as best she could for the events that might take place that evening.

Ormus had shown his appreciation to Strawberry by leaving a gift in her bedroom, which she found when she returned home from the shopping trip. She had entered her bedroom to see a splash of deep purple draped across her ivory satin bed cover. Picking up the dress and holding it to her face, she knew at once that it was made of Chinese silk. The colour was most complimentary to her dark grey eyes and rosy complexion. Shaking the dress gently, she hung it on the wardrobe door. On the floor beneath the dress were gold silk slippers embroidered with peacock tails of turquoise and blue. An evening bag that matched the slippers lay upon the bed, as did a black box that contained gold earrings, a bracelet, and necklace set with the most powerful of all healing crystals, amethyst stones. Ormus had chosen the amethyst gift for two purposes: one, to show his appreciation, and the other, to protect Strawberry from the negative energy she would encounter during the gruelling challenge ahead. Ormus had thought this to be a wise choice, especially while his attention was taken up with Lia. As for Glas . . . well, Glas could look after himself; his instinct for survival was excellent.

During her time spent with Strawberry, Lia had learnt many things about the behaviour of those she was to meet at the Ball. People had come and gone in the Cavil household, some just to peer and some to sneer. Some were friends, and some were most definitely not. All in all, Lia had come through with flying colours, thanks to the long hours of tuition that Strawberry had lavished upon her. Lia, whom Strawberry had grown very fond of, now stood confidently at the top of the stairwell, looking down at her friends who stood in the hallway waiting for her. All were attired in their finest. As they looked up at Lia, they were in no doubt that she would be the most beautiful woman at the Ball that evening.

In the soft light of the hallway, the flowing chiffon gown gleamed like the gossamer wings of a butterfly. The tight lace bodice encrusted with tiny pearls emphasised Lia's tiny waist and long slender body, to perfection. As she descended the stairs, the chiffon floated about her, revealing the delicate satin slippers upon her feet. The vision before those waiting was nothing less than perfection. Lia's beautiful dark hair was piled high upon her head and held together by a comb of pearls and diamonds, a Cavil heirloom that held memories of the days when Strawberry had been a young woman coming out into society. The pearl necklace purchased with the dress now adorned Lia's long, slender neck to complete the picture. Beautiful was an inadequate word to describe the woman that stood before them.

After some time, Strawberry broke the silence. 'You look beautiful, Lia.'

'Yes, yes, indeed you do,' said Ormus.

Glas remained silent for some time, being overwhelmed by the transformation in Lia. After a moment, he said, 'You *do* look beautiful Lia; I am so proud to be escorting you tonight. I'm sure I'll be the envy of every man at the Ball.'

Lia smiled, but not coyly, for she knew she looked beautiful, and with this knowledge had come a new-found confidence that matched her appearance. Lia was not aware that her self-confidence was of Ormus's making; the perfume he had given her was a potion. The Stargazer Lily perfume was a magical potion and a challenger's companion, as it stimulated a state of fearless courage for the traveller who entered the other-worlds. Tonight there would be many challenges for Lia, and at times very little help from him or the others. Ormus trusted that she had used enough. When the night was over, and if she was successful, Lia would never have need of the Stargazer Lily potion again. The reward that tonight's challenge would afford her was the knowledge of a 'wise one' for always. And failure – Ormus closed his thoughts to that outcome. Hafnium and the Masters of the Four Directions had given their word that it would not be Lia's failure, only his – and that he could accept.

The four companions left the house, with Strawberry's cousins Lilly and Joseph looking on, their silhouettes framed in the light of the doorway as they watched them leave. They were both spell-bound by the grace and beauty that Lia now emanated. Quietly, they whispered their good luck, as the one in gossamer chiffon disappeared into the waiting taxi, followed by her three companions. Lily turned to Joseph, the soft light of the porch lamp showing the concern upon her face.

'Joseph, I do hope she will be all right.'

'Do not worry, Lily Stargazer, Lia Dubar will face her challenge tonight with the courage of a lioness, and she will come through triumphant. Of that I am certain, for her future is blessed. It is Ormus I am gravely concerned for. I feel that he knows it is his destiny to lose and that this challenge is his sacrifice for Lia and mankind, for their future in a world that will be brought back to reason and stability for all.'

'We agree with you, Joseph' murmured the flowers, rustling their petals.

'What do you think, Great Oak?' said the Great Pine from his home on the central reservation of Matlow Street.

'I am of the same opinion,' said Great Oak. 'All the years of knowledge that is held within my roots tell me that Ormus's time with us is nearing an end.'

Oak's aged roots spread out many miles beneath and away from the street that had been his home for hundreds of years. His branches hung low in solemn acknowledgement of Ormus's demise.

Great Oak and Great Pine had been planted by Strawberry on the centre green when she was a child, and they had grown together, listening to many stories of the world, especially from Ormus.

'My dear friend, Ormus,' the deep voice of Great Oak sent ripples along the roots beneath him. 'I remember the wonderful times when he and Strawberry sat beneath my branches for protection from the sun and rain, talking of their many adventures. I will wish for those times again. Perhaps if we all wish for those times again they will surely manifest.' But in his heart Great Oak knew there was no going back; the fate of plant life on Earth, like Ormus's fate, was inevitable.

The taxi disappeared into the night, and the front door of the Cavil residence closed amidst the sounds of 'Goodnight, Oak,' 'Goodnight, Pine,' and 'Goodnight, everyone.' The light in the porch vanished, and stillness settled over the Cavil household.

On the central green, the stillness of a suspended existence became evident for all that were now attuned to the four companions and the challenges that would be played out that night. Two winged stallions of pure white appeared in the sky, their noble heads rearing and bucking. Mounted upon their backs sat the challenger knights heralding the colours of Hafnium and Aspheseuos: one dressed in silver and the other in blue. The knights made an awesome sight seated on trappings of gold with silver bridles. The knights rode towards each other across a dark night sky lit only by the radiance of their beings, each knight holding his colours high. This night the stars were veiled, and the moon was shrouded in darkness. The knights rode towards each other, their lances held low as if to attack, and then, as they approached one another, they held their lances aloft, and their radiance became as one. Each extended an arm, and their gauntlets met in a clasp of friendship.

'May the best knight win the challenge,' said Hafnium's knight to his brother. The knight of Aspheseuos returned the gesture. 'May the best knight win, my brother.'

'Indeed, brother. May the fear of the many be seen for the mirage it is. Be sure – the test for tonight will be of immense duration, and the outcome is not in our power to see, which makes the task in hand all the more challenging.'

'May the power always be challenged,' they lifted their voices together as two cups filled with golden liquid appeared before them, which they held aloft to toast the coming challenges. The two winged stallions reared up in the night sky, their flying manes releasing shooting stars into the darkness around them, and then, as silently as they had come, so they were gone, and all was dark and tranquil once more.

Great Oak said a prayer for his dear friend Ormus before entering a troubled sleep.

Outside the Hall of Chequers, Ormus stood by the open taxi door waiting for his companions to alight. Lia stepped out into the eerie shadows of the evening and gazed upon a flight of stone steps flanked by an elaborate balustrade, with lions mounted at the top and bottom. The life-sized lions stared back at Lia as if to warn her not to mount the steps between them, which made her step back to stand closer to Ormus. The taxi driver's nervousness was showing; he did not like this part of town at night and wanted to be on his way. Ormus sensed the driver's agitation, and, turning his attention from Lia, he paid the driver and allowed him to leave.

The four companions stood together at the bottom of the steps. Glas, knowing that Ormus wished to be alone with Lia for a moment, offered his arm to Strawberry, and they began to mount the steps together. Ormus studied Lia's glowing face, her cheeks flushed by the excitement of the evening to come.

'My dear, I am so proud of you, and I want you to know that – whatever you face tonight. Remember, you cannot lose.'

'But, Ormus, what am I to face, and how will it affect the future?' Lia looked into the craggy old face that she had come to trust.

'If I say to you it is of no importance that you know right now, but that in the near future you will know and understand all, will you trust me and accept that answer?'

Lia paused looking deeply into the solemn blue eyes. 'I will,' she said.

'Good,' he replied lightly. 'Then we can go and have some fun.' Ormus put his hand into his coat pocket and withdrew the ring that he had placed there.

'Here is the ring I bought you, Lia. You are to wear it at all times while we are inside the Halls of Chequers. Do not let it slip from your finger.' Ormus placed the ring on her right index finger.

Lia looked down at the ring of diamonds shaped like a dove, the flames of white fire flaunting the translucence of the centre pearl. Lia lifted her face to Ormus and placed a kiss upon his cheek. 'Thank you,' she said. 'I will treasure it always.' Lia withdrew the tiny package that she had put in the evening bag she carried. 'I've bought you a gift as well, Ormus, and I hope you will cherish it as much as I will yours.' Lia undid the wrapping, and a ring with a blue opal stone set in the centre of a wide band dropped into her hand.

'How unusual – a blue opal set in pewter. It is beautiful, my dear.' Ormus slipped the ring onto his finger and gave Lia a warm embrace, 'I think it is time for us to catch the others up, for we must all enter the doors together.' Ormus held out his arm for Lia to slip her arm through his, and they began to mount the stone steps, the lions watching them solemnly as they ascended.

Chapter 16

The Dance of the Neophytes

Ormus gave each of them a warm and encouraging smile, as the four stood silently together beneath the great stone mantle over the doorway. They held their hands in a clasp of friendship; it was a moment they would remember evermore, and then Ormus released his hold and knocked on the huge oak door.

The great doors opened and they were motioned forward by Mercer, who had been waiting for them, 'Let the games begin, my friends,' he said as he ushered them through the grand entrance. Mercer greeted Strawberry with a bow, 'So nice to see you again, Madame.'

'Thank you, Mercer!' Strawberry answered curtly, having very little time for the man.

'May your evening be pleasant,' Mercer replied as he turned on his heel and beckoned them to follow.

Ormus nodded but made no comment, as he followed with Lia on his arm and Glas and Strawberry bringing up the rear. No more was said, and they were left in the sanctum of the Outer Halls, while Mercer took away their cloaks.

As soon as they were on their own, Strawberry remarked, 'That man, well really! I wonder if he starches himself while doing his laundry – such a pompous individual. I find him quite exasperating.' Strawberry swished her gown furiously from beneath which the silhouette of a tail was plain to see at that moment.

'Now, now, Strawberry, do not get so fraught. You need to remain calm and keep your wits about you. If a little thing such as Mercer's manner is going to upset you, how can I rely on you through the challenges of the evening? And tuck that tail in.'

'Yes, yes, you are right, I know. It's just nerves, and I apologise for my behaviour.'

Glas remained silent, for he knew that the challenges had already begun and that they were being watched right now for their weaknesses and their strengths. As far as he was concerned, the less said the better. Ormus, who was listening to Glas' thoughts, knew he was right. He also knew he could rely on Glas for his shrewdness and brilliant – if a bit over the top – tactics amidst the enemy.

Lia was about to go to Strawberry's defence and console her for her outburst, when Mercer returned and requested them to follow. They headed for the staircase leading to the Inner Halls. The doors at the top were open, and Lia could hear the sound of raucous laughter and the tinkle of glasses, as though a party were already in progress . . .

Before Lia had dressed that evening, Ormus had joined her in her room to acquaint her with what she might expect on arrival at the Halls, who would be there, and the manner in which they might engage her. The information had been a warning for her to err on the side of caution at all times.

Ormus listened to the noise coming from within the hall. The party tactic had come as a complete surprise and was now making him feel uncomfortable, especially after his talk with Lia. Ormus knew that anything could happen, and the best he could do was to expect the unexpected.

Glas was listening to the thoughts masked behind the laughter coming from within the Inner Halls. He stopped and turned, saying 'I believe Lia is my escort, Ormus.' Glas winked at him, while taking Lia purposefully by the arm and gathering her onto the step beside him.

Strawberry stepped down beside Ormus, who immediately took her arm.

'Ready when you are, Ormus'

'Ready as ever I will be, Glas.'

They locked eyes in a gesture of, 'Good luck.'

Lia mounted the last step, her gaze now drawn to the scene before her: a vast ballroom bathed in shimmering light from the crystal chandeliers that hung from a baroque ceiling. The ceiling was covered in paintings of cherubs, neophytes, and figures of beautiful women and handsome young men dancing together, all dressed in the most resplendent clothes. Upon the walls hung large ornamental mirrors painted silver and gold, which reflected an unnatural pallor upon the silver wood of the ballroom floor. The floor was so polished and smooth that to dance upon it would be nothing less than a dream. Upon the ballroom floor, the poignant scene of dancing figures floated by, emanating a haze of silver and blue, as in the shadows of a dream. As they stepped upon the ballroom floor, the doors of the Inner Halls closed silently behind them.

The ballroom was crowded with people, the waiters moving among them with silver trays filled with glasses of champagne. The whole scene was set for an evening of fun and laughter. As Lia gazed at the people in the room, she wondered why their clothes of silver, gold, and blue were in keeping with the ballroom décor. She noticed a young couple who were beautifully dressed in black but looked out of place, and then she realised that it was her sister, Ette and Edward. Lia gave out a cry of delight and started forward. Mercer held out an arm to restrain her, telling her quietly that she must be introduced first. Lia stepped back, the first flush of embarrassment upon her cheeks. Quickly, she mumbled an apology, and Glas squeezed her hand to reassure her. However, there was no time to dwell on the matter, for, within a moment, Mercer was announcing their arrival, and Ette and Edward were almost running towards them across the ballroom floor. Greeting each other with hugs and kisses, they were unaware that the dancers had stopped to look on.

'I'm so glad you're here,' Ette said dramatically. 'I don't know how much more of this I could have stood without your coming.' Ette paused for a moment, waving her invitation in front of Ormus. 'Not a soul has spoken to us since the announcement of our arrival; even the waiter did not acknowledge my 'thank you' for the champagne. What is this place, and how did we get an invitation to this evening?' Ette looked boldly at Ormus.

'My dear,' Ormus held out his hands to Ette, his welcome warm and genuine, 'how lovely to see you again.' He placed his arms around her waist and they embraced.

Ette had only known Ormus for a brief time, but she felt she knew him as an old friend. 'Well, thank goodness you have turned up, as now the night shows promise.' Ette giggled, having completely forgotten the question she had asked Ormus.

Having forgotten her embarrassment, Lia giggled too. 'Let me introduce you to my friend, Strawberry, and Glas,' she said to Ette and Edward. 'Strawberry, this is my sister, Ette, and my dear friend, Edward,' she said brightly.

Everyone exchanged greetings.

Edward, who had said little up to this point, joined in the exchanges. His attention had been taken up with Lia, who he thought looked amazing. Edward was so pleased to see her again, and yet he found it strange that he could not remember when they had last been together or why she was here with these people. As the introductions were exchanged, Edward held Lia's hand for a moment in greeting and then her hand slipped away again. For Edward it had seemed an age, as though they had conversed at length, but then he seemed to be in a dream in which Ette, Lia, and Ormus were taking part. *Am I in two places at once ... what am I thinking?*

Ormus's voice broke into Edward's thoughts; *do not concern yourself with your whereabouts now, my friend. Just keep alert to what is happening, and know that there is a real danger here for Lia, Ette, and for you, Edward – in fact, for all of us.*

Ormus moved away, leaving Edward to listen to the conversation going on between Ette and Strawberry. Strawberry was telling Ette that whilst they were at the ball they must keep an eye on Lia, and that all would be explained later. Ette agreed with pleasure, as now the evening was looking to improve. Ette could see beyond them to the banqueting hall, a room not unlike the one they were in. The table was laid with a sumptuous feast, a different scene altogether to the ballroom. Here the only sign of silver, gold, and blue was on the long tables that were covered with a delicate china dinner service, crystal glasses, and the silverware set upon them. Here was a feast to make anyone's eyes widen. The pure white tablecloths were hardly visible beneath the delicious food that adorned them. All manner of food was on display, both sweet and savoury; there to be sampled as much or as little as one could manage. Ette beamed with delight; her taste buds were already anticipating the banquet to come, her sense of smell attuning to the delicate aromas drifting through the open doors of the banqueting hall.

'Wow, doesn't that look good! But first, a drink … I feel like champagne,' cooed Ette, looking at Glas. A waiter was at her side in an instant, and everyone took a glass of champagne.

'To a night to remember,' said Ormus as they raised their glasses to toast each other.

Those assembled in the ballroom raised their glasses silently, mimicking the toast. The music began.

Edward took Lia's arm and asked if she would like to dance. Glas, who was enjoying Ette's company, did the same, leaving Ormus to ask Strawberry onto the floor. The three couples began to whirl around the centre of the dance floor to the tune of a lively polka, while the other guests danced around them in a merging circle of silver, gold, and blue, as faster and faster they danced.

Ette leaned towards Strawberry as they passed by each other. 'Who are they and what are they called?' Ette whispered furtively.

'Well, my dear, you are in the dreamtime, and they are the creatures that create its existence.' Strawberry realised that Ette would not understand and changed the subject. 'Ette is such a beautiful name,' continued Strawberry. 'It implores you to dance, as you are dancing. Ette; you are the dancer of the ball.'

Ette beamed with pride, as she was whisked away by Glas, although she was completely mystified by Strawberry's nonsensical reply.

Lia, on hearing Strawberry's remark, began to laugh nervously at a smiling Edward who was whirling her round the dance floor with such expertise. Round and round they spun, with Lia gazing on the faces of the strangely grotesque guests who had now slowed down and did not seem to be enjoying the wonderful music or the company of their companions. *In fact, they seemed to stare without expression, as though they were marionettes.* Lia's friends were dancing nearby again, and she cast aside her thoughts of dancing puppets, intent on enjoying the evening and the companions she was with.

'I'm so glad Ette is here,' she giggled, the champagne beginning to take effect, 'and you, of course, Edward.' Lia smiled brightly as Edward gathered her in his arms, ready to dance another polka.

As the music began, a man dressed in black evening attire stepped onto the chequered dance floor and approached the dancing couple. Touching Edward on the shoulder, he asked if he might dance with Lia. Edward released her into the arms of the stranger, who then danced Lia away, leaving Edward to watch from the edge of the dance floor. Ormus, who was immediately alerted by the appearance of the stranger, danced Strawberry towards the couple on the floor. He wanted to be near them, to take the stranger's place should Lia need his help.

Lia was now having the time of her life whirling about the floor. Her new escort had not given his name, and she had not asked. The stranger danced her around the floor so swiftly that her feet did not touch the floor. His voice drifted softly about her, as he told her that the ball was in honour of the young seeds of the masters.

'They are here to celebrate their "coming out",' he continued.

'Their "coming out"; what do you mean by that?' she asked.

The stranger replied, 'The young neophytes are now ready to learn the wisdom of the universe, albeit under the watchful eye of their masters, the first of these being the Masters of the East.'

'How long is their apprenticeship?' Lia asked.

'For as long as it takes them to master the knowledge of the universe, my dear,' was his answer, and he said no more.

Lia began to feel uncomfortable. She was not offering information about herself, and yet, by the very presence of this unknown person, she felt that she was being drained of all her strength and knowledge. As the thought entered her mind, a hand tapped the stranger on the shoulder and Ormus replaced him.

Lia felt her energy surge and return to normal. 'Thank you, Ormus. Who is he?'

'He is the 'Inquisitor"; he came to test your knowledge and strength, but his information is incomplete, and he will try to dance with you again. Beware Lia. Remember our conversation and avoid that character at all costs. Do not dance with him again.'

A 'voice' rang out above Ormus's, and all around became silent as the voice continued, although no one could be seen. The tone of the voice was low and respectful.

'Welcome to the Neophytes' Ball; welcome to those of you who have experienced the event many times before, and, for those of you who are honouring us with your presence for the first time, welcome.'

With the opening ceremony over, the ballroom fell into silence and Ormus's small gathering of friends felt an iciness enter the hall, for, when the music stopped, so did the laughter and gaiety. They realised it was their presence alone that had filled the ballroom with a warm ambience.

The voice continued, 'It is with great honour that we have invited the seedlings of the future to celebrate with us.' The voice could be heard to turn direction as it continued to address, first the east wall, then the south, followed by the west and finally the north. 'I thank you for, and am honoured by, your presence with us,' said the voice, addressing each direction in turn.

The mumbles of acceptance echoed around the room.

'Now my friends, it is time for the parade of neophytes, so let us honour their presence.'

The voice faded and a lilting tune began to play. Lia felt ill at ease with the familiar melody. The tune was melancholy – not light and lively as it was supposed to be played. From a doorway to the left of the ballroom came the first neophyte, followed by another and another. Out they rode on their winged white ponies.

'How bizarre,' Lia whispered to Ette.

'Most odd,' Ette replied, not wanting to stand and look at these peculiar individuals a moment longer. Ette was getting very hungry and an enticing array of food could be seen clearly through the open doors of the banqueting hall. The food on display was such an inviting choice when faced with the pale coldness of the neophytes' clothes of silver, gold, and blue, with their faces painted to match. The spectacle was all too much for Ette, who, always acting on her basic instincts, was about to head straight for the banqueting hall.

'Oh, lovely; don't they look wonderful,' said Ette unconvincingly, while turning to Glas to grasp his arm and persuade him with, 'I am famished, Glas. Shall we pass into the banqueting hall?' Without waiting for an answer, and with one heave of her strong slender body, she moved forward, taking Glas with her.

Glas found himself unwittingly heading towards the banqueting hall.

'Yes, let's,' said Lia, following her sister's example as she pushed Ormus towards the open door. Edward followed with Strawberry, having no option but to go, as to stay would mean giving way to his thoughts about exactly what was afoot tonight.

Safe in the warm glow of the banqueting hall they began to relax again. From the hall beyond, they could hear music and applause as, one by one, the neophytes joined the parade, each one being applauded for their appearance and degree of learning achieved. The strange celebrations, whilst eerie for a 'coming out' ball, did not seem as sinister from where they now stood as when they had been in the ballroom among them.

'What is going on, Ormus?'

Edward spoke to Ormus in a curt manner; he could not believe that they had been brought here for the sake of a night out. The whole set-up seemed fraught with danger, and he could not understand Ormus wishing to bring Lia to such a place. He would never have brought Ette here if he had known what to expect; he did not realise that they had entered the dreamtime freely in order to attend.

'I know you are concerned and upset, but please understand: in the long term, we will come through. In the short term, we must all pull together to get through tonight. I cannot say any more than that. I don't know what to expect myself.'

Glas spoke up. 'You have no idea what is at stake here, and, therefore, please listen to Ormus and do as he asks.'

Edward did not protest but went to stand by Lia. She was looking beyond the open door at the strange pageantry as it continued in the ballroom. The neophytes had found themselves partners and were now dancing. Strangely, their partners were not among those who had danced while Ormus and his companions were on the dance floor. They were, Lia realised, the figures from the baroque ceiling come to life, and now they were prancing and springing their way around the floor with their partners, the white figures of the cherubs a ghostly complement to the painted faces of the neophytes.

Lia's face was as pale as the cherubs'; she had known to expect the unexpected, and yet nothing had prepared her for this. Her body felt as bloodless as the face she showed to the world. Edward put his arm around her, his warmth giving her comfort and strength.

'We are all worried, Lia, but, like all things unknown, with time they become apparent,' Edward said reassuringly.

Lia nodded in agreement, somewhat comforted by Edward's composure.

Suddenly, a scream of disbelief came from the direction of the banqueting table, causing Edward and Lia to jump nervously. Edward swung around, taking Lia with him. They were now facing into the room and looking at Ette. Her face was now a mixture of anger and disbelief. In her hands was a plate piled high with all manner of delicacies selected from the table with the help of her keen sense of smell, which had told her the food was mouth-wateringly delicious. Poor Ette! As the first morsel of scrumptious-looking food had entered her mouth … there was nothing, absolutely nothing. It was only air and just as tasteless. Ette had let out a scream of disbelief at the cruel joke that was being played on her.

Ormus was by her side in an instant. 'Sorry, Ette, the food is not for eating,' Ormus spoke the words quietly into Ette's ear.

The plate of food that Ette had selected now lay upon the tablecloth, its contents splayed across the white linen. Ette was hungry and, having been tricked, she was now very angry. Her perfect white teeth appeared beneath her top lip, as she hissed, 'Just what is going on here, Ormus? I assume the invitation to dine was from you and your friends.' Ette pointed angrily towards the door.

Ormus was taken aback by Ette's reaction over the buffet. Rarely had he any interest in food; his only need of sustenance was for survival in the physical, and his taste buds were so old and worn that his sense of taste was almost a memory.

'That is correct, Ette. The invitation was of my making, and I apologise for not warning you that the banquet would be illusory before entering the hall. My mind had been occupied with other matters. In fact, they have kept me very busy! All I can say is that I am very sorry for your disappointment.' Ormus's reply was equally curt.

Ette shrugged and pushed the plate further onto the table, a gesture of defiance at her disappointment. She watched as, right before her eyes, the table resumed its perfect arrangement, the upturned plate and contents returning from whence they had come. Ette jumped back from the table and stood next to Glas, shocked at the sight her unbelieving eyes had just witnessed.

Glas, unlike Ette, was having a ball; his mirth at her disappointment was about to explode to the surface. With great control, he put his arm around Ette's shoulders and said sympathetically, 'Never mind, bumpkin, perhaps we can rustle up a nice cheese sandwich for you.'

Ette glared at Glas; her displeasure very obvious.

Ormus, ignoring the banter, strode towards the door and stood beside Lia and Edward.

'Why are they dressed in such a manner, and what is this strange dancing called?' Lia asked Ormus.

'Lia, think carefully. When would you see these images?' Ormus paused to allow Lia to absorb the scene thoroughly.

'It's bizarre … and Ette and Edward are here. Dreams; yes, a dream, that's where these images would appear normal, in the realm of one's dreams.'

'Yes, Lia, dreams are as real as the so-called waking hours, which can also seem unreal in times of stress and pain. Remember the adages: "Is this for real?" and "I must be dreaming"? Right now, you are living in real time, and yet it is so unreal, so unlike your so-called conscious moments. It is your mental and spiritual thoughts that have brought you to this place, and therefore, it *is* real. What you must do is interpret what you see into logical reasoning, just as you do when the conscious mind is in control. At this moment you exist in the binary world where the substance of dreams is created, and it is part of the challenge that you are engaged in.' Ormus became conscious of a transformation about to take place. 'Come, we must re-enter the ballroom.'

Ormus's statement seemed strange, as though they were leaving one stratum to enter another. Ormus and Lia moved forward to step over the threshold of the doorway, leaving Edward behind, while the bizarre scene within the ballroom faded away to be replaced by a chequered floor of silver and blue squares within a hall of granite masonry. They had re-entered the Inner Hall where the four directions existed. Ormus and Lia now stood in the dwelling place of the masters.

Lia now understood who the neophytes were: they were the seed of all dreams that grew in size and strength with every thought of them. Each mortal deliberation adding to their credence and reality, be it fear, hope, inflexibility, or inspiration. Each seed grew in wisdom of its 'kind', to evolve from beginning to end within the halls of eternity, in an ever-moving circle from beginning to end and back again.

As Ormus and Lia had stepped through the doorway, the ballroom had vanished and the light from the banqueting hall had disappeared, leaving nothing but blackness behind them. Ormus could hear Glas' thoughts and knew that all was under control. Glas, Strawberry, Ette, and Edward were there in the blackness and could see Ormus and Lia and the changes beyond the banqueting hall doorway.

The granite walls of the inner sanctum dappled and faded, revealing an extraordinary universe lit by the beauty of the stars. For Ormus and Lia, the floor of sixty-four silver and blue squares was all that anchored them to the darkened cosmos.

Chapter 17

Chiron: Back to the Source

The sudden changes to the ballroom announced that the twelve masters of the first 'other-world' – the rulers of men's souls – and Chiron, master of the challenges, were about to appear. Ormus stood motionless; there was nothing to do but wait and make his moves as the game presented itself.

Lia stood anxiously waiting – for what, she was not sure. She began to pray, 'Thank you for everything that I have received today and everything that I have been able to give to others in return. I am trying very hard to resurrect the happy, trusting child from within, while letting go of all that no longer serves me, in order to heal myself both physically and spiritually, and, in doing so, not to judge others, including myself.' Lia's words tumbled into the cosmos.

Ormus listened to the prayer that Lia recited each night before falling asleep and squeezed her arm reassuringly. She felt the strength return to her body and took a deep breath in anticipation of what was to happen.

If it's only a dream, I've had dreams before. I've had nightmares before in my waking and sleeping hours. Lia smiled at her thoughts and began to laugh, her laughter becoming louder and louder until she was laughing uncontrollably. Ette, who stood in the darkness behind her, began to laugh too; they laughed at the sombre faces that appeared to come from nowhere, their heads mounted in the darkness like hunting trophies upon a wall. The sisters continued to laugh at the bizarre situation they found themselves in, laughing loudly together, each one trying to speak but unable to get the words out.

'How f ... funny they look,' Ette stuttered uncontrollably.

Within the halls, there was no other sound except the sisters' laughter; they were both laughing at the bizarre contrast to reality as they knew it, laughing in defiance of their fears.

The masters of the twelve tribes of man made their entrance onto the silver and blue chequered cosmos, followed by the seeds of Hafnium and Aspheseuos, players that were dressed as chess pieces, two kings, two queens, four bishops, four knights, four rooks, and sixteen pawns. The two ranks of players faced each other across the universal chess board, their fine porcelain features staring forward without animation.

Lia and Ette had ceased their laughing, fascinated by the new entrants.

Puzzled by their appearance, Lia asked Ormus, 'Who are they, and why are they dressed as the pieces on a chess board?'

'They are the seeds of mankind's souls, who take part in Hafnium's challenges on behalf of the twelve tribes of man,' Ormus answered reverently.

Lia, still in a playful mood, asked. 'And, the one with the purple onion on his head; who is he?'

Ormus answered her sternly, 'Lia, that is Chiron, master of the challenges, and you must begin to take this seriously. Your dreams are as important as your times of consciousness, and, if you ignore them, it can be hazardous to your physical body.'

Chiron moved forward to address the throng and, greeting them, he said, 'Welcome to the Challenges.' Then, turning to Ormus, he said, 'Greetings to you, Ormus, "wise one"; you are here to take up the challenge again, and we welcome you back to the Halls. Your steadfastness in the quest to help mankind is admirable. Of course, you have a personal quest to prove yourself where you have failed in the past ... Let us hope that you will succeed.' Chiron turned to Ormus's companions. 'Each one of you is here to champion Ormus and Lia Dubar, who is to take up mankind's challenge alongside him. Let me explain to you why Universe Four cannot continue to evolve if the challenges are not met and mankind is allowed to continue ignoring the spirit-soul within his mortal body.' Chiron paused, as a mutter of agreement filled the hall from the spirits gathered there, and then he continued, 'Many of those who have passed through physical death are manifesting on the psychic plane as though still in the physical body, their mortal mind in denial of their Earthly death, while their ghosts terrorise the mortal living. The psychic plane is the first other-world, where man goes to heal the physical body when he sleeps during his Earthly life.'

A hologram appeared beside the silhouette of Chiron. Within it could be seen the first other-world: the psychic plane surrounding the Earth, a place of dreams and nightmares and of exceptional struggle. Within the hologram they could see people aimlessly wandering through their dreamtime, each one refusing to acknowledge the four separate aspects of his or her psyche and the purpose of their life upon the earth.

Light filled the hologram, revealing the four elements of the human psyche: the higher self, the ego, the shadow self, and the duality of the anima (feminine emotion) and animus (male logic).

In the first spectrum they could see the ruins of a stone temple with twelve supporting pillars; ten lay broken, and only two remained from the beginning of mankind's existence. The pillars were the symbol of man's soul – mankind's higher self, of which ten were forgotten, but not lost to him.

Within the second spectrum, there stood a child with an animal, which symbolised the ego and the basic urge for action; at the beginning of mankind's existence, the basic urge for action created a spiritual desire and ambition to return from separateness to the *one* within Universe Four. This goal was lost when mankind's basic aspiration for action turned from spiritual to material desire.

In the third spectrum, which hung heavy with dense undergrowth, stood ten decaying trees, a symbol of the knowledge of the Initiators – forgotten by man in the darkness of his shadow self and the limitations of his mortal life.

From the fourth spectrum, the stone temple rose up from the wilderness, with a man and woman in the centre to symbolise equilibrium of the anima/animus – knowledge that man had chosen to forget.

Ormus and his companions watched, as from within the second spectrum of the human psyche a light began to manifest. The life story of those who had recently passed from physical death to the psychic realm was revealed to all watching, and it was obvious that nothing had changed in their passing. Men and women were still gossiping and quarrelling, always pious, always right, their surviving mental energy confined within the spectrum of the ego. Souls that were still labouring with the prejudices buried deep within their shadow-selves. Intolerance was nurtured by a lack of knowledge, which could have set their souls free. Another soul was voicing his ideals, calling out to those who passed by that he had always been fair and had never taken sides, so why was he in this abysmal place? Lia knew the answer at once: the soul had been unable to speak out with courage and commitment when challenged to make choices. All aspects of his psyche had engaged the easiest options during his mortal life.

'Man is thus imprisoned,' Chiron's voice echoed softly above them. 'Compassion, fairness, and tolerance are now latent in man, and scarcely does remorse come to fulfil and nourish his soul ...'

The lost soul continued to voice his ideals, appeasing all, offending none, his impartial attitude bringing him no challenges. So it continued: the mental thoughts of the disembodied jumbled and twisted, sometimes making headway but most times not, and with only a few listening to the wisdom of Chiron.

'... This place is the psychic realm that divides Earthly life and the continuing journey of the soul. It is the first step that man takes after death to continue his journey to the higher realms where none other than good can exist. In order to journey to these spiritual realms, the soul must first forge through the psychic world, where, as upon Earth, darkness and light can exist together. The psychic plane is a place without physical matter, where many souls remain trapped in an illusionary world of their own making and where their psyches exist within a ghost impression of their deceased Earthly bodies. If these souls do not evolve, they will lose the energy to exist, and, like stars, they will eventually burn out. Death releases the soul to the psychic plane, where it manifests on the same level of consciousness as it manifested upon Earth. The one passing through physical death may not believe there is a continuing mental energy held within the soul; as a result, when the soul enters the psychic plane, it refuses to believe its physical body is dead. When the misguided soul becomes aware of this delusion, it can then move on to the next level.'

Glas, having heard it all before, began to fidget, while the others listened attentively. Chiron's voice was becoming tedious to Glas, and he wanted closure. *A change of scenery would be nice,* he mused.

Chiron continued. 'The spirit-soul is given a perfect body, a vehicle in which to learn and evolve. That vehicle does not separate the soul from the *one*. It is always a part of the *one* and must be fitly joined at all times to the *one*, in order for the universe to be complete and perfect.'

Glas nodded in agreement, hoping the end was nigh!

'Mankind has forgotten his soul and no longer challenges his spiritual development. Material advancement, power, and wealth are the deities of mankind now. The time has come for these wrongs to be righted.'

Chiron ceased speaking, much to Glas' relief. The hologram faded, and Chiron's silhouette disappeared.

From the darkness two voices rang out, 'Ormus, you have taken up mankind's challenge for his continued existence in Universe Four. So be it.'

Above them, in a dark velvet cosmos strewn with stars, two knights appeared, signalling the start of the challenges. Lia looked down at the silver and blue chessboard floating in the universe with Ormus and herself standing on the brink, teetering on the edge of eternity, and wondered why she felt anchored and unafraid. Hafnium's knight came forward and handed her the chalice of the seeker.

'Drink from the cup, Lia Dubar.'

Lia drank the glowing golden liquid.

'You have started on your quest as the seeker and the wise fool,' said the knight. 'From here on, you will seek and find the quests played out on the chessboard, and, as you challenge each quest, we will succeed or fail. We of the light will win or lose to Aspheseuos's knight and his players. The games will continue until we reach the final quest and checkmate! Find your way carefully across the universe of endless knowledge. Return as the talisman, the teacher of future youth. Come back with the wisdom and humility to bring stability back to the twelve nations of mankind. Good luck!'

Lia could see the wilderness of the first spectrum and the assembly of the masters of men's souls. Above them, within a circle of multi-coloured light, stood the twelve angelic forces of the second other-world, each one ruling thirty degrees of the sphere. Their magnitude was encircled within the dynamic of their colours; each one had been a god or goddess long before man stood upon the Earth. Within the first symphony of colour stood Aries, Taurus, Gemini, and Cancer, their flames of burnished orange representing the era of mythology. Then noble Leo appeared, representing the era of the sun kings and queens within the radiance of golden yellow sunshine, Leo being the heart and will of all matter. Virgo and Libra came next, dazzling and shimmering, their beauty manifest within their Earthly colours of green; both represented early civilisation. Scorpio was next to emerge, her luminosity soft and mysterious in the transmuting colours of a velvet blue night, and representing the dark years of the Middle Ages. Sagittarius, sheathed in the colour of a clear blue morning sky, was next to appear, followed by Capricorn in a mantle of cerise, whose responsibility it was to keep heaven and Earth joined together. Aquarius and Pisces followed, embellished in flames of crimson; these last four represented the ages of individuality. All twelve were responsible for guiding mankind.

Below them, on the psychic plane, a wheel of light hung suspended to support the twelve tribes of man. Countless rays flowed into space, each ray thick and heavy, representing the tribe's evolution throughout the ages. Each tribe was weary from carrying the burdens it was responsible for. Mankind was shackled with the oppression that his loss of the ten strands of first knowledge had brought him: mankind's spirit was repressed. The vision slowly dissolved, and the light began to darken. Lia gripped Ormus's hand tighter as she began to tumble, frightened of what was to come . . .

Lia stood with Ormus, Glas, and Strawberry at the front door of Chequers. It was as though it had all been a dream. Mercer was saying goodnight, and the taxi waited below. Ormus, who had never let go of Lia's hand, drew her gently down the stone steps to the waiting taxi, and, when all were seated inside, Ormus asked the driver to return them to the Cavil residence. On the journey home, no one spoke of the events of the evening, and when safely inside the house, the four said only a brief goodnight and retired to their rooms. Tomorrow was another day in which to discuss all that had taken place. They were exhausted and needed rest.

Lia lay in bed staring up into the blackness. Where were Ette and Edward? She felt a pang of loneliness, and, turning on her side, she brought her knees to her chest and folded her arms around them. A tear ran slowly down her face onto the pillow, then another and another, until the pillow that she lay on was wet and uncomfortable.

Go to sleep, Lia. Ette and Edward are safely tucked up in their beds at the Hotel Renoir. On hearing Lia crying, Ormus had sought to console her by sending healing thoughts in his soft and kindly way; his voice so soothing to her troubled mind that before long Lia was asleep. Only then did he leave her to her dreams.

Chapter 18

Ormus and Lia Return to Tintagel

The guests of the Cavil residence were awoken by the smell of hot croissants and fresh coffee. Downstairs in the kitchen, Lily and Joseph had been busy preparing breakfast. Joseph stepped out from the kitchen to strike the copper gong standing in the hallway, indicating that breakfast was about to be served. The resonance hung in the empty passageway for some time before the four companions appeared at the top of the stairwell, robed in their dressing gowns. Only a few hours ago they had said their brief goodnights; now, as if no time had passed at all, they were together again. Without a good-morning or an apology for their attire, they filed downstairs and into the breakfast room. Still without a word spoken, the four set about consuming the breakfast laid before them. It was a while before anyone spoke, the first being Glas, as he took a large bite out of his third croissant, filling his mouth with the flaky, buttery-sweet confection.

'Well, this beats eating fresh air, doesn't it?' Glas mumbled as he tried to eat and talk at the same time.

With that, the silence was broken, and they all laughed together at the memory of Ette and the banquet.

Once they had completed breakfast, bathed, and dressed, the four faced each other across the breakfast table once again. The breakfast room was light and airy and a good place for them to get to grips with any future plans. Strawberry and Glas had assumed they were to be included and were not prepared for what

Ormus was about to tell them. They both assumed they would be escorting Lia wherever she was going next.

Ormus began hesitantly, 'I will be taking Lia back to Cornwall . . .' he paused, '. . . alone.'

'Alone?' echoed Strawberry and Glas.

'Yes, Lia must now become versed in the same practices and knowledge that we three are somewhat experienced in. It is essential that she learns to use her senses as we do; if not, she will be lost in this Earthly world of double standards. Only when she can distinguish the truth by listening to the thoughts of others as well as to their words can she hope to accomplish any of the challenges in front of her. With both of you to lovingly nurture and protect her, she will emerge from her chrysalis stage an imperfect butterfly. It is essential she need not rely on your help or prompting.'

Lia listened to Ormus's words, while her heart sank to her stomach. She began to think of the caves to which Ormus had taken Glas and herself; the thought of spending more time there without Glas and Strawberry to cheer her up made her feel numb.

'Ormus, are we going back to the cave for long?' Lia asked.

'We will not be going back to the cave, Lia. Being there would not produce the results that we need; we will go where needs must.' Ormus was giving nothing away. Wanting their destination to remain a secret, he closed all knowledge of it from his mind.

'Now, my dear, go upstairs and pack your belongings, except for your ball gown; that will stay here for now. We will be leaving shortly.'

Surprised by the short notice, Strawberry stood up to help Lia pack.

'No, stay here, my dear. I wish to speak to you.' Ormus put his arm around Strawberry's shoulders. 'Strawberry, do not worry about her. You will be with Lia throughout the next challenge. Let that knowledge be your strength now.'

Strawberry gave a half smile, the tears spilling from the crinkles in the corners of her eyes. 'I do understand, Ormus. To give her strength, we must also give her independence.'

'That's right, my dear, that's right.'

Glas had shot upstairs with Lia; he was aghast that she was being taken away and just when they were beginning to have so much fun, but mostly because he was going to miss her so much. Lia was part of his life now, and he was not happy at this turn of events – not happy at all.

'I can speak to Ormus for you if you really don't want to go, Lia. Ormus could teach you here. Strawberry and I would keep out of Ormus's way; we'd be no trouble, no trouble at all,' Glas scrambled through his statement.

'It's all right, Glas. I understand why I must go, and I am not unhappy, truly I'm not.' Lia turned to Glas and gave him a big smile, 'I'm sure I will be back here with you and Strawberry in no time at all. It's up to me, really. If I learn quickly, well, then I will soon be home.' Lia realised she had said the word *home*; this had become her home as much as the one she knew and loved. 'I will be back in no time, Glas. I am determined to learn the knowledge of the ancients as fast as possible.'

'Well, that's fighting talk.'

Ormus and Strawberry stood in the doorway smiling at the two young people.

'Are you ready, then, Lia?' asked a more relaxed Ormus. He had not looked forward to telling them his plans, and, now they had been accepted, he felt much better. 'Glas,' said Ormus, 'after we have gone, Strawberry will give you a clear picture of our future plans. You will be working alongside Lia very soon.'

Glas nodded an acknowledgement, still not entirely happy with Ormus's decision. They were about to leave, when Ormus posed the question: 'When do you feel best about making a decision, Lia?'

'Well, I always listen to other points of view first, but usually I find, if I sleep on it, when I wake up in the morning I have the answer,' Lia replied brightly.

'A wise way to make important decisions, my dear; very wise.' Ormus gazed ahead, trying to justify a visit to the wise ones. Sometimes they can teach her in a night, sometimes in a week, and, at her most obstinate ... what has it been in Earth years, oh yes ...

oh well. Time is nothing within the universe. Ormus gave thanks to Hafnium for his patience and generosity and for all the wonderful life he had created within Universe Four.

Chapter 19

The Causeway

Two months had passed by since Lia's return to Tintagel, to Ormus's cottage where the village's history included much of his own. The cottage, which Ormus had occupied for centuries, was hidden away down a rough, potholed single-track pathway, lined by lofty hedges and evergreen shrubs, which stopped at the entrance gate to the garden. Beyond the gate, a wild and grassy backdrop extended out towards a ledge on the rugged cliffs, one hundred and fifty feet above the Atlantic Ocean.

At the beginning, Lia was eager to learn quickly, so that she could return to London, but gradually she began to feel at home with the easy way of life and the people who, although always friendly when passing the time of day, never delved too deeply into why or how she came to be there. Lia had learned many things in the short time she had been in Ormus's care and was now completely absorbed in the knowledge that he was teaching her. She no longer felt alone or homesick, and her independence was growing stronger each day. Lia had become hardly recognisable as the girl her father had brought to London. The awakening Lia was now becoming an independent adult with a mind and strength of her own.

It was autumn, a time when the coastal tides most days were whipped into a whirling fury that pounded the rugged coastline remorselessly. Lia closed the back door and walked along the pathway which led back towards the cliff-top or down towards the garden steps and the weathered rock platform below. She would most mornings take a walk along the cliff-top to watch the birds racing and circling on the wind's currents above her and to feel the energy of the ocean below. As she turned back towards the cliff-top, she wondered when she would be able to fly like Strawberry and Glas, whom she thought of often – every day, in fact. Lia gazed at the horizon. *How wonderful it would be if I could fly on my own,* she thought, her mind willing her to be on the horizon.

The trees dotted along the top of the cliff edge were shedding their leaves, their colours magnificent in the late morning sun; the greens were now turning to gold, red, and burnished orange. How magical life was. Ormus's words came to mind: *Always look at life with an artist's eye, and you will always find beauty.* His words were so true: many people's thoughts turned to winter when autumn showed itself, never truly appreciating autumn's beauty or the fact that winter, like all seasons, had a beauty of its own.

All things being relative to one another, Lia murmured, a warm glow of happiness rising from within. *Every level of life sharing the same cycles, each cycle being common to all levels of life.* She was beginning to see the world from a new viewpoint, one that she now welcomed with openness. Turning, she made her way back to the cottage.

The Causeway now looked bare without its cloak of summer flowers. The painted green shutters and doors were firmly closed against the cold autumn wind. Lia's morning routine was to take a walk after breakfast and then return to the cottage to study the ancient knowledge of the Holocenes, with Ormus. As she approached the gate, she stopped to look at the cottage, which was so small on the outside and yet so roomy on the inside, with its welcoming open fire and the old kettle that was always steaming on the front of the hearth. It was one big room, with everything you could possibly need for comfort, and it was home for her now. Lia would look out from the window in her tiny bedroom at the top of the stairs and watch the ocean rising and dipping like some huge being breathing slowly in and out. She loved Tintagel: the name sang to her; it was alive and magical. When she had arrived, the shutters and doors had been open to the sun and the garden amassed with flowers of every colour and shape. Lia recreated them as she closed her eyes against the salty wind, her mind chasing the memories. Many species of birds had already flown to the warmth of the southern hemisphere and no longer sat on the thatched roof calling out their song. 'But it doesn't matter,' she reminded herself. 'They will return in the spring, and the cottage is still as beautiful, even in an autumn coat.' Lia pulled her cloak about her and hurried down the path. She knew better than to keep Ormus waiting, as patience was not one of his virtues.

Chapter 20

The Globe of Living Energy

Inside the cottage, the old kettle whistled merrily on the stove. The table had been laid with scones, jam, and clotted cream. One of Lia's favourite treats was experiencing the delight of a Cornish cream tea, and, as far as she was concerned, that could be at teatime or any time of the day.

'Come along, my dear; take your cloak off and get by the fire. Tea's brewed and we can eat, after which we can get down to some work.'

Lia took her cloak off and hung it on the door hook, and then, crossing to the table, she sat on the chair nearest to the fire. Rubbing her hands together, she sat enjoying the warmth, her face aglow with health and happiness. Ormus poured the tea and they sat and ate in silence, enjoying the good food and each other's company. Later, when the table had been cleared and Ormus and Lia were sitting comfortably, Ormus began the lesson for the day.

Ormus intended to explain to Lia the meaning of 'being out'. Unlike the dream state that was entered by sleeping, 'being out' was achieved by entering a deep meditative state while still awake, and it was necessary to empty the mind of random thought in order to achieve a tranquil state prior to being out. Ormus realised that to accomplish this would not be easy for Lia. Unlike formal learning, learning to meditate would need a shift in her consciousness as well as an understanding of the method. Lia was making steady progress with his teachings, although she still had a long way to go, and he would not hurry the process. Ormus peered over Lia's shoulder as she read from the little red book in front of her. On the opened page was a diagram of the human body with a double helix spiral, which formed a central column from the crown of the head to the base of the trunk. The spiral column contained seven loops, each loop signifying part of the continual spiral of unseen energy that connected man's physical body to the influences of the Earth and the universe. Lia would find this information useful when mastering the breathing technique needed to achieve a state of meditative consciousness.

Disregarding the open book in front of Lia, Ormus began his lesson. 'Let's begin with the Globe of Living Energy ...'

Lia was disappointed; intrigued by the drawings, she had hoped Ormus would explain their meaning to her, but Ormus felt uncomfortable when explaining textbook information, formal teaching not being one of his best skills or favourite pastimes.

'You can read it later; it is self-explanatory,' Ormus said, reading her thoughts. He stood in front of her and began altering his body to a state of vaporous transparency.

Lia's thoughts of the book were forgotten as a light appeared and entered Ormus's crown. It then continued down the twelve spirals that had replaced his spine, stopping at each of the seven loops within the spiral. Lia immediately recognised Ormus's strange torso as the picture drawn on the page in front of her. She started to laugh, as each time the light merged with a loop it changed colour and was accompanied by a ding! By the time the light had reached the base of Ormus's torso, Lia was in fits of laughter. She had calmed down by the time the light had filtered out around his silhouette and finally passed through to the floor beneath him. The light now anchored him to the floor and ceiling, with his body cocooned in the centre. Lia began to clap, so enthralled by this method of teaching.

'Much more entertaining than reading a book, don't you think?' Ormus said with a twinkle in his eyes. 'The next page explains how to draw in energy by imagining your breath is entering through your crown and moving down the pathway of your spine to the base of your body. This allows the light energy to flow, and then you begin to relax, to meditate – simple.' Ormus continued without waiting for Lia to ask questions. 'The void of zero energy is created from within the Globe of Living Energy. From this energy Hafnium created everything within Universe Four. Energy never dies but continually transforms in substance, matter, and shape, which can be in the form of physical death and rebirth or metamorphosis; there are many ways that the transformation of energy can take place. The structure of energy is this: when all changes have taken place, the form will be ready to return to the *one* and be reabsorbed within the Globe of Living Energy.' Ormus wondered if he would be able to make Lia understand. He continued, 'For the soul-spirit, an Earth life is an experience within the physical body, and, as you know, when the physical body sleeps, the soul-spirit withdraws and enters the psychic plane, the first other-world, to seek guidance in the affairs of his earthly life. What you do not know is that the soul-spirit may also journey to any of the other-worlds beyond the psychic plane, if the soul is sufficiently knowledgeable to permit entry to one of these levels. Energy, light and bright, or dark and sludgy,' Ormus smiled as he began to relax. 'Life has many dimensions played out simultaneously on *all* levels and *all* continually changing.' Ormus turned to the book and pointed to the loops. 'What is important is the energy that flows within the loops, energy that gives life to all material form. Do you understand so far, Lia?'

'Yes, I think so,' replied Lia, realising that the seven energy loops were placed in most of the same positions as the hormone glands of the physical body, including the base and crown, which were the entry and exit points of the flow of energy.

'Good ... .' Ormus paused to allow Lia to absorb what she had learned before continuing in another direction. 'All souls have journeyed to the Halls of Learning, where the twelve master teachers reside. They are the teachers of the universe and convene to give advice and guidance to all who seek a way forward, as do many more. Twelve light and bright and, of course, one dark and sludgy, who is never, never allowed access above the psychic plane.' Ormus smiled, 'Aspheseuos, the thirteenth initiator of darkness, who continually attempts to slip his sinister little fingers into the other-worlds above his own world of learning. Thankfully, he fails miserably. Aspheseuos is the creator of man's desire and will compel his spirit not to resist him. The challenge, of course, is *not* that man's spirit-soul will resist the knowledge of darkness while evolving, but how long it will take him to concede, and how extensively ...' Ormus paused briefly, deep in thought about his own dabbling. Suddenly he continued forcefully, 'Therefore, I question: is there free will for man on his journey back to the source, to the *one*, the Globe of Living Energy? There are twelve master builders of the other-worlds who take charge of our present existence on Hafnium's behalf. They are responsible for bringing balance to the universe and, decide when we pass into the dreamtime for guidance. Try refusing your need for sleep, Lia. Where is the freedom in that?' He stopped, shocked by his own words. Ormus had looked through a window of bitterness, and, like a fool, he had stepped beyond.

'I'm sorry,' he said quietly. 'We will continue.' His words were spoken softly, as if to rid himself of a hidden guilt. 'The master builders, the master teachers, and the Initiators, masters of men's souls – they build our dreams and tear them down again. That is the law of Universe Four. Four seasons, four directions, and so on; the number of the grand plan is four, which transforms like the movement within a kaleidoscope, forever playing out trillions of mathematical responses to the addition, multiplication, and division of the numbers one to four and each one of us is an important part of that mathematical plan. Man has outgrown Universe Four, having split Hafnium's perfection when he split the atom. Man now vibrates to the energy of six; therefore, change must come, and man must begin his shift towards the sixth universe. Very soon, he will have opened his awareness to his journey to the sixth universe,' Ormus paused, watching Lia's face with deep concern, '... but first he will journey to another world in this universe – he will leave the Earth. Do you understand?'

Lia nodded and cleared her throat. 'I understand,' she said clearly. 'Man has come through five major changes in his evolvement, the last one having been wiped from the face of the Earth to the bottom of the ocean, and now he must prepare to move forward a sixth leap ... and, if I have understood you correctly, first beyond the fear of physical death and psychic entrapment.'

'Well done, Lia! That is a very good appraisal of the sum,' said Ormus. 'You see, my dear, everything that exists in Universe Four vibrates on a magnetic field of energy, and that field of energy rotates in never-ending cycles, although to those living a physical existence they appear to have a beginning and an end. Flowers, etc., appear to grow and die each year, which, in truth, is the illusion of the universal hologram going round through four cycles or points: east, south, west, and north. Imagine a butterfly's wings, Lia; imagine the slow circular rhythm, and you get an idea of how the hologram shifts the seasons around and around in a circular motion. Man, like a flower, only changes when new illusion is added to the hologram ... man, and then woman ... then man, woman, and child. Man is evolving rapidly, and this change is extended to all other composites that make up Universe Four. Heat, light, water, vegetation, man, and animal – they are all evolving within the hologram of planet Earth, and the master builders must keep all within Universe Four consistent. Within two hundred years, man will no longer exist upon Earth but in Universe Six, as a non-physical being' He stood up and walked towards the window, wanting to give Lia more time to absorb his words. Ormus looked out at the darkening sky, the rain lashing at the glass. Returning to his seat, he continued, 'Through the illusion of thought, we can cut into any cycle from the past or daydream the future. Through thought in the present, any condition can be changed back and forth. That is the power of mental thought; however, always remember that thoughts are real, even though they lack physical creation.'

Lia interrupted Ormus, 'So, when I dream I am flying, the real me, my spirit-soul, is flying?'

'Yes, Lia, but not your physical body, and when you have dreams of other lives, anywhere, then you have existed there. They are also the real you, the spirit-soul that is you, continually evolving in the universal hologram. You are the evolved spirit-soul of your ancestors, from the first to descend into the physical, and you retain every experience within each one of those lives. *All* is contained in the soul; however, remember, there are ten lost strands of humanity's knowledge, consumed by the darkness that is Aspheseuos. This knowledge is lost within the darkness of the psychic world and can only be regained when mankind begins his final one hundred years upon the Earth.'

Lia pondered on the awesome truth that Ormus was telling her, but her mind was also on another subject. Lia felt cheated and suddenly blurted out, 'Because I am human, will I never be able to fly?'

Ormus watched her ego body materialise. 'Flying is not a diversion for the ego, Lia. We fly for a purpose and for that reason only. Many humans have lost their lives through the ego's need of amusement and have used dangerous substances to achieve that goal. You can only fly within the binary world, which is a parallel world to this one and accessed within the dreamtime.'

Now that Lia understood, it didn't seem to matter. Matter held within gravity was the one world in which she could not fly. 'I am beginning to understand why I exist. I am but a drop in the vast ocean of universal thought, one atom of energy held within a physical form. This energy is so real and so unique that I have to exist, to be, in order that the kaleidoscope of the whole, Universe Four, remains in perfect balance.'

'That's right, my dear,' Ormus sighed with relief as Lia's ego shadow disappeared. 'Thought is reality, as is the energy of the spirit-soul real, although, in truth, mankind has forgotten this.'

'Now I understand why you say *all* is perfect always, no matter what is happening,' Lia repeated the words that Ormus had said to her many times. 'Everything that ever was . . . everything that is . . . and everything that will be . . . is already manifest and part of the collective whole.'

Ormus smiled back at her, his wise blue eyes like those of a child, innocent in the simplicity of truth. 'You have learned a great deal today, Lia. You have understood the concept of my teaching, and your energy centres are waking without conscious effort. You have made a giant step towards being out, entering the binary world in your waking state. Close your eyes, Lia.'

Lia closed her eyes to hear Ormus's voice guiding her away from the cottage and out over the cove where two dolphins played near the ledge beneath the cottage garden. The names Millie and Max entered her thoughts before she fell asleep . . .

While Lia slept, Ormus's thoughts drifted to mankind's tampering with nature and his putting the Earth more and more at risk. He smiled to himself while remembering how magnificent it had been when he first came to Earth. His thoughts drifted through the wonderful times he had experienced alongside the disappointments. Suddenly Lia cut into his thoughts; she was returning.

As Lia awoke, she remembered the dolphins and the blueness of their eyes, but nothing else. Her mind was now rested, and she wanted to continue.

'Why are the loops of coloured energy and the hormone glands placed in the same position?' she asked attentively.

'The celestial energy is fluid and flows in and out of many energy centres within the physical body, giving it life. At the same time, the hormonal secretions created within the hormone glands have the specific function of keeping genetic tissue healthy, also in order to sustain physical life. You will learn much about the combined human and celestial body, Lia. It will be necessary if you are to become a healer of the spirit-soul and the physical body. The celestial energy plays a vital unseen role in energising what would otherwise be inert form. Celestial energy that is, you might say, the nucleus, the power of your being and keeps your physical body healthy. What you sense and experience also reins in on your physical body, causing it to remain healthy or become unhealthy. But that is enough for today, Lia.'

The clock in the hall chimed five times.

'Time to put the dinner on,' Ormus said thankfully – to a non-responding Lia, who was already deeply absorbed in her book.

Chapter 21

The Dolphins: Millie and Max

As Lia sat eating breakfast with Ormus, she decided to say nothing of her early-morning swim with the dolphins, Millie and Max. She sat thinking about the incident that had come about while she was with them and the dream of the past night that had woken her so early . . .

Lia had laid awake, tossing and turning, into the early hours, her thoughts with Edward and the events that were moving her life along at breakneck speed. She had eventually fallen asleep to find him in her dreams, the meeting having been strangely polite, which had left her with a feeling of melancholy on awakening. With all the incredible events that were happening, she still found the need to dream of him. A longing to be ordinary entered her thoughts, taking the pathway of marriage and a family. It was at that point that she realised the dream had manifested her guilt at leaving with little explanation as to why.

René had many times, after the news of Ette's pregnancy, warned Lia to leave marriage as late as possible, as the bliss at the beginning was short-lived, after which followed a wonderful journey of family life that was often contentedly humdrum until an unpredictable event came to shatter the harmony. René would often tell Lia that her life would encompass many unusual experiences, which would require her taking a road of solitude for long periods at a time. Marriage and a family would often have to take a back seat, and she would need an understanding partner to survive such conditions.

Lia had risen at sunrise and wandered down to the rocky ledge. The dolphins were waiting to encourage her into the ocean where she would sense, breathe, and experience the Earth's watery womb. As she reached the ledge, Max appeared from below the waves. Lia sensed no fear as she slipped into the icy water, the stinging sensation of the salt water awakening her like no other sensation could. With Lia holding onto his fin, Max began to swim out to where Millie, his partner, was waiting. They began to dive and resurface, staying close, encouraging Lia to breathe deeply as she swam between them, holding on to their thick rubbery fins for support. Lia began to relax, paying little attention to the depth that they were diving, her troubled thoughts of Edward still with her. At first she had been conscious of the coldness of the ocean, of the seagulls and the changing sounds about her as the dolphins dived and resurfaced, the vastness of the ocean that surrounded her, pulsing in her ears as she submerged. Slowly she began to unwind, and a feeling of complete peace engulfed her, her troubled thoughts melting away as she drifted, cushioned in the strength of Gaia's watery womb. It was just a little while later that she realised Max was teaching her something new. He was urging her to take deeper breaths as he and Millie stayed down for longer. Lia began to feel just a little afraid. As they resurfaced, she opened her eyes and realised they were much further round the cliff face, and the rock ledge and steps to the cottage were no longer in sight. Millie, feeling Lia's unease, moved closer to her, the deep blue eye of the beautiful female dolphin looking deeply into Lia's own. Lia's apprehension dropped away, and she closed her eyes, taking deeper breaths as the dolphins dived again and again ...

Lia opened her eyes to the sound of the dolphins crashing through water to emerge at rest inside a large underwater cave. Max pushed Lia to the ledge, urging her to climb from the water. When Lia was sitting upon the ledge, the dolphins swam backward and then came towards her again. They were leaving her. Max and Millie disappeared beneath the darkness of the water, and Lia was left alone. A feeling of numbness spread about her body, followed by the hammering of her heart as she realised she was trapped beneath the water line where the tides never receded. Lia looked around the cave, her instinct for survival urging her to find a way out.

From the middle of the pool ripples appeared, as the water began to part and Millie surfaced. Lia stared at the bright blue eye, as the face of the dolphin changed to the face of a female with delicate features and waist-length hair of such incredible yellowness that flowed about her in the water. Lia noticed the long, scaly tail of a mermaid, as another surfaced beside her. It was Max; his torso was dark, and his hair was the colour of jet and curled about his neck and shoulders, contrasting starkly with the blueness of his eyes.

'Do not be afraid, Lia. We are known to Ormus and are of the Mer race.'

Before Max was able to explain further, Lia was gone. She had noticed an opening in the rocks and had scrabbled through. Up she climbed, not even feeling the sharp rocks that dug into the soles of her feet when she was beyond the slippery soft wetness around the pool. Some time later, she emerged above the ledge where she had entered the water with Max. Pushing through the gorse undergrowth, she scrambled onto the steps leading up to the cottage. Once inside, she ran upstairs to change out of her wet clothing and then quickly back down to where she knew Ormus was waiting for her with breakfast prepared.

'I must have been mad getting into the water with the dolphins.' Lia realised she had spoken aloud.

'Well, my dear, you have to take these things on trust. If you had waited for them to explain, you would have found the experience fascinating. Go back down after breakfast and see what happens. Ormus rose from the breakfast table and began to prepare for their study time. 'Time for your walk, isn't it, Lia?'

Lia made her way down to the ledge to find Max waiting for her. She had felt a mixture of anger and hurt that they had left her beneath the ocean – she had trusted Millie and Max implicitly. Lia caught Max's eye, and the thought came to her that she was to find her own way back to the cave. There she would meet with those who were going to help mankind survive the coming disaster.

Coming disaster! It was then that Lia realised she had turned and run from the cave, not in fear of Millie and Max, but of what they were about to tell her; instinctively, she had wanted to remain unaware of man's future plight.

Max turned and began his journey out to sea. Lia realised, with a touch of guilt, that Max was disappointed with her reaction; this was a setback and must not happen again. She had missed an opportunity, but, fortunately, the meeting with these helpful creatures would still come to pass.

Lia found her way through the gorse to the opening and scrabbled down the roughly hewn stairway to the water cave. This time she had come prepared, and her feet were well protected. The cave entrance widened out in front of her, and she went and sat by the water's edge, waiting for someone, or something, to turn up. Lia's thoughts drifted back to the Mers that had been present at her transformation, but she found it difficult to recall them as anything other than shapes of bluish energy with strange, watery voices. 'Anyway,' she said aloud, trying to boost her courage, 'they meant only good, and I must show myself to be worthy of their loyalty.' Lia wished that Ormus had come; he had treated the incident with such confidence that she wondered if, in truth, he knew the outcome already.

Lia jumped nervously as Millie surfaced and came to the edge of the pool. One heave and she was perched skilfully upon the ledge, her extraordinary beauty making Lia feel plain by comparison, 'Hello, Lia, are you ready to learn of mankind's future now?'

Lia nodded, feeling a little embarrassed.

'It is all right, Lia, there is no point in pretending it didn't happen, but you have faced your fear and have decided which action to take in order that the worst scenario is spared you.' Millie smiled reassuringly at Lia.

Max appeared in the water, his Mer figure as large as his dolphin form. Lia could tell immediately that his disappointment with her was now a thing of the past. Behind him surfaced another, who, when introduced to Lia, looked very much like a half-cat, half-fish being and whose name sounded like Catfish.

Lia wondered if she had misheard. 'I beg your pardon – your name is?'

'You heard correctly. I am as Ormus and yourself, a Holocene by ancestry and very proud of it, but we must get on. You have much to learn, and the easiest part is telling you that within the next few years mankind will finally reach his undoing, and it is vital that those who are awakening are lifted beyond the coming disaster to survive elsewhere as the collective one tribe of man. Those who are learning the esoteric teachings of self-mastery over the mind, body, and spirit are to become the new race of man . . . It is as simple as that.'

Lia wondered again if she had heard correctly, as Catfish stared back at her with unblinking eyes.

'Your part will be to help those like Ormus who are leading a race against time to prepare the lightworkers for their journey to the Mer world. They will need leaders like yourself to persuade them in their waking hours as well as in their dreams. Remember your fear in this cave today. Those that survive will have to live beneath the oceans in the world of the Mers for many years until the Earth's surface is again habitable.

Lia stood up, her mind in shock. *Surely I'm dreaming and this is not going to happen!*

'I'm afraid so,' said Catfish, his large green eyes still staring at her without blinking, 'Man has sown his seeds, and they will soon be ready to harvest. In a while, you will be taken to the underworld to see for yourself and to experience the travelling procedures, which most humans will find distressing. No parting of the waters for man of the twenty-first century; no, indeed, he is going to have to trust the idea of drowning.'

Lia thought of her anxious journey with Millie and Max and the enormous effort that would be needed to get people to walk into the ocean and submerge themselves freely in subterranean waters without breathing equipment, even though the journey would begin in the dreamtime. Man had long believed that death by a fall or drowning in a dream meant never awakening from one's sleep.

Ormus appeared beside Lia and put his arm around her

shoulders, 'Lia, you have done extremely well,' he said proudly. 'I had my doubts whether you would re-enter the cave, but you have shown you have what it takes to get on with the challenge in hand. Well done. Now it is time for your studies; you have learned enough of the Mers and mankind's future for today.' Ormus placed his hand upon her forehead, and, moments later, she was sitting in the cottage at the table, with her book opened in front of her, ready for the day's work to begin.

Chapter 22

Raphiel

Having finished the day's lesson, Ormus and Lia sat by the fire relaxing, while the evening meal gave forth an appetising aroma from the kitchen. Lia sat reading her little red book, while Ormus sat quietly entering a meditative state from where he could access the binary world of being out. Ormus wanted to speak to his old friend Raphiel and decided to invite Lia to join him.

The words on the open page became a blur as Lia eased herself from the physical by visualising Catfish's face. First his large green eyes appeared and then his turned-down ears, which made his chinless face resemble a cute pixie. Lia had tried many times to merge into a meditative state but without success. It was not until her fear of the unknown had diminished, and she realised how uncomplicated life could be, that her thoughts were transformed and the universe opened out to her.

Lia's energy centres began to open, as the healing light filtered through the crown of her head and down her spine. Catfish's face began to disappear as Lia fell into a whirlpool of hypnotic green eyes and beyond, spinning and floating as she slipped further into the meditative state that would allow her to communicate with the other-worlds. The connection to her physical body disappeared, as the light surrounding her began to ebb and flow, streaming out into the universe about her. She began to see and hear the inhabitants of the other-worlds without the assistance of her mentor, Ormus.

Raphiel entered the room and greeted Ormus. *Good day to you, friend.*

Ormus returned his greeting.

Hello, Lia, many blessings to you. Raphiel bowed ceremoniously in her direction.

Thank you, Raphiel; it's good to see you again. Lia felt euphoric. She was with them independent of Ormus. The light of the healing globe surrounding her begin to fade. Immediately she returned her concentration to the light, and it grew strong again.

Ormus advised her not to be too adventurous on her first time out and to observe more than participate, in order to retain her concentration upon the light. *The practise required is similar to driving a car; there needs to be a very dedicated kind of relaxed concentration that, when mastered, becomes as natural as breathing.* Ormus turned his attention back to Raphiel to announce that Lia was ready to face her next challenge. In the morning they would travel to the Château Dubar to spend Christmas with Lia's family. After that they would be returning to London, where the next challenge would take place.

Raphiel did not comment. He sensed the weariness in Ormus's words and tried not to let this be communicated to him.

You have nothing to say, Raphiel?

No, my friend; I am happy to go along with your decision for Lia, and for all of us. Edward and I will join you for Christmas and we can continue our conversation then.

Ormus nodded in agreement, pleased that Raphiel had accepted his decision.

Lia drifted peacefully while listening to the conversation going back and forth between them, not minding in the least the decisions being made for her. She observed her thoughts floating in the orb surrounding her, the conversation between Ormus and Raphiel at times penetrating her space but not so that they made any lasting impression upon her. Suddenly, she became aware of Raphiel's departure; he was saying goodbye to her. Lia acknowledged his farewell and continued to drift in the stillness until she heard Ormus calling her back to the physical.

As soon as Lia was safely back, Ormus left the cottage to take a walk before dinner. Lia sensed that he was troubled about something but did not venture to ask what. With a cup of hot tea to hand, she sat by the fire to read, but before the tea was cooled she was fast asleep.

Raphiel entered Lia's dream as she stepped onto the silver and blue chequerboard spinning slowly in the universe. Hafnium's knight was winning the first moves of the game because of the determination of those who wanted him to succeed, the positive thoughts keeping the knight ahead in the challenge for mankind's continued existence. Above the universal chequerboard, the colours of the twelve star tribes ebbed and flowed unceasingly, while the masters of the other-worlds looked on with compassion at the lost souls bound within the psychic plane. The masters waited in hope, praying that compassion would win the day and they would be released from their unending burdens.

Raphiel wanted to speak to Lia about his concern for Ormus. *I must speak now,* he thought. *It is the only time I might find her without Ormus by her side.* Raphiel waited while the images of the universe drifted through Lia's dreamtime, waiting until her sleep became dreamless again.

Raphiel entered Lia's dreamtime to tell her of his concerns. He believed Ormus was having troubled doubts about his freedom of choice, of self-will within Universe Four. Raphiel knew his old friend well. Ormus would find it hard to exist in the physical world without the belief that he *chose* for himself. For Ormus there could be no compromise to the purpose for his Earthly existence. Ormus believed he had returned to Earth to redeem himself. If Hafnium had forgiven him, why was he so racked by guilt? Choice was so much a part of life as he saw it, and Raphiel knew that Ormus questioned why he alone was troubled by these doubts. It was becoming a problem and an enigma for Ormus. Raphiel knew only Ormus could forgive himself.

As Lia listened to Raphiel, she began to hear sounds all about her that had no recognisable meaning other than as random musical notes. The sounds became louder, making it difficult to hear what Raphiel was saying. Ormus appeared in front of her, warning her to listen to his words carefully.

'Read the clocks and remember the nature of the seasons. The game, the challenge, is to free space, in order to stop the light of the universe being absorbed unto darkness. Mankind must seek stability. He must break free of the delusion that he can control nature. He must return to the old beliefs, in which he will find a way forward that is beneficial to all. Nature demonstrates the way in which all things can survive together by allowing free space. There must be harmony, Lia. It is when the free space is taken, blocked, or controlled that it stagnates, as it does now.

Lia felt the urgency in his voice.

'The seasons are not transforming and being reborn; they are becoming compounded into one. Like man, they are holding onto the past and dragging it forward into the present, leaving no free space! The opposite to *live* is *evil*, the opposing force that denies life and happiness, and where there is no longer free space, there cannot be fresh creation.'

In front of Lia appeared a mountainside with three circles hewn into its vertical rise. When Lia looked closer she saw that the circles were sundials, each with the numerals one to four at every ninety-degree turn. Light moved slowly across the three dials, one turning clockwise and representing Earth time in the present, the next anticlockwise and representing future events, while the last one remained static, representing the past: each one was a consequential reflection of the other.

Lia listened carefully to the voices in her head, not wanting to mistake what they were saying. Ormus had vanished, and she felt alone and afraid, wishing it was his voice she could hear. *And where has Raphiel gone? Nothing remains unchanged here for long,* she thought. *One moment secure, the next vulnerable – each moment a conflicting reflection of the one before.*

Stop! The word exploded inside her mind, her instinct for survival warning her from within. She was standing at the edge of a ravine, below which there was nothing but a void. The mountain face had split apart and the three dials were cracked and misshapen. In front of her, a rickety bridge swung precariously against a howling wind that showered sleet across the deep divide. Two dials remained upon the side where Lia stood, while the third was on the far side. To cross would be dangerous, and who knew what was on the other side? The page of an open book appeared in front of Lia; it contained the numbers one to nine and the symbols of the star tribe. The symbols and numbers were mounted upon a zodiac wheel that was waiting to be pressed. Lia heard a sequence of numbers being repeated in her mind, but each time she tried to press the correct numbers she could not remember them. Again and again she touched the wheel, but nothing changed. It all seemed hopeless, and she gave up. As the sleet cascaded down upon her, Lia remembered the Mer angels in the cave and the rhyme that they had taught her. With renewed hope, she began to recite the words, and they appeared by her side.

'Lia, do not waste your resources – think. To stay in the past is difficult and pointless, and yet humanity spends most of the time living with the memories of the past to the expense of the future, which stagnates while they linger. Do you want to take the hazardous journey back to the past, reliving all your mistakes and making them part of your present and future, always dragging the past forward with you? Or do you want to go forward into the future unhindered?'

'Forward of course,' Lia responded brightly, relieved that this journey was one she was not meant to take.

'Then leave the past behind you. Do not try to connect with it. Believe in what you are today, not what you were yesterday. What did Ormus tell you?'

Lia repeated his words. 'Read the dials and remember the seasons. Go forward unhindered' Two of the dials were once again in front of her, and she knew what she must do. 'I do not want to loiter in the winter of the past,' she said loudly as if adding force to her decision. 'I choose to go forward to my favourite time of year, spring.' The book appeared in front of her again, and this time she heard the voice clearly. Lia sprung forward and pressed the sequence that would take her into the future. The light upon the two dials moved forward one quarter, and immediately winter on the bridge transformed to spring. The bridge disappeared, and the mountain became one again. The sounds of spring could be heard. Life was continuing again.

Lia crossed into the time of spring, and when she arrived on the other side, she entered a landscape very much like that of Earth from space. Lia held her hands aloft and the surge of Holocene power flowed into the world before her, turning the Earth's mountainous regions to gold. She saw her father, a man with deep financial worries, sitting in his study, trying to make good his business accounts. Lia realised she had a choice to make. Drawing the golden energy back towards her, she watched the scene transform as her father realised that he had enough money to clear his debt to the bank. For a moment Lia's happiness was complete, but the Mer angels appeared again.

'Now look further into the future, and see how your powers cannot change destiny.'

When she looked again, although her family were unhindered by debt, their home in France, Château Dubar, had been razed to the ground by a fire that had engulfed the surrounding region.

'You see, Lia, you can only use your powers to help the future if that is how destiny will allow mankind to free space for further creation.'

Lia now understood that freeing space was to balance creation, and it was in the hands of destiny. Lia resignedly undid her desire for stagnation. Life for her father and his family would – must – continue upon destiny's pathway.

The Mer angels continued, 'Life is a game in which you must learn to be a champion player of the present in order to become part of the future. We bid you farewell, Lia. Good luck!'

Raphiel had continued with his concerns for his dear friend, Ormus, without realising that Lia had been away. 'Well, my dear, we will have to wait and see what the outcome will be; it's no good fretting about it. We need to get on with the future.'

Lia replied distractedly, 'Most definitely, Raphiel.'

Raphiel, unaware of Lia's experience with the past, present, and future, wondered if she had been really listening to his concerns. 'You must return to a dreamless sleep now, Lia. But before you do, remember what Ormus taught you.' Raphiel disappeared from her dream.

Lia thought of Ormus's teachings and his face appeared just long enough for her to visualise the cloak of light that would keep her from the dreamtime. Before she had time to say thank you, Ormus had vanished. Lia gathered the cloak of light about her and drifted into a restful sleep.

Chapter 23

Château Dubar

On the psychic plane, the hologram of consequences was breaking up the seasons and melding them into one another.

Strange weather patterns had been gradually changing the seasons upon Earth for years. The New Year was just days away, and yet the weather was unusually warm, so much so that the traditional log fires at Château Dubar remained unlit during the Christmas season.

Ette was disappointed when the weather did not turn cold enough for snow. She had decided to marry, Andre, her fiancé, and dreamed of a snow-laden winter wedding during the family gathering at Christmas. The wedding had been arranged for the morning of the twenty-sixth of December, when a small gathering of guests assembled at Château Dubar. René's friends, the astronomers, Edward's family and local people, and friends and neighbours of the Dubar family all came to celebrate the civil ceremony. The day went splendidly, and, apart from the disappointment for the unlit log fires and lack of snow, Ette's day was just as she had imagined it to be, including her twin sister, Lia, being her bridesmaid.

As the evening began to draw in, the wedding party drifted into the garden that in winter's early darkness had become strangely temperate, almost as warm as a summer's evening in June. René and Ormus did not show their concern, but when most of the guests had retired to bed, René and his friends, the astronomers, made their way to the glass-domed building that housed a large telescope and other instruments for plotting the movement of the universe. The twelve astronomers sat round the large, circular table beneath the giant dome, their places mapped out by the thirty-degree sections of the twelve astrological signs of the zodiac. Ormus took up his place at (120–150 degrees) Leo, whilst René placed himself at (270–300 degrees) Capricorn. Gradually the seats were taken, until all were occupied.

'It is time for your life's work to be taken from here, René.' Ormus had risen and was addressing the gathering. 'Aspheseuos's force is gathering, and soon this whole region of France will be devoured in his fire.'

The others agreed with him. They had been observing the planetary signs and realised that disaster was imminent for the region of France in which Château Dubar was situated.

Ormus continued, 'Within the next few days, I will return to London with Lia and Edward. René, when we have gone you must gather all that is meant to survive this time of fire and transport it to London. Once it is there, Raphiel will see it safely to Tintagel and deposit it beneath the causeway, where it will remain safe for the future.

The astronomers rose from the table and climbed the stairs to the dome; there, upon a giant revolving chair that seated twelve, they sat watching the planetary gathering that Aspheseuos had been planning for months. René felt his stomach twist as the information before him revealed with certainty that many children, adults, and the wildlife of the region were to perish in the flash of searing heat that was to come. In the last few days, he had watched the migration of birds and animals that were not domestically tethered to mankind. René felt Ormus's unseen hand upon his shoulder, which he had placed there for strength. René turned to look at him and felt comforted by his reassuring smile.

'It will be over so quickly they will not realise death has taken them, and by the time they do, the lightworkers will be there to guide them to the psychic plane and further if they are ready . . .'

The next morning at breakfast, Ette felt somewhat deflated. Her golden day was over and her father's friends had departed, 'What a shame they had to leave so urgently; they are such exciting company,' said Ette to her father while feeling a little bored.

That morning when Lia entered the breakfast room, her eyes sparkled with pleasure. She had been up early and, having said her goodbyes to her father's friends, had taken a walk with Edward. For her the day had begun with promise, and Ette's unsmiling welcome was a blot on her happiness. 'What is it, Ette? Why are you so down? You should be on top of the world! You have a wonderful new husband and a beautiful child. What else could you possibly need at this moment?'

'I just wish father's friends had stayed a while longer, that's all. I love our conversations with them, especially when they speak of the planets surrounding Earth. It's as if you travel on their words to the places that they speak of.' Ette spoke dramatically, while her face remained unsmiling.

'Well, maybe so,' said Lia, 'but cheer up. Ormus and I leave for London tomorrow with Edward, so you had better make the most of today. Which, may I add is only going to give you a couple of days to sort yourself out before you, your new family, and father join us in London for the New Year. Really, Ette, don't be such a down-in-the-mouth,' Lia chided.

With the mention of the New Year's celebrations, Ette bounced back. 'Come on,' she said brightly, 'let's take the baby out for a walk.' Ette was still not acknowledging motherhood with a name for her child. 'Come on, I'll race you to the nursery.'

Both girls rushed from the room, pushing each other aside to reach the staircase first. René remained seated at the breakfast table, watching them fool around together, and it was then he decided that both Ette and her family would leave Château Dubar with Lia and Ormus. There was too much at risk, and even he was not sure how much time was left. Better to be safe. Besides, Ette would only hamper the exodus of his manuscripts and other important documents, as she was far too astute not to realise something was amiss. René made a note to order a large bouquet of flowers for his wife's grave. The realisation that he and the girls would never return to Château Dubar meant that they must take the flowers that afternoon. His daughters would be able to say farewell to their mother without them knowing the truth.

René walked to the domed conservatory hidden deep within the grounds of Château Dubar, and, on entering, he stood looking up at the spiralling staircase mounted on the inside wall. He saw the stairs begin to turn, until they were spiralling into a whirlwind of raging heat, debris, and choking acrid smoke. In the middle of this inferno, he saw Château Dubar explode and the area disappear into a crater of nothingness … Aspheseuos would conduct his symphony: the atomic plant near the coastline would implode, the intense heat beneath its structure now barely contained; this gave reason to the uncanny weather and the migration of the wildlife from the region. The unusual weather gave a warning of the coming devastation that mankind would not heed. As the radioactive cloud plumed in the sky, a miracle, although small, happened: a strong northerly wind began to rage, sweeping the cloud of poison out over the sea and away from the provinces further inland and, fortunately, away from the western tip of England. Cornwall would be safe for now. Mankind was nearing the brink and would soon tip the balance beyond where it could return to normality. 'Thank God,' René uttered, relieved that the looming devastation would be benevolent. Ormus had been right; his manuscripts would be safe in Cornwall.

Chapter 24

Hotel Renoir: The Twelve Food Merchants

Ormus's thoughts were with his home, Holocene, and being among the wise ones again. What did he have to lose if he failed this time? Ormus knew that, if he failed, he would not return to Holocene and thereafter would have to begin again at the foundation of existence, which was an option he most certainly did not desire. 'I am a Holocene from the ninth universe, which is where I belong and want to return … I must not fail.' He said the words slowly, knowing it to be the truth.

Ormus loved the Earth and the memories he held of its radiance at the start, when the prospects of helping mankind to evolve had seemed so easy a task. The possibilities had been immense then. Now all he could hope for was that the plans being made would save the Earth and mankind from extinction, after which he would return home to Holocene. With this one thought in mind, Ormus continued his journey towards London and the Hotel Renoir, where the next challenge would take place …

Lia sat looking out at the mass of cars surrounding her as Ormus drove slowly in the congested traffic. With the journey through the Channel Tunnel behind them, she had begun to relax and a sense of relief drifted over her. Lia had never liked journeying through the man-made tunnel beneath the sea that divided the French and English coasts.

Ormus had noticed the change in her body language as soon as they re-emerged into the pale winters light onto English soil. Lia now appeared more settled, and he decided that it was as good a time as any to continue their conversation, which had ceased as they entered the tunnel in France.

Ormus began, 'Returning to our conversation, Lia. As the Earth's hologram slows down, time speeds up and mankind remains within the dark forces of his nature for longer, and his abominations become more malevolent and threatening. Wars continue for longer and become more destructive, as mankind's awareness of the difference between good and evil becomes less obvious. This situation can only end when this way of living changes and mankind ceases in his excesses, especially the unnecessary restrictive practices that are forced upon those who are weaker.' Ormus stopped to ponder on the excessive number of foods that were manufactured by tampering with nature's harvests. Intense animal farming caused pain and suffering to the animal kingdom, the results of which were destroying the health of mankind. He continued, 'Mankind has been unknowingly destroying his physical body for years with too much sugar and processed food, which is consumed as a substitute for love, which brings me to your next challenge. Tomorrow, there is to be a meeting between your father's associates, the wine merchants, and the world's twelve most powerful food merchants, men who are responsible for enhancing their products with addictive compounds in order to increase their wealth. The meeting is scheduled to take place at the Hotel Renoir, and you are to take your father's place alongside the wine merchants. When your father arrives in the morning, we will sit awhile and speak of the people you are to meet.'

Lia had, in her early teens, learned to deal skilfully with unwelcome tradesmen at the Hotel Dubar, when, in her father's absence, she had been left to deal with them. Lia listened to Ormus's announcement without concern; her father's friends she knew well, and tomorrow would be soon enough to learn more about the food merchants. Lia pushed the thought of them from her mind.

Once free of the multiple lanes of traffic, they made their way towards London, with Edward's car in front and Ette's behind. Lia continued to listen to Ormus until; finally, she could concentrate no longer and fell asleep.

On the first evening home, Edward was able to spend time alone with Lia, while Ormus went out on business and Edward's father, Ralph, entertained Ette and her family. It had been a wonderful evening for them, and, although it was chilly, they had walked along the river to dine at one of Edward's favourite restaurants. Lia was in love and at that moment longed to abandon the journey that had started with Ormus's appearance – but she knew there was no going back. Edward, on the other hand, could see nothing in their way and intended to ask Lia to marry him at the New Year celebrations.

Early the following morning, Ormus waited with Lia for Raphiel and René to arrive with their associates, the astronomers, who, like René, were notable wine merchants. The meeting with the twelve food merchants was to take place at ten o'clock, which allowed ample time to discuss the situation with Ormus and Lia, who was to represent her father in the dispute over the proposed bid for most of the French wine market.

Breakfast was served in Ormus's suite, after which the waiter withdrew, leaving Ormus's guests to enjoy their breakfast. Lia was not hungry and was beginning to feel nervous at the thought of meeting the twelve food merchants, a group of black-suited influential businessmen whom she had seen arriving earlier. Although she would be in the company of the wine merchants, it did not ease her unexpected nervousness. Having learned how influential they were, she was now convinced that they would take little notice of her words while consuming another slice of the world's food market – all to satisfy their insatiable appetite for world dominance.

The wine merchants' cause was a worthy one: they wanted to continue trading freely, without restraint, in the world markets, and Lia was expected to speak for them. *But where was she to find the words?* Before breakfast, Ormus had gone on about balancing the universal hologram with not a word of help for her speech.

'You are not going to give a prepared speech, Lia' Ormus said, reading her thoughts. 'You are going to talk to these people and try to make them understand the folly of their ways.' He studied her pale face thoughtfully, 'When you face them, the words will come; believe me, they will come. I have every faith in you, Lia. Now, have some tea; it will make you feel better.'

Lia took the cup held out to her and took a sip. It was the nectar from the challenger's cup, and she felt her strength renew. 'I'll get ready now; I must be downstairs in a while,' she said, getting up to leave the room.

'Yes, yes, my dear, go and prepare yourself,' Ormus replied distractedly from the comfortable armchair where he sat with a freshly ordered breakfast balanced on his lap and the morning paper spread out on the small table beside him.

The wine merchants had left Ormus's suite almost an hour earlier, and it was time for Lia to join them. He chuckled genially at what he knew would come to pass and said, 'The situation looks favourable for you, Lia.' *Destiny*, he thought, d*o you really give us a choice?*

Lia descended the oval staircase in the Hotel Renoir knowing that the wine merchants were now trying to ward off a takeover bid by the food merchants, the latter having forced shares to tumble, after which they speedily bought them up. They now owned a formidable share of the wine market. The wine merchants had asked Lia to delay her appearance for an hour, and, as she reached the bottom of the stairway, she felt none of the anxiety she had been suffering during that time, which allowed her to think that perhaps now all was going well for the wine merchants. Lia had been a guest at many of her father's business meetings, but this was the first time as his representative and she was pleased that he had trusted her.

The Hotel Renoir had always been her favourite place to stay in London, and the people employed there were always so friendly and willing to help. She felt confident, on home ground, as she went through her father's account of the men she was about to meet.

The twelve food merchants who now waited for Lia to appear on behalf of her father were the most powerful men in the world. Unobserved by social structures globally, they were able to control all events that took place in the food markets, the health and leisure industries, and many more; internationally, their control of the world's monetary policies could send the markets crashing with one strike. As they waited for the one remaining wine merchant's seat to be occupied, they talked with ease in their comfortable surroundings, assuming that their conditions to devour the wine market would eventually be met. The wine industry had managed to remain elite, and the global market was shared between the world's vineyards, *shared* being a word of blasphemy to the food merchants. Good wine had always been a commodity that was hard to falsify, which had helped it to remain one of the last free markets, and today's meeting would decide whether it would remain so.

Feeling composed, Lia stepped into her role. She knew her words would not be of her choosing and that her message would come from a far higher source of life. Lia reached the last step and turned towards the waiter who was approaching her.

'Madame, you are expected in the drawing room. Would you please follow me?'

Without looking up at the waiter, Lia followed him, her composure having dissolved with his words. She was alone and without preparation, and her heartbeat had gathered momentum. Lia remembered the pearl ring that Ormus had given her, now pressed hard in her clenched hand. A voice cut into her thoughts and, amidst the pounding of her heart, she heard Ormus's voice. His voice flowed quietly through her mind, assuring her that all she needed to do was trust in order to complete the challenge, and to remember that *all* would be supporting her throughout the task in hand. Ormus's voice faded, and Lia was listening to the waiter again.

'This way, Madame,' the waiter repeated his request.

Lia took a few deep breaths to slow her racing heart as she followed behind the waiter. They walked across the rich, soft carpet towards the doors that would bring her face to face with her challengers. The waiter opened the double doors wide, and Lia crossed the threshold into the room. This time, unlike her previous visits, her gaze took in little of the elegant drapes, the antique furniture, and the soft lighting that fell upon the sumptuous décor. Before today, she had found it a pleasure to wander through the Renoir or to dine in the magnificent restaurant, where afternoon tea or dinner was always presented with such joie de vivre. Today, however, these pleasures were out of sight and she dismissed the thought from her mind.

Lia held out a hand in greeting to the first of the twelve food merchants standing before her. The waiter had left as she entered the room, his withdrawal removing the comforting barrier between her and those that challenged her. Boldly Lia faced the men in suits of black, the likeness making their appearance seem superior and overwhelming. Taking one last deep breath, she greeted each one amiably as the introductions began along the row of merchants standing in a half circle to her left, while the eleven wine merchants stood in a half circle to her right, the twelfth, her father, René, being absent. As the introductions continued down the line, she felt her nervousness begin to lift and a feeling of certainty enter her mind.

With the introductions completed, the waiter reappeared and placed a chair of pink brocade behind Lia, inviting her to sit down. The waiter positioned a small table beside her, upon which he placed a delicate china cup and saucer and a small dish filled with cocoa beans covered in fine, dark chocolate.

'Coffee, Madame?' asked the waiter.

'Thank you,' replied Lia.

The waiter poured the coffee and left.

Lia felt the hushed merchants' eagerness for debate, as twelve pairs of eyes remained focused on her every move; it was not a pleasant feeling. Their gaze, although not hostile, most certainly showed impatience, as they waited for her to speak. The food merchants wanted to seize the world's wine industry, their goal to be the primary vendor of all worldly commodities, including the world's cocoa and coffee markets, which they now virtually owned.

The wine merchants of France, having made their case, had informed the food merchants that their answer was no, and they would never cease to resist their control. Now the food merchants waited to hear from the daughter of René Dubar, daring to hope that they might yet gain Château Dubar because of René's financially stretched situation. They had noted his absence with surprise and amusement. If they gained Château Dubar, one of largest vineyards in France, it would give them a sound foothold towards their eventual goal.

Lia started to speak, allowing her thoughts to flow. 'Thank you for inviting me here today, gentlemen. I am not certain how we can help one another, as I feel sure *our* vision of the world's future,' Lia motioned towards the eleven wine merchants, 'is not in step with yours. However, if there is any way in which my father and his associates can be of help to the world and its inhabitants by keeping open the free trading markets, then they will do their utmost to help, as I hope you will. My father's role is that of spokesman for the wine merchants, and they have given you their answer, which is no, as I do on my father's behalf, and there is nothing I can say to alter their decision.' Lia paused, as immediately there was a refusal to accept her answer.

The master of the food merchants countered, 'But if the takeover bid was to go ahead, we would be able to improve our productiveness. And with the cooperation of the wine industry, who, in turn, would improve their wealth, we would be helping the world population by offering even more low-cost products, oil, and other merchandise – at affordable prices, of course!' The master merchant smiled confidently, as along the half circle there was agreement from the eleven men who now sat muttering among themselves.

Lia listened to the grumbling businessmen, who were obsessed with a need to do better, to become stronger, and to rule the world. She sat quietly until they had ceased complaining and then said, 'May I say, gentlemen, that perhaps you are looking at this from the wrong angle. Try reversing the situation somewhat. Where human food consumption is concerned, if you were to cease producing food products containing addictively high levels of glutamate and flavour enhancers, then immediately the world population's desire for those products would decrease, and they would eat less – and the Earth would not be stretched to produce so much. It is with the same regard that the wine merchants wish to produce good wine – not volumes of cheap, chemically laden alcohol.'

There was a roar of disapproval from the food merchants, 'What nonsense!' they screamed. 'We want more production, not less. We want to find ways that will produce more from the Earth. Not less!' An angry silence settled over the group of businessmen, and their eyes bored angry, resentful holes in Lia's beleaguered form. The food merchants were becoming restless and nervous at this woman's approach to the execution of their business.

Although not evident to those watching, Lia swallowed somewhat nervously before continuing, 'Gentlemen, you stand at the edge of a precipice, and yet you want to move forward in the same futile direction, which is endangering every species upon Earth. If you continue along this pathway, the Earth will cease to support mankind. You must listen, or we are lost forever.' Lia turned her gaze upon the most powerful of the men, the master of the merchants, whose global power controlled so much of human life. Speaking to him directly, she said, 'Tell me, sir, who or what does your empire stand upon? What is the most powerful ingredient of your success?'

The master of the merchants, whose primary wealth had amassed from mankind's love of chocolate confectionery, thrust himself to the front of his chair. His energy field was strong and powerfully charged by his successes; he was a man who felt he could not lose and who would never look at failure as a possibility. To himself, *he* was the almighty power.

His voice thrust through the quietness. 'My empire is built on my ability to succeed, my ability to mould a workforce into perfection – and those that cannot think and do as I and my empire commands, they have no place within it.' He continued, his voice becoming louder, 'I use my genius to utilise the Earth's resources to the optimum efficiency of production. That is what my empire is built on – MY INGENUITY!' the master roared.

The food merchants gave the master merchant a roar of approval.

'We are the world's master merchants!' he roared back. 'The ultimate force, who intend to conquer the Earth and make it an Eden to live in; more food, more buildings, more roads, and more cities. We will build our empire bigger and more magnificent than you could ever dream of, Mademoiselle Dubar.'

'Yes! Yes!' his associates bellowed.

'And what of mankind, of all living things upon the Earth – have you taken their thoughts and feelings into account in your plan?' Lia asked.

There was a stony silence as they glared at her. How could this young slip of a girl dare to tell them how they should behave! After all, humans beneath *their* level of genius had no right to a say in such things; they were worker humans without opinions and just another commodity, like all other resources on Earth, and just as expendable.

'What rubbish you talk!' one said aggressively.

'Hear, hear!' said another.

A voice cut in, a voice as cold as steel; it was Lia's. 'I give you your answer, sirs. It is not your money. It is not your food empire, or even your controlled workforce that gives you your power. It is this ...' Lia reached across the table to the small dish of coca beans that the waiter had placed with the coffee. Taking one, she held it aloft for all see, '... this tiny seed of nature has built your empire, master merchant; this tiny seed for which you have so little regard.' Lia's voice had become soft and low as she drove her point home, 'And what does this little bean rely on for its life, for its nourishment?' Lia paused again, making sure they understood her. 'Why, the energy of sunlight, rain, and the airstreams upon the Earth, of course; these necessary elements provide natures freedom to proliferate, which you are continually disrupting as you drive relentlessly on in your desire for wealth and power.' Lia looked into the eyes of each of the twelve food merchants, finally coming back to the master merchant to whom she had posed the question, and, as their eyes met, she placed the tiny bean in her mouth. The sound of the little bean being broken into many pieces drove the meaning home.

The Earth's energy fields were beginning to shatter and would eventually manifest catastrophe for the planet's inhabitants. Now uncertainty replaced the arrogance in the food merchant's eyes, for never had any lesson been put across to them with such meaning; they had realised much in a very short time: Hafnium had given them his warning through Lia. They must release their control on the Earth or take the consequences.

Lia stood up, 'Gentlemen, the authority that sustains the Earth cautions you to alter your way of thinking and the means by which you generate your products. The warning signs are there for all to see in the rapidly changing patterns of nature and the movement of wildlife.' Lia stood up as the waiter returned to her side, and, moving the chair away, he invited her to follow him. Nothing more was said and no goodbyes were offered as she turned and left the room.

As Lia turned to follow the waiter, she realised that he looked familiar, and, as they reached the doors, he turned slightly and smiled – it was Glas.

'Well done,' he said excitedly. 'Well done!'

Lia could hardly contain her relief as she walked towards the staircase. Her heart felt so much lighter now that her ordeal with the food merchants was over. Reaching the stairs, she ran up them, taking two steps at a time, wanting to tell Ormus all about her adventure. As she knocked on the door of Ormus's suite, a woman dressed in black with a neat white apron tied about her waist opened the door. She stood beside Ormus, holding out a tray on which stood four glasses of champagne; it was Strawberry. Glas appeared in the doorway behind Lia, and together the four companions raised their glasses in celebration of Lia's first success as a member of her father's circle of associates, the wine merchants and astronomers.

'We raise our glasses to your success,' Ormus said, his blue eyes deep and serious. 'We toast success today. However, I speak with absolute sincerity when I say that the change which is coming needs far more than today's success will bring to mankind. Lia, my dear, you have helped to plant a small seed today that will grow and bear fruit with some of the merchants, those who are not happy with their life and the world around them. They, in turn, will also plant seeds and the crop of change will bear fruit. Mankind will harvest a new set of values with which to nurture the Earth.' Ormus raised his glass and gave a toast, 'To the precious gift of life upon Earth.'

Lia was happy to delay her studies in Cornwall or her learning with creatures from the other-worlds, while she was able to spend the New Year celebrations in London with her family and friends, and especially Edward. The knowledge she was acquiring was presenting her with a new role in life, one that would allow her to live out her human destiny upon Earth and be part of the challenge afforded to her own kind, the Holocenes. Lia's life had changed in ways that not many could ever hope to experience, except perhaps the caterpillar, whose transformation into a butterfly is also uniquely sublime.

Edward, Lia, and Ette roamed the city by day, visiting the beautifully decorated stores filled with gifts and exotic food, some of which the girls had never seen before or had any desire to sample. By night, they marvelled at the brightly lit capital and the boats upon the river Thames, which snaked its way through the heart of the city; even man's destructive genius could not dampen its beauty.

On New Year's Eve, Lia watched from the hotel window as the boats passed by on the river. The human race had not completely forgotten the wise ones' hopes for them that mankind could be united in a bond of love for one another, if only for a short time. 'Let there always be a time of giving in the human heart,' Lia whispered. 'That's my wish for the new year.' Lia listened to Big Ben strike the old year out, and then an enormous wave of sound erupted all around, as the people cheered throughout the city. Everyone around her was wishing each other a happy new year. *What will it bring?* Lia wondered as she kissed Edward and wished him a very happy new year.

Edward celebrated the New Year with Lia, but at Ormus's request, he did not ask Lia to marry him as planned, and the engagement ring he had bought for her remained in his jacket pocket. They dined and danced with their friends and family, observing mankind's season of good will. For Lia and Edward, life had taken on a magical presence where only a future of happy-ever-after could exist.

Chapter 25

Lia Dreams of Emily

New Year's Day: it was the beginning of a year that would remain in mankind's memory forever.

That morning, Ormus had invited René and his family for a late breakfast in his suite at the Hotel Renoir. They sat chatting about the delights of the past evening, while the day's news bulletins flashed across a television screen in the corner of the room. The pictures on the screen showed the usual global revelry that mankind indulges in at that time of year, when suddenly the mood changed, as reports of a major disaster began to filter through. The details were unclear, but it was being reported that a region of France, near to the coast and bordering Spain, had disappeared beneath an enormous blast that had devastated the surrounding towns and countryside for miles thereabouts. René showed no sign of emotion as the girls listened to the report without realising where the devastation was. The nuclear energy plant near to the Château Dubar had finally vaporised, revealing the cause of the wildlife's flight.

René had been extremely angry with Ette the day before her return to England. On returning from a walk, the girls had found flowers he had placed in the hallway for their mother's grave. After lunch, René had asked them to accompany him to their mother's grave in remembrance of the wife he had loved so dearly. Ette had decided she needed the afternoon to pack for their trip to London and wanted to stay behind. René, who would normally conceal any frustration beneath a calm and even manner, had become furious, so much so that Ette had changed her mind immediately.

Now, as the girls realised where the disaster was taking place, they understood his reason for the visit. Ette and Lia looked at their father's pale, tense features and knew he had been giving them the opportunity to say a permanent farewell to their mother's remains.

René waited for one of them to speak, but they remained silent.

Lia, although numbed by the reality of the situation, could think of nothing but her father's work, his manuscripts.

Ette began to cry, and, turning to her father, she flung her arms around his rigid form. René softened at the warmth of her tenderness. His daughters, his only family, were alive, and that's all that mattered right now. Ette felt so ashamed now that she understood why her father had been so angry with her. She wanted his forgiveness as when, as a child, she had been stubborn and later realised she was wrong. Lia came and held them both; all three comforted by the nearness of each other.

'But what of your life's work, Father?' Lia said. 'Your manuscripts, they have been destroyed, and what of our friends, our neighbours,' she added, 'are they . . . ?' Her voice faded away.

René answered soberly. 'The manuscripts are safe, and our friends and neighbours were warned of what could happen and heeded the warning. They have left the area, but throughout the region there will be many missing.'

News of the disaster continued with little clarity, as military troops sealed the region off to civilians and reporters. The news moved to another topic, but they remained watching in the hope that it would return to the disaster in France with more information.

Ormus was the next to break the silence. 'We will stay here today, but tomorrow we must go our separate ways. This event is the beginning of the change to come. René, you must return home to begin the sale of the hotel, and Ette and her family will accompany you. Lia will come with me to continue her studies. Raphiel, Strawberry, and Glas have other plans. I'm sorry, my friends, the festivities have come to an end.'

Edward entered the room to hear the last of the conversation, which meant that Lia would be leaving him. Edward wished he could ask her to marry him, but one glance from Ormus told him he should not.

Raphiel, while listening to Ormus, had been paying attention to the remainder of the news bulletin. A new party was making itself known in the political arena as the voice of the country's electorate, and the number of members was growing daily. Raphiel listened to the leader of the new and popular party, a doctor working in London who was determined to bring change.

The candidate continued to speak with confidence of his party's manifesto. 'There exists a lack of cultural identification that has been brought about by an open border policy here and, indeed, across Europe. We are bordering socially on a downward spiral of major proportions and must return to a system that monitors all movement in and out of our country. Only when this is in place can we return to managing our living standards properly. The public must make their anxieties known before we lose control of our cities and our country. The British public are being slowly disabled; believe me, I witness it every day.'

Raphiel felt concerned at the panic this man's revelations were causing among the nation but knew it to be true.

The speaker continued, 'The present government assures us that they are putting more funding into the health service than any other government before them, while, in truth, they make it their guiding principle to enforce a policy of withholding hospital referrals for those in urgent need of treatment. They say they are dealing with the removal of toxic chemicals from the public's food chain, while subversively they introduce genetically modified foods to our markets, against the wishes of the public. You must not put your trust in this government. It is time for change …'

The news moved on to a disturbing report regarding a virulent disease transferred from infected cattle to humans, for which medical science had yet to find a cure. The disease was capable of destroying both animal and human brain tissue and was escalating alarmingly, causing death in both animals and man.

Ormus noticed Raphiel's attention to this piece of information and remarked, 'Mankind's lack of knowledge when tampering with the natural feeding of livestock has resulted in a lethal genetic mix-up, which is endangering the lives of many humans as well as the herds.'

Raphiel agreed with him.

For the rest of the morning they sat listening to the constant news bulletins, forgetting the joy of the previous night. Lia and Ette stayed watching the screen in the hope that something they recognised near to Château Dubar would appear, but nothing did.

During the confusion of the morning news, Lia had absorbed the same tragic story as Raphiel had. The families of those who had recently died from a disease transferred when they ingested the meat of infected cattle were speaking of their deep loss and the ensuing court case. She was, however, too numb with grief to think further than the comparable pain and suffering of the grief-stricken families.

Ette had left Lia with Ormus and Raphiel to take a walk by the river with her husband and baby, while Strawberry and René went downstairs to talk with Edward. Raphiel and Ormus remained with Lia, waiting for her to drift into sleep.

Raphiel said quietly, 'Ormus, we must make her aware of the tragedy that the cattle disease is creating for mankind. His genetic structure is already fragile, and the transference of this disease must not be ignored.'

'Yes,' Ormus replied. 'When she enters the dreamtime, we will give her direction.'

Ormus and Raphiel disappeared onto the bank of twilight to support Lia as she entered the world of another, one whose family was the first of millions to be affected by the virulent genetic cattle virus, commonly known as mad cow disease.

In the dreamtime, Lia awakened to autumn daylight. Beneath her lay a blanket of woodland grass and above a clear blue sky filtering through the branches of a giant oak tree that shaded her. The morning sun felt warm, as though it were still summer, but the trees gave the season away. Overhead the branches were almost bare, with just a few brightly coloured leaves left to fall. Lia watched as one left its place upon the branch, ready to become part of the Earth again. The leaf floated down towards her, the skeleton showing clearly within the fabric of the foliage. Lia pondered on the miracle of nature, life, and death.

Ormus appeared before her. 'Good morning, Lia. We have moved you into the open, so that you may draw strength from the sun as you rest. So much has happened to you in such a short space of time, which cannot be good for your health and contentment. Today you will rest and play.'

Lia repeated his words, "Rest and play'. I haven't played since I was a child,' she smiled and stretched with pleasure. 'What a lovely idea.'

'Look over there,' Ormus said, pointing to the far side of the bank, where the river appeared from beneath a waterfall.

Lia followed his direction to where the sound of laughter came from behind the cascading water. She sat up and was trying to peer further into the curtain of water, when a young girl appeared from behind it. Lia stood up but began to sway; her body felt weak, and she sank back to the ground.

Ormus came and sat beside her, 'Remember, Lia, you are sleeping because you have been through an ordeal and need to rest.' Ormus held out a cup of steaming liquid to Lia, and when she had taken it, he produced some food.

Lia was not feeling hungry. Her body felt weak, and she had no desire to eat, but once her lips touched the cup she felt renewed and began to eat hungrily.

The young girl sat down on the far riverbank and began trailing her fingers in the flowing river, the disrupted flow sending water splashing up against her hand and over her outstretched arm. She seemed absorbed by the droplets flowing back into the river, droplets that seemed determined to become one with the river again. Raphiel appeared beside her, and they began to talk.

'Who is the girl with Raphiel?' Lia asked.

'Her name is Emily, and she has come to know Raphiel well while remaining in the dreamtime. Emily never awakens from her dream state and spends most of her time here by the river.'

Lia watched Emily play with the water; she was a pretty girl of tender years, perhaps ten.

Ormus continued, 'Emily remains in the dreamtime while her mother and father sit by her bedside waiting for her to wake up.' Ormus waited, as Lia was disturbed by the noise of the breakfast remains being cleared away from the Renoir suite, and then, as quietness settled again, she returned to the dreamtime.

'Lia, do you remember I told you of the young girl that remains here in her dreamtime?'

Lia nodded. 'Emily,' she answered.

Ormus continued, 'We are in her dreamtime, but she cannot see us from the other side of the river, which is a condition of her choosing. Look at the river, Lia. Can you see the line that divides it in the middle?'

Lia realised that the view of the river looked a little strange, and then she glimpsed what Ormus was seeing. There was a dividing line similar to a reflection in a pool of water that, when disturbed, breaks up and returns when all is still again.

'I feel the need to talk to her. I might be able to help her,' Lia said, feeling sure she could help Emily.

'Then you must make her accept your presence,' Ormus replied. 'Close your eyes and wish yourself beyond the river's divide. However, do not be put off if she appears unwelcoming,' he told her.

Lia did as she was asked and found her way to the far side of the river.

Raphiel disappeared as the young girl stood up and came to look at Lia. 'Who are you,' she asked, 'and why are you in my dreamtime?'

Lia remembered Ormus's advice that Emily might not be welcoming.

'My name is Lia,' she answered calmly, 'and what is yours?'

'My name is Emily, but you know that.' Her voice softened as she gazed at the beautiful woman with waist-length black curls towering above her. 'Would you like to play with me?' she asked.

Lia remained silent as her attention was taken by something else. A large shard of crystal appeared from under the waterfall, carrying a small boy upon it. The boy remained motionless while the shard of crystal glided towards the river bank and came to a stop alongside them. Lia and Emily, without invitation, climbed aboard, and the crystal moved out into the river again, slicing through the central divide to land at the bank alongside Ormus. The boy helped Lia to step onto the grass but Emily was left to step out unassisted, and then the crystal drew back into the water and disappeared.

'Who was that?' Lia asked Emily.

'He is my brother, but he doesn't speak to me, even though I desperately wish he would.' Tears flowed down her cheeks from his rejection of her.

Lia looked enquiringly at Ormus, but he did not speak. Emily went and sat down beside Ormus. They appeared to know one another and were soon deep in conversation. Lia joined them, wanting to find out more about Emily's brother. The young girl was now listening attentively to Ormus, while he explained to her that her brother had brought her across the river to encourage her to leave her isolation and find out why she could not communicate with him. Emily had locked herself away in the dreamtime, and to be free she must face the fact of his death.

Lia sat waiting, eager to join in the conversation, wanting to ask Emily why she remained in the dreamtime. Moments later there was a pause, and she seized the opportunity. Emily remained silent for a while, as if ignoring Lia's question, and then her words tumbled forth.

'I'm unwell and remain asleep,' she said. 'The doctors cannot find anything wrong with me, other than to say that I may be in shock at the loss of my brother.'

'How did your brother die?' Lia asked, beginning to understand the boy's presence in Emily's dream. Lia realised that if Emily could understand what kept her in the dreamtime, she would be able to move beyond the tragedy of her brother's death. She would become well again and leave the dreamtime.

Emily continued her story. She had resented her brother. He was younger than she was which had made her feel very jealous. It had rested upon Emily to look after her brother while both their parents worked. They had spent much of their time in each other's company, which she had deeply resented, having friends of her own that she wanted to be with. One Saturday morning, Emily had been feeling bored and angry because she had been left to look after her brother while her mother went shopping. She had decided to read her six-year-old brother a story that she knew would frighten him. Emily repeated part of the story she had read to him:

"Man's cruelty to the animal kingdom had passed beyond any reasoning or caution to the danger that was looming for mankind, who considered himself above the laws of nature. Forgotten was the herd's sacrifice, made for man in order that he might survive the ice age. Hafnium, creator of the universe, brought the herds together and, with a sad heart, told them that Aspheseuos, the dark angel, had won the minds of mankind. There would be no return of peace between man and the herds without a great deal of pain and sacrifice. The herds would suffer a terrible disease in order that man would learn his lesson. The disease would come upon the herds, and man would destroy many of them because of it, but the disease would also reach out to man, and he would be greatly afflicted. Hafnium told the herds it was the only way that mankind would learn their lesson." Emily explained, 'I told my brother it was only a fairy tale when he became frightened and started to cry.' The young girl stopped talking as tears ran down her cheeks. 'I didn't mean to frighten him, not really, but it was as if he had glimpsed the future and could not be comforted.' Emily looked at Lia, her eyes wide and pleading, 'I didn't know what was going to happen, did I . . .?' After a while, she stopped sobbing and continued, 'We didn't know anything was wrong at first, although he was always complaining of being very tired and would not play with me. My parents started to tell him off for being lazy, which they had never done before. Then, as he became weaker and weaker, they realised something was wrong. The doctors could not help him; they said there wasn't a cure for his illness, which they said came from the cattle – which I did not understand.' A look of bewilderment settled upon Emily's face as she brushed away her tears. 'After that, I never left his side. I felt so guilty. It was a warm summer's day in June. Mum and Dad . . . we were sitting in the garden enjoying the sunshine. My parents thought my brother had fallen asleep, but he had gone away. I told my father he had been carried away by the angels who were waiting for him. I saw them, but Father didn't believe me. After he died, I came here to be with him, but when he does come he doesn't talk to me.'

Lia was not a child, yet she felt afraid. Would the cattle disease affect her or her family, and when would that be, if ever?

'Lia, come out of this mode of thinking,' said Ormus who was listening to her thoughts. 'Can't you see that you are being challenged? You must help Emily back to her world, where she will grow up understanding the reality of man's folly, having experienced such a tragic loss.'

Lia understood how the denial of strong emotions, which breed within family life, can cause serious illness to the physical body and that Emily's reluctance to wake up arose from the guilt of her jealousy towards her brother.

The young girl stood up, 'If he would speak to me and tell me he was happy, I could leave the dreamtime. I want to wake up and be with my parents, but I cannot stand the pain when I'm awake, for I feel as though my heart is broken in two.'

Ormus stood up and gathered the young girl into his arms. Cradling her, he began to soothe her. Lia felt the word *guilt* form in her mind again and recognised that Emily's guilt for her brother's death would eventually be the cause of her own. Lia's thoughts turned to those who could help Emily awaken; her own fear was now forgotten.

The Mer angels rose from within the river's divide to enter Emily's dreamtime, and with them they carried Emily's brother. They stepped onto the riverbank and held the little boy out to his sister. Emily gathered his weightlessness to her like a little mother, drawing him close until they were wrapped in each other's arms. For a while they held each other close, and then he reached into his pocket and held out a gift for Emily, while releasing himself from her embrace. The child unfurled to reveal an adult whose voice she did not recognise, a voice full of wisdom.

'Emily, to stay immersed in any human emotion for too long can destroy your life. Because of your guilt, your cycle of Earthly experiences ceased when you would not accept my death. Your future continues to stagnate whilst you hold onto the past and will not allow you to continue with your life until you let go of me. As you can see, I still exist, but in another dimension. We must all experience loss, which is a part of our earthbound existence. Rise above your guilt, and let go. Unconditional love is all we need, but that is rarely achieved outside of the *one* existence beyond physical life. And if we should discover this truth while living a human existence, then we have found a priceless treasure.' Opening his sister's hand, he placed a crystal heart inside it. 'You have your heart back, Emily. Leave the dreamtime and teach the experience of your sorrow to the world, and never be afraid to speak of love. Offer mankind a choice for change.'

Emily flung her arms about him and then let go as the Mer angels eased him from her embrace. Smiling at Lia and Ormus, she turned to say goodbye. 'I will try to remember you on awakening and hope that we will meet again.' Emily began to fade from the dreamtime, as she started her journey back to consciousness.

Ormus called to her, 'Remember the crystal heart and always keep it near to you, for it will encourage you to reach out and help others with your words.'

John and Mary were spending another hopeless day at the hospital. All their prayers for their daughter's return from her unconscious state seemed to go unheeded, and they were resigned to losing Emily as they had their son. As Mary straightened the covers over her daughter's fragile body, a thing she did so many times a day, she noticed the crystal heart tucked in the top of Emily's nightdress.

'What is this, John?' she asked.

John bent forward to look, and, as he did so, Emily opened her eyes.

Having met Emily, Lia now understood another danger that was threatening mankind and the herds and, on awakening was still anxious as to what the outcome would be.

Later that day, Lia prepared to return to Cornwall. After finishing her packing, she went to sit with her father. She felt anxious at being separated from him, but her journey into the dreamtime had softened her grief and given her new strength. She also sensed a release of guilt which she had carried unknowingly for her mother's death during hers and Ette's birth. This anxiety would always appear alongside her father's unfathomable melancholy.

'You have done well, Lia,' René told his daughter proudly. 'I love you so much, and I am very proud of you for helping Emily to return from the dreamtime. Emily will, in time, become a strong ambassador for mankind.' René held Lia close. 'And you as well, my dear, but for now you must return to Cornwall to continue with your studies,' he said not wanting to let her go. René now understood why Lia had taken his place at the meeting with the food merchants; she would one day take his place as one of the twelve astronomers, but when that would be or how it would come about, he had no idea. René let all thoughts of his daughter's future drift from his mind.

A knock at the door interrupted anything further René was about to say. Lia threw her arms around her father's neck and hugged him tightly. It was time to say goodbye. Without explanation, Ormus was leaving immediately.

'Come along, Lia. We must be away tonight.' Ormus had entered the room and stood waiting by the open window.

Lia gave her father a last hug and ran beneath Ormus's cape. In moments, they were above the city. She watched London become a dot below them as they circled out over the river towards the ocean. Lia felt instinctively that they were not going back to Cornwall.

'Where are we heading for, Ormus?' she asked.

'All in good time, Lia, but I will tell you this: It is an extraordinary place within Earth that only those who have "the gift" know of.'

Chapter 26

The City of Memories: Zrsiofour, King of the Ocean People

'Within . . .? The gift . . .?' Lia wanted to know more, but for now she would let Ormus's comment go. Below them she could see a dark blue coastline towards which Ormus appeared to be descending. They glided downward until it was plain to see that the coastline was not dark blue at all, but flooded with a thick, dark oil spill discharged from a half-submerged shipping tanker that lay grounded nearby.

'Look at what has happened!' The sight of stranded birds covered in oil and struggling desperately to lift off from the sticky mess that held them, made Lia feel distressed.

Ormus's reply was curt and angry: 'Man has again worked his mischief upon nature. The ship is spilling its cargo of oil into the sea and will destroy the seabed and marine life for miles around.' Ormus held back his anger with choking breaths, 'Lia, if man only knew what he was doing! His greed for money and power has gone beyond all reasoning and compassion for nature. There will follow one disaster upon another. I wonder at the reasoning of my kind to be involved in this world of chaos.' Ormus's emotions felt raw; sometimes he wanted so desperately to be back in his world, where civilisation had advanced far beyond the corruption of mortal gain.

Lia looked down at the stranded birds and sea lions that had little hope of freeing themselves from their situation.

'Look over there, my dear,' said Ormus, pointing along the

beach. Ormus's voice had lightened as he caught sight of a small army of people with large buckets and cleaning materials descending upon the beach to lift the stranded birds and small mammals to safety. 'They will clean them up and make them well enough to return to their habitat,' Ormus said with relief.

The sight of people gathering on the beach cheered Lia up a little. The half-submerged tanker was like a monster rising from the ocean, and seeing the disaster for real, as opposed to viewing it on a television screen, had made her shed tears. 'They will be all right, won't they, Ormus?'

'Most will survive. But there will be a next time. It will continue until the pyramid of power is turned upside down. Only then will it stop.' Ormus flew on, lifting them far above the ocean until they could no longer distinguish the shoreline, his thoughts so deep that at first he did not hear Lia's question.

'What is the pyramid of power?' Lia asked.

'It is a metaphor for the power of an elite few who ravage the world's resources and control the masses of every continent upon Earth. It is so named after the legend of the ancient pyramids that were built by the enslaved masses for their masters, those who were looked upon as gods. Now, the pyramids are built on financial power, and the enslavement of mankind remains the same.

'What will happen to mankind when the pyramid of power is reversed?' Lia asked.

'Man was meant to live upon the Earth in small communities. When the time of the "masses following a few" was established, the civilisation of man began to die. The spirit-soul of mankind is meant to follow one, and that is Hafnium. Mankind was meant to follow his instincts and function independently of his fellow companions, while accepting the gift of difference that he found in others. If mankind had remained that way, there would not have been the need to support the multitudes, and shipping of the magnitude we have just seen would not exist. Mankind would have found another way to evolve without destroying planet Earth. We all have a destiny, and there are many roads to the final goal. Mankind chose the wrong way, and it is too late to turn back. He must continue on the road he has chosen to the bitter end. And remember, those who listen to their instincts not to follow the same path, though it is a difficult choice to make, will benefit at the outcome.'

Lia felt numbed by what she had seen and heard. Having left her family and Edward, it was as if she had no say in her life any longer, as if it had been taken over by Ormus and the challenges.

Ormus, having become aware of Lia's anguish, let his thoughts become hers. 'You must bear these circumstances with resolute strength, Lia. Before long, you will have command of your life again – and in ways that you never did before. These experiences will give you such vision that you will never see any situation in the same light again. Trust in those who have shown their love and support for you. All will work out at the end.'

Ormus and Lia continued on their journey far above the great oceans that merged into each other, as they travelled over the centre line of the Earth. Lia had been deep in thought when suddenly Ormus gave out a scream of pain and let go of her. Immediately she began plummeting into the darkness below. At first, she could not accept the fact that she was hurtling towards the vast ocean below. Murky shadows of immense depth seemed to be reaching up to engulf her. Just below her, Lia could see Ormus spiralling downward, his body plunging, turning, and twisting in a state of unconsciousness. Lia's last memory was seeing Ormus's body hit the water and disappear, and then all was dark ...

Lia awoke to the sound of gently splashing water, and then her stomach tensed at another sound, an eerie kind of music. Lia relaxed after she realised it was the calling of dolphins and whales communicating to one another across the ocean. Slowly the past events came back to her, as she remembered what had happened. Lia realised that although she was on the seabed, she was breathing. She could see the ocean floor from where she lay on a small ledge that formed part of the opening to a large cave. Ormus's words came back to her: 'the ocean bed is just like the valleys and mountains you see on land, other than they are covered by water. Plants still grow and kingdoms survive, although of a watery nature, and these kingdoms of the vast, deep oceans are all part of the underworld.'

Lia moved her body to a standing position and found that she drifted as much as she walked. She was relieved to find that she was not hurt from her fall. As she explored the cave further, a shaft of light appeared overhead from an opening high above her, which she hoped meant that the surface of the ocean was not far away. She decided to swim towards the top of the cave, hoping desperately that someone or something friendly would turn up and tell her where she was. Surprised by her calm, she felt strongly that if she had survived, then so had Ormus. She swam towards the top of the cave where the light was stronger, until the ceiling of the cave became a pool into which she surfaced.

Lia swam cautiously towards the edge. The cave surrounding the pool displayed a cosmic spectacle of light from the walls of amethyst crystal. Lia blinked to clear her eyes. She could see Ormus's still body laid upon a large oyster shell, the size of which she would not have thought existed. He lay covered in a white pearly substance, his face as white as his shroud. Worried by his lifelessness, Lia hurriedly climbed from the pool and went over to him. Placing her hands upon his face, she was relieved to feel some warmth there. It was then that she noticed the mermaids at the back of the cave, beneath a gentle cascade of steaming water.

'Come, sit with us, Lia,' said one. 'My name is Tamelia. We did not expect you to wake so soon.'

The mermaids beckoned her over to where a cascade of steaming water flowed down the crystal surface of the wall, sending shimmers of purple and turquoise across the cave's interior. The water cascaded gently downward on its journey to the pool, its soothing rhythm one of the sounds that Lia had heard upon waking.

'Touch the waterfall, Lia.'

Lia did as she was asked and found it pleasantly warm.

'Go on, get into the waterfall and revive yourself.' The laughter of the mermaids echoed around the cave.

Lia stepped in, feeling happy to do so, as her body was still cold from shock. The water felt comfortingly warm as it foamed and splashed over her limbs. 'Where does the heated water come from?' she asked.

The mermaids told her there were many hot springs gushing from the Earth's volcanic crust, which kept areas of the ocean at a comfortable temperature for those living in the underworld.

'Those that live here in the underworld?' Lia said politely, knowing a little of the answer but wanting to know more.

'The Mer race and those who are not by nature part of it,' they replied.

Lia listened fascinated as they told her of the humans who, with the consent of King Zrsiofour, had come to start a new life in the Mer underworld.

'Lia, come and look!' Tamelia beckoned her to follow as the mermaids spilled from the ledge into the pool and swam down to a lower plateau of the rocky terrain. From there they crossed a volcanic crater, where the white molten lava spilled out so far below them that the heat was barely noticeable. The mermaids continued to move rapidly downward, as if descending a vast mountain, until they reached the summit of another. Lia began to feel extremely tired, and her body began to float downward of its own accord. The silhouettes of two entwined dolphins appeared beneath her and held her as she drifted into blackness. When Lia opened her eyes again, she was being carried along by Max, who swam behind his companion, Millie. Lia felt safe as her eyes focused on Millie's waist-length yellow hair flowing out around her in the water. Just below them, beyond the curtain of yellowness, the seabed levelled out to a vast flat plain on which stood a city of pristine whiteness.

'What is this place?' Lia asked breathlessly. The coldness of her body and the iciness of the water had left her, and she felt warm and strangely comfortable. She had no idea where she was or how far down, but still she breathed.

'This place is called the City of Memories, and it is home to the new tribe of man.'

Lia remained still, her thoughts on the beautiful, but ghostly, city below. Beneath her in the watery depths lay a silent city of pure white. The only colours reflected upon the walls were those of the brightly coloured marine life that transposed the ever-changing matrix: city walls of shimmering white, which reflected a myriad of hues into the surrounding underwater currents. The city's beauty was far beyond description. One pinnacle after another reached towards the unseen sky, the white marble buildings untouched by the ravages of the salty ocean.

Lia could not see beyond the gates or see any signs of life within. 'How long has the city been here?' she asked.

'The City of Memories was hidden here a long time ago,' they replied.

'Why was it hidden?'

The mermaids told Lia the story that was well known among their race. 'Ormus has told you of his people, the wise ones, the Holocene race from Universe Nine?'

Lia answered with a nod of her head.

'The wise ones, when they came to live on Earth with man, built the City of Memories to live in. The City of Memories was to be the centre for teaching mankind. It was to reflect the nature of the world where the Holocene race exists. For thousands of years, their being here on Earth worked well. Man embraced the spiritual teachings of the Holocene, but eventually many returned to the old ways, and, when this happened, many of the Holocene wise ones returned home. Hafnium had foreseen this, that mankind would again be ruled by those without the potential to advance his celestial development. After he allowed the Holocenes to leave the City of Memories, he had it taken from the Earth; for he would never agree to give the city of the divine into man's keeping. The city disappeared beneath the ocean, as mankind's fifth world disintegrated into dust. The city was sent to the world of King Zrsiofour, to be hidden in the underworld, and so it fell into the ocean – never to be seen again by man until now. The City of Memories was built some ten thousand years ago, when the Holocenes arrived. Many who remained, as Ormus did, were greatly saddened to see it go to the bottom of the ocean – including the custodian, King Zrsiofour.'

Lia suddenly realised she had not asked after Ormus and turned to ask Tamelia. Before she had spoken the thought, she was beside Ormus again. In front of him stood an old man with flowing white hair, his magnificent robes of deep blue seaweed glistened in the light of the amethyst cave.

Zrsiofour stood looking down upon his old friend Ormus, knowing that soon Ormus's work on Earth would be complete, and with this thought he felt great joy, as he believed it was time for Ormus's release from the Earth. Ormus had done a great service to mankind, and it was nearing the time of his homecoming. He turned around to see sadness in Lia's eyes and felt the reverse of his joy reflected in her face. Zrsiofour broke the silence, his words forming sounds that resembled oxygen bubbles struggling to surface. 'Ormus is tired and his old heart is weak, but he will be with you until the challenges are over.'

Lia nodded. She felt unable to cry or to feel anything; all she could think of was what would happen to her after the challenges. How long would it be before they ended?

Tamelia took her hand, 'You must rest now, and, when you are feeling better, Zrsiofour will travel with you to the ocean kingdoms, for he wants you to understand what is happening between our two worlds. By the time you have learned what you need to know for the future, Ormus will have recovered and you will leave here together. Ormus was bringing you here, Lia. It was unfortunate that you arrived in such an unexpected manner. Come by the warmth of the waterfall and drink.' Tamelia held out a seashell.

Lia, suddenly aware of her thirst, drained the shell of its familiar golden liquid. Her body felt warm again, and her thirst was gone. Contentedly, she lay down to sleep.

When Lia awoke, she felt at peace and restored to good health. She slipped over to where Ormus lay peacefully; his face was flushed and his gaunt cheeks looked rosy. Lia touched him and he opened his eyes and smiled at her. She felt better knowing that he had stirred, if only for a moment.

Zrsiofour appeared in the water, 'Come with me, Lia, we must leave Ormus in the care of those who can heal him.' With one graceful movement of his mighty tail, Zrsiofour's body turned into the flow of water and disappeared beneath the ledge with Lia following.

Zrsiofour and Lia swam down through the channel of connecting caves to the ocean bed below, where a Viking longboat was fastened, its painted sides rolling against the water's undercurrent. Aboard the longboat, the waiting oarsmen each held a giant shell horn, and, as King Zrsiofour and Lia approached, a loud fanfare rang out: Zrsiofour was bringing Lia, the seeker of knowledge, to the ocean people.

Zrsiofour took Lia on a journey across the great oceans to show her the devastation that mankind's pollution was causing and the destruction of the ocean floor marine life that none on land could see. 'Spilt-oil slicks and toxic waste have damaged the oceans' coral reefs and the sea creatures' habitat beyond repair. Many of these areas have become contaminated, and the fish are unable to produce future generations.' Zrsiofour looked on sadly as he opened Lia's mind to the devastation within his kingdom.

Lia felt ashamed at the suffering inflicted upon his kind by man.

When their journey was over, the oarsmen set sail for the City of Memories. The magnificent Viking longboat moved swiftly through the water, cutting its way through the strong ocean currents. The longboat, a tribute to mankind's inspiration, had been lost to the ocean in one of the many battles of mankind and now served the king of the ocean people, Zrsiofour.

Lia sat quietly watching the ancient elder in front of her, not hazarding a guess as to his age. Zrsiofour had been one of the first of the Holocene race to appear on Earth. He had travelled at that time to establish a spiritual awakening among the Earth's underworld people, which had been achieved. Zrsiofour was half man and half fish, as were the Mer people. His body was the colour of dark blue petroleum, all the colours within that spectrum glistening within the one. His eyes were sapphire blue, bright and piercing, and they would bring any secrets to light from those who tried to hide them from him. His body shifted shape from man size to colossus in the flicker of a thought. The king of the ocean world was a sight that all fishermen dreaded to see, for they knew if they saw him they had committed a wrong against the Mer race and would perish.

The great ship neared the subterranean valley where the City of Memories lay. Zrsiofour told Lia about the first migration and the humans who now lived there. He spoke of the time when Hafnium had asked him and his people to receive mankind into their world – those who were to become the one tribe of man. He and his people had agreed, knowing that the Mer race would also develop while living alongside the humans. 'The time is drawing near for the main body of lightworkers to migrate here. The wise ones, such as Ormus, are entering their dreamtime to instruct them and assure them that they will return to the surface when forty-five years have passed. When that time comes, the emerging one tribe of man will leave our world to re-establish communities around the world.' Zrsiofour went on to tell Lia why some had found their way to the City of Memories before the mass migration.

Lia was aware that mankind's inevitable downturn had long since begun, and, as Zrsiofour gave his explanation, Lia knew it to be true. The numbers of teachers educating the young had fallen rapidly, forcing places of education to close. The media had blamed the crisis on the intimidating behaviour of a minority of the young and the government's lack of support for the teachers. But as the situation worsened, public opinion was that something else was responsible for their disappearance.'

Lia leaned towards Zrsiofour, listening attentively to every word he spoke.

'While the situation remains contained,' Zrsiofour said gently, 'the rebellious children remain happy. They have no respect for their elders, their parents, or their teachers, and life without school is a gift beyond joy for them. However, for those wanting an education, the future is distressing, terrifying, and soul-destroying. A life without purpose, without expectation! It is these young people who protest. They realise their future is clearly fated without those who can educate them.' Zrsiofour sighed, the gravity of the situation heavy on his heart. 'The time is approaching when an era of nature's worst aggression will be inflicted upon mankind, and many will die.

Within a few Earth years, the God of Fire, Hafnium, will initiate a holocaust upon the Earth to rid her of mankind, after which a tsunami will rise from my kingdom to cover her scorched surface and heal her wounds. That is the plan.' Zrsiofour cried in anguish, 'The younger generations of man were born to save the Earth. Where are they – what has happened to these lost souls? May Hafnium have mercy upon them, for there is still time for them to unite with the spiritually awakened?' Zrsiofour fell silent. Like Ormus, he was tortured at their failure to bring mankind forward without such devastation, but it appeared that they had failed. They had revealed the future to all of mankind when in the dreamtime; some had heeded the warnings, and many had not.

Lia had always believed that the creator of Universe Four was untouched by evil and of a gentle nature, and she had agreed with Ormus when he laid the blame for mankind's suffering at his own door, but Raphiel's words of warning were also in her mind: 'Hafnium has a stick to beat us with.' Hafnium was the God of Fire, and he would use mankind's ingenuity to bring about his downfall. There was truth in what both had told her.

Chapter 27

Pythagoras

The first of the migrant lightworkers to enter the City of Memories had purposefully reconciled themselves to their new way of life. They accepted their exile from the Earth's surface, with the belief that their children would develop a natural sensitivity to both the Mer world and the one they had left behind. The migrants kept their vision on the future, when they would return to the Earth's surface as a new civilisation of man that would be wiser than the one about to be taken.

In the City of Memories, Lia was seated among a small group of lightworker migrants in the Halls of Legislature, a vast, circular building that rose on the midpoint of the city, and where those such as Hippocrates, the founding father of medicine, would appear from the other-worlds to inspire and teach. Zrsiofour was explaining to the migrants the laws by which the Mers structured their daily lives – and which the future mankind was expected to abide by.

Zrsiofour continued to address the assembly, explaining the difficulties the Mers faced with the intolerable behaviour of a few humans. 'The mermen patrolling the perimeter of the city have found the remains of cannibalised marine life. The slaughter of the marine life must end. This offence is causing much distress among the Mers. They fear for their environment and the peaceful existence that they share with the ocean dwellers. The final migration is nearly upon us. Then the Mer world will become home to three times as many humans, all trying to adapt to living in the

Mer world and by Mer law, which means never taking another life, no matter how insignificant it may appear to them. Those among you who have disobeyed our law will be forgiven this time, after which they will be returned to the surface if caught taking the life of a marine dweller.'

The spokesman for the migrants argued that most were vegetarians on arrival but that some still ate fish, and that within the Earth's oceans most marine life survived by feeding upon another.

Zrsiofour replied, 'That is so, but not the Mers or, indeed, mankind, if he is to become part of the one tribe of man. There can be no lenience in this matter. Man, in order to comply with his destiny, must obey Mer law.'

Lia decided to ask the question that was foremost in her mind, and those about her whose attention had been fixed on Zrsiofour began to pick up her thoughts. An elderly man in white flowing robes mounted the steps of the dais beneath which Zrsiofour reclined in the watery depths of a natural pool. The elder standing before them was a teacher whose life philosophy had been recorded for all time in ancient Greek script. After mounting the steps, he stood observing Lia for a moment. Zrsiofour greeted Pythagoras warmly, for he was held in high regard. He was a scholar whose teachings, like so many of his kind, had left their mark upon the history of mankind.

'Pythagoras wishes to speak.'

Those assembled in the white marble hall murmured their approval.

Pythagoras began by acknowledging Lia and then voicing her thoughts. 'Lia, you would like to know how the lightworkers, those who are to become the one tribe of man, journey here to the City of Memories. I will explain.'

Pythagoras held his hand aloft and a hologram appeared in the centre of the hall. Within the hologram, two sets of the numbers one to nine flowed ceaselessly along the lines of a double helix. Suddenly, the strands separated to form two triangles with a set of numbers inside. The number one filled the point of each triangle, below which sat the numbers two and three. The next row held the numbers four, five, and six, and on the last row were the numbers seven, eight, nine, and zero. Each number was positioned over one of the nine planets orbiting the sun, whereas the zero was mounted over a fathomless opening. The triangles began to spin, each reflecting an image of the other, and then they merged together to form the shape of a diamond.

'What do you see, beyond the obvious?' Pythagoras asked.

Lia looked at the triangles within the shaft of light. She began to panic – then to concentrate. Lia's reasoning told her that the two triangles contained the secret language of all physical and spiritual life within Universe Four. The answer was straightforward enough. She was positive the answer was simple and she was not to look for problems. She gave her answer. 'The two triangles contain the digits of basic mathematics, which hold the codes of all physical and spiritual life within Universe Four, each life form having a unique code that, when applied ...' Lia's words ceased as she realised she had the answer. Her father had taught her all there was to know about the codes of birth that were held within an astrological chart. How had she not realised before?

Pythagoras agreed with her, saying, 'Straightforward, was it not?'

'Yes,' Lia answered simply.

Pythagoras repeated Lia's explanation of the triangle's code. 'The triangles hold the code of each living thing within Universe Four, and all other universes, and each combination is individual to the one 'being'. Any 'being' wishing to journey within Universe Four, or beyond, could do so by visualising his or her code and so, as with the magical genie of the lamp, their wish would be granted. That is, if they know of its existence, of course! Most do not. The code holds the conditions of the life form's destiny, which is contained within the date and time of the birth. Within the triangles of physical mass and spiritual energy are contained the units one to nine, nine being the one number that contains all numbers: one and eight, seven and two, six and three, five and four. You may include or leave out the number nine when reducing a sum to a one-figure number, as both answers will always reduce to the same sum. The number nine, whole or incomplete in division or multiplication, represents all elements within all universes and is the source of all life forms in existence. Hafnium created Universe Four from the mathematical fragments of his being, because it is his domain. Nine is the energy vibration we call unconditional love, which powers all universes from the Globe of Healing energy, and to which *all* is returned. And then, of course, there is zero energy, the 'moment' at which each universe begins and ends. Zero energy – the void within the binary world where physical matter enters a non-physical existence, which is the gateway to all universes, a space that mankind calls black holes or places of the unknown.'

Pythagoras paused, allowing Lia to rest. She was struggling with so much to absorb, but her mind was buzzing with interest.

Pythagoras continued, 'When the plan to create the one tribe of man was under way, the lightworkers were awakened to the use of healing energy to help the sick and emotionally unwell. They began to teach their ways to groups, which was part of Hafnium's plan. They found themselves teaching people who were also disillusioned and, like the teachers of the young, they were turning away from their professions. Groups of lightworkers began to manifest all around the world. It was at that point that the wise ones began entering their dreamtime to show them the future and the part that they were to play in it. In answer to your question, Lia, the life of man is held within the numbers of his date of birth and the exact time that he is born into the fourth element, matter. From the flesh of the mother an infant is created, to which is added at birth the trinity of consciousness, love, and – most importantly – the spirit-soul. The potential of that being is manifest at the moment of birth. To dream of the fusion of a square and a triangle . . .'

'It is man perfected,' Lia responded. 'I have seen it in my dreams and have been told – it is man perfected.'

'That is so, Lia,' said Pythagoras. 'The twelve-number code needed for the light-workers to take their journey contains eight digits for the day, month and year, and four digits for the hours and minutes, including the zero, where a digit does not exist, which is of great importance. When the time to journey arrives, a wise one will be with them to light the way. The two symbols that represent the lives of each will be revealed within the binary world, and the Gate of Triangles that bars the entrance to the City of Memories will open, and those who are to be received will find themselves within.'

Lia asked, 'I have seen many numbers in my dream but not my time of birth. Is it because I am not ready to make my journey yet?'

'That is so. To see any numbers in your dream prepares you for the time when you will see your code clearly shown upon the triangles. Then your journey will begin. Remember, Lia, you are a soul fragment of Hafnium. When correctly balanced, the soul fragment that is part of Hafnium creates experiences for the good of all. Many soul fragments created by Hafnium are now destructive. To begin with, there were twelve fragments to each soul; now there are only two. Ten fragments of knowledge have been lost to man because of his weakness for evil. The migration will weed out that evil from mankind, and prepare him to receive the ten missing strands of knowledge.'

Lia had barely heard Pythagoras's last words before she thought of those she loved who might be left upon the Earth's surface.

'I cannot know the future in whole, Lia,' Pythagoras said, reading her thoughts. 'Therefore, I do not know if your family will continue within the evolution of man. I do know that man is set upon a pathway of self-destruction which cannot be avoided. Man has caused his own tragedy and will reap his reward. Those who are not intuitively open to the coming danger will be in the wrong place as the disasters happen, and many will perish. But then, many are perishing on Earth now, and man accepts this tragedy as commonplace.'

Lia listened numbly to his words of desolation that would be borne, not only by man, but by every living creature upon Earth.

Pythagoras sat quietly waiting for Lia to collect her thoughts, and, when he felt she was ready to go on, he said, 'A time was chosen when the lightworkers could enter the oceans around the world without feeling the stress of drowning. At certain times of the year, when the moon is in shadow, the triangles are put into force and released into the dreamtime. Those who wish to depart the land are drawn to the oceans in their dreams, where they enter the binary world to emerge as the celestial body of both man and angel. Only those who have worked in the light, those who have listened and acted upon their dreams, can use this method of travel, for their bodies have become transmutable. Many will come to the City of Memories, where they will work to build a new and spiritual life for mankind while healing the living Earth. It is an important time for the Earth's evolution.' Pythagoras ceased to speak.

Lia's attention was drawn back to the triangles rotating slowly inside the hologram. She did not know her time of birth, her mother having died when she and her twin, Ette, were born, which her father never spoke of.

'Of course you know, Lia!' Pythagoras prompted.

Lia felt an intensifying force pass through her body, as her soul energy began to emerge from the crown of her head. The light danced hazily above her and then moved swiftly towards the two triangles within the hologram. The hologram's space grew in size to fill the auditorium, revealing to those assembled the nine planets orbiting the solar star. Above the triangles, the twelve stars of the astrologer's zodiac rotated slowly upon the three-hundred-and-sixty-degree wheel of Earth-time. Within the triangles appeared the year, month, day, and time of Lia's birth, her code captured in time and space for always. The star Scorpio, under which Lia was born, was emblazoned in the heavens at the time of her birth, which was sunrise. This was her Earthly blueprint, the nucleus of her physical life. Her time and date of birth, emblazoned in a changing pattern of colour, seemed to speak to her. She realised that the numbers also represented the points at which the nine planets – Mercury, Venus, Earth, Mars, Jupiter, Saturn, Uranus, Neptune, and Pluto – were fused upon her wheel of life to give her the challenges that would manifest in her lifetime and compel her towards her destiny.

The books upon the dais fluttered and opened before Pythagoras. They were the book of the Ephemerides and the Table of Houses, books of calculation that were a mystery to most of mankind. 'Lia, you now understand that the two triangles of numbers reveal how the universe reproduces itself with the four elements that sum up a kaleidoscope of equations, where everything may appear haphazard, but will, in reality, connect and, above all, balance the existence of Universe Four.'

Lia thought about the work involved to balance such a vast organism. She also realised that to those like Pythagoras, it was no great thing, as easy as two plus two. Another thought came to her, and she remembered that Ormus had taught her that nothing was ever lost; it just entered the void to be transformed into another life form. He had told her this so many times that it was permanently etched upon her mind. Surely she would never forget.

Pythagoras smiled at her thoughts, 'Lia, let me tell you more about how the universe expands. Remember when you stood upon the squares of the universal chequerboard. Well, each one is a time equation, and the number two is the bridge between the building blocks of four.' The universal chequerboard appeared inside the hologram, displayed in such a way that he hoped Lia might understand. Pythagoras stood back and began to explain the sum, 'The universe you live in is made up of a trillion, trillion squares; that is its nature. This equation holds all atoms together by the force of gravity, and, if the equation were smaller, then life would not exist in Universe Four. As the universe expands and life develops, so the universal computation expands, and the game plays on. In the future, this expansion of the universe will alter the destiny of mankind radically.'

Lia looked at the diagram of squares expanding outwards, each square bridged by a void that was the gateway to the next, corridors of space through which the Holocenes had travelled to find Earth. Lia's mind raced to absorb the information displayed before her.

Pythagoras continued, 'There are many codes that unlock the void of zero energy, and they are held within the symbols of the planets within each universe, of which there are nine. But, of course, the consciousness of life is expanding all the time and could become a new universe. I think that is all you need to know for now, Lia.' Pythagoras wished her well with the challenges before leaving her alone to study the hologram.

Later, when Lia looked up, the gathering had disappeared; only Zrsiofour remained.

'Ormus is waiting for us, Lia.' Zrsiofour beckoned her to enter the pool before disappearing below the water.

Lia slipped into the pool to follow him, leaving ever-widening ripples upon the pool's surface to indicate their departure from the tranquil whiteness of the Halls of Legislature.

Ormus held out his arms as Lia ran to hug him, his slight body appearing taller to her because of his slender form.

'Are you well again?' Lia asked, concerned by his frailty.

'Yes, yes,' said Ormus warmly, dismissing the seriousness of his ill health. 'You have learned all you need to know for now, Lia, and we will be leaving here shortly.'

Lia listened to the weariness in his voice and wondered how many more times she would hear those words spoken before the challenges were over.

'Say your farewells, my dear.'

Tamelia came forward to say goodbye. In her outstretched hand was a pearl, which she placed in Lia's palm, and, closing her hands around Lia's, she said, 'Take this gift, Lia, and when you arrive in the City of Memories, it will bring me to you.'

As Tamelia held her hand, Lia saw a vision of the lightworker migrants as they entered the City of Memories. She wanted to ask the time of this event happening to her, but she knew she would not be given the answer. Lia thanked Tamelia and stepped into the boat to sit beside Ormus. The boat moved swiftly away into the bluish depth of the underworld. Both of them remained silent until they reached their destination. In the pitch-black depths of the ocean, the boatman steered towards the shore with a shoal of luminous ocean dwellers swarming about them to light the way. Beneath the boat two triangles of light appeared upon the ocean floor. Ormus thanked the boatman, and he drew Lia close to him as they stepped from the boat to stand alongside the two triangles.

'Hold tight to the pearl that Tamelia gave you,' he whispered and, covering her shoulders with his cloak, he walked with her between the illuminated triangles into the binary world of zero energy that would transfer them from the underworld to the world above. A moment later, Ormus and Lia appeared on the surface of the Earth. He laid Lia on the sand-covered beach, knowing that she would not be conscious for some time, not until her body had become used to breathing air again.

The oarsman turned his boat in the direction from whence he had come and waited for the group of lightworker migrants who were due to appear inside the triangles from the binary world.

Ormus stood silently breathing in the cool night air. He sensed the fear of those in the dreamtime who were about to migrate to the world below. Their watchful eyes were full of apprehension as they looked for reassurance to Ormus, the wise one who had appeared to light their way.

'Enter the void. Do not be afraid. Transformation is the most natural phenomenon within the universe and not to be labelled with the finality of death.'

With Ormus's reassurance, the cargo of migrants slipped into the void and reappeared within the lighted triangles. The boatman's consignment was safe.

Ormus raised his face up to the unlit night sky. For a moment, he caught a glimpse of the lightworkers making their journey to the City of Memories with the boatman who been waiting to welcome them. All had gone well. Ormus gathered Lia into his arms and flew into the darkened night, his thoughts with the recent events of his failing health and his deep concern that he would be unable to safeguard Lia. *Was destiny to repeat itself,* he wondered. Ormus's spirits dropped a little, and then he heard Strawberry's voice.

'Remember, Ormus, Hafnium has guaranteed her safety while she is challenged. After that, she must take her chance in the hologram of life, as do *all*. For now she is safe, and you will be with her to complete the challenges. You must put those thoughts from your mind, for they are part of the challenge and will distract you from your goal. Have you forgotten, 'gifted one'?'

Strawberry's fading laughter was left implanted on his mind, as he smiled at her obviousness. Ormus's mood plunged again as he remembered what lay ahead. Man had destroyed nature and now nature was to destroy man. It was time for the female energy to rise again, to balance the scales of creativity. Ormus focused on the blackened sky and then down at his charge resting peacefully in his arms, 'How strong will the female energy be when you are an elder of the one tribe of man living deep within the Earth's oceans?' Ormus spoke the words wistfully, knowing he would not be with her.

'Let's go home to Cornwall,' he said softly.

Chapter 28

The Gifted Ones

Lia felt the cold morning air penetrating her body, even though she was wrapped snugly within Ormus's cloak. Opening her eyes, she recognised the coastline of Cornwall below them. Ormus began to descend as they flew over Land's End towards Tintagel. He brought them down at the back of the Causeway, so that Lia would not see the car parked at the front of the cottage. That would give the game away.

'Why are we going in through the back door, Ormus?' Lia began to laugh, knowing something was up. She sprinted past Ormus to the front of the cottage, where the open-top sports car was parked in the road. Immediately she recognised the car as Edward's. Ormus had caught up with Lia and was pretending to fumble with the key amid her shouts of excitement.

'Give it to me. Give the key to me!' Lia demanded playfully.

Ormus pretended to be serious, 'Hold on, Lia! Patience now; I can't see what I'm doing – move back.'

Lia stepped back and saw a shadow passing by the window.

'Let me in!' she shouted amid bursts of giggles.

The front door opened, and out stepped Strawberry and Glas, her father, René, Ette and her family, and, finally, Edward. Lia was ecstatic! The two sisters jumped up and down with delight and hugs and kisses followed.

Glas shouted above the din, 'Why are we standing out here? Let's go in and sit by the fire, and then we can talk.'

A moment's quiet fell as in they filed in and closed the door behind them, Lia and Ormus dropping their cloaks on the nearest chair as they entered. The room felt warm and cosy. They all sat down around the large kitchen table while Strawberry laid the meal. She had kept herself busy cooking enough food for an army, having thought of everything including one of her red-and-white checked tablecloths. Strawberry had dusted and polished that morning until the cottage shone, wanting Lia's homecoming to be perfect. The kettle sung upon the hearth, sending streams of white vapour into the air, while the pungent savoury smells that drifted from the oven mingled with the smell of home-baked bread cooling by the window, making everyone feel hungry. Strawberry placed the bread and savouries upon the table and, when the tea was made, she sat down and invited them to eat. They needed no second invitation. Conversation ceased, as the clink of cutlery mingled with their pleasurable sighs as they ate Strawberry's good fare in the warm Cornish kitchen.

Late into the evening, when all the news had been exchanged, they settled down in front of the fire to hear of Ormus and Lia's journey to the world of the Mers, while Ette and her family, and Edward, slept peacefully upstairs.

'Do you know of the world below the oceans, Glas?' Lia asked.

'Yes,' said Glas.

Strawberry and René answered the same.

'Why do you ask?' enquired Ormus.

'Because, you told me that all wise ones knew of the Mer world, and I wondered if Strawberry, Glas, and my father were wise ones.'

Ormus sat looking into the flames of the fire. 'Would you like me to tell you more about the history of the wise ones, Lia?'

Lia nodded, 'Yes, I would like that.'

'Very well, then,' he answered, 'but first; let me explain that your father is not a Holocene, as are Strawberry and Glas. He is a wise one of the Saturnian race, whose work as an enforcer of universal law is very important to the Earthly quest. The Saturnian's are working alongside the Holocene race to bring about a positive change for mankind, and they will continue to do so for as long as is necessary.

Ormus paused to sip his drink. 'The wise ones . . .' Then he began his tale. He talked long into the night of those who had come to Earth to bestow upon man the gifts of spiritual life. The Holocenes had travelled across many universes, exploring many galaxies to observe other life forms. During that time, they had joined allegiance with many, including the Saturnian's.

While voyaging in Universe Four, the Holocene race came upon Earth, and a new era began for mankind.

'Sesome was the first leader of the earliest Holocene voyagers to enter Universe Four. His was the first ship to land upon Earth, some ten thousand years ago, at a place called the Eye of the Eagle, by the Dead Sea in the east. It was there the wise ones initiated Hafnium's plan for mankind's future. Sesome could see the potential of the developing Earthman beyond that of an animal and, as requested by Hafnium, requested a colony of Holocenes be sent to Earth to live among the race they named humankind. Sesome realised that to liberate the Earthman's animal nature, they would first need to win his trust, and so they decided to take on his physical form. The plan was to imbue humankind with the Holocene intelligence and spiritual nature in order to bring the Holocene and the Earthman together within a new race. There were to be twelve tribes that would repopulate the Earth over thousands of years. The task began in selecting twelve Earth women who were the gentlest-natured of humankind. The Holocene travellers then took them as wives. The change in man's nature had begun.

At that time, the gradual thawing of the ice age was making the Earth's climate more amenable. The Holocenes' plan was to teach man to grow crops, encourage him to live from the newly emerging land, and reduce his dependency upon the animal herds. The wisest teachers, the greatest builders, and the finest craftsmen were chosen to colonise Earth and use their highly evolved skills to create a change in mankind. For the Holocene travellers, the challenge of integration was immense and dangerous, as over time the primordial earthman began to attack the twelve new tribes of man on a major scale. By that time, Sesome was a father of many children, having taken many wives during his seven hundred years upon Earth. When it was decided that a culling of the primordial earthmen was necessary to safeguard the race that had been created, Sesome's wife, a wise woman of the first generation, prophesied that it would fail.

Ormus ceased his story while Strawberry poured him tea. Lia sipped her tea, eager for Ormus to continue.

'Man continued to evolve rapidly, and, over the next ten thousand years, he and his developing intelligence achieved greater and greater things. But all was not well. Over that time, the primordial earthmen flourished, as they took the women of the new race to create a new race of their own. The genetic impregnation from the wise ones was not enough to extinguish the insidious brutality that remained the dominant part of their nature. Their unique powers among the animal world delivered forth a material world of great intellect, wherein the influence of the spirit could not flourish. When the wise ones could no longer commit themselves to the Earth experiment, they returned home to Holocene, leaving a few to remain as advisers to mankind. These, such as Raphiel and I, have returned many times to prepare mankind for the pending challenge by fire. This must happen, because man is now exploring the galaxy surrounding him. Another era has begun, one that threatens Universe Four with mankind's insidious aggression. The time has come to separate the lightworkers from mankind in order that they may continue evolving towards Hafnium's goal, which is to unite mankind with other races within Universe Four. If the lightworkers are not separated from the family of mankind, they will perish.' Ormus became silent, his story almost told. He would not tell them that he would be leaving the Earth before the destruction began or that Lia would take her place among the elders of those chosen to survive.

Ormus's mind rolled back over the changing years of mankind and his part in it. He had been on Earth at the time when man would no longer accept the words of the wise ones. Man had lost sight of a future that included a peaceful Earth. Mankind began to elect spiritual leaders to replace the Holocene wise ones; many of them were eager to be rulers of men. At the beginning, some governed well, wanting a good life for their people. Others wanted only power and travelled to other lands to kill, conquer, and rule.

Ormus remembered those, like him, who had stayed and remained loyal to the new rulers of the Earth, because the challenge had been prophesied. They had continued to teach the ancient wisdom, and most were revered – but some were in the service of powerful and evil kings and were given inestimable rewards for their knowledge of the future. They, too, were gripped by the pleasures of Earthly life and, like Ormus, eventually lost their powers. Ormus suddenly felt a heavy burden for those once placed in his care, those he felt he had let down badly, naïve and loyal people who had followed him on the path to destruction. Ormus pushed his thoughts aside and continued with his story.

'The spiritual nature of humankind had brought a natural magic to the Earth. The first-born females of the twelve tribes were endowed with magical powers that were passed on through the females of her kin. These gifts went unquestioned for thousands of years, until man proclaimed these women sorcerers and witches of evildoing.'

Ormus had looked on passively as the Holocene gifts of empowerment diminished with each new millennium. In the name of men's new faith, religion, the female gifted ones were tormented and put to death. Eventually their numbers were few, and the mystery was hidden beneath a shroud of secrecy, in order to keep it alive. Without the wise ones to guide them, the wise women forgot the powerful gifts bestowed upon them, the ten strands of knowledge that were lost to mankind forever. Ormus had turned away from his purpose, which was to protect them. It had been men's free will to do as they did, he had told himself, while the women, by birthright, had the power to stop them.

Without the female human's power to endow the Earth with spiritual life forms, man had brought destruction to the land and destroyed the kinship of magic and man that was created in the union of woman and Holocene.

'Was it because of my love for the life I had chosen, because of my power? Did I . . . did I have a choice, with destiny making the moves?' Ormus spoke the words as if only to *himself*. He continued, 'Many of the wise ones returned to our world beyond Earth's universe, never wanting to return again to the task of teaching mankind and his kings that which had become an impossible task . . . From that time, those who had journeyed here named this place Hell on Earth. That is the story told of how the wise ones came to Earth,' said Ormus. 'At first they wanted to help mankind bring about a new humankind – to help them evolve and live peacefully in this Eden of colour and sound.'

'Is there really a place called Hell?' Lia asked.

'In truth, Lia,' Ormus replied, 'Hell is within the mind, for that is where the thoughts of evil first manifest. Hell is a place where the spirit struggles to flourish, as a plant struggles without light.'

'And what of the humankind that survived those times. Are there many?'

'There are many, Lia. Many of them are the lightworkers who are working to bring balance to the planet. When most of the wise ones returned to Holocene, the lightworkers replaced them, in order that Hafnium's plan would continue – although at a much slower pace. Once started, the challenge between light and darkness must continue. Mankind had begun his evolutionary climb to level six, and the struggle of light and darkness is essential to its continuation. Therefore, it was decided that the future children of humankind would continue to be born with the spiritual light of the wise ones, but their special gifts would remain dormant, waiting for a time when the hidden mysteries would be restored. These children always have the choice to generate light into the world through some field of work, and those that follow the light become the 'chosen ones' – and there are many of them,' Ormus smiled, and he ceased speaking.

The fire had died down, and the room was beginning to lose its warmth.

Strawberry stirred from her slumber and got to her feet, 'I'll put the kettle on for a cup of tea. Then I think it will be time for our beds.'

Chapter 29

Catfish: The Keeper of Souls

The following morning Edward was up early, preparing for his journey back to London.

Lia went out to speak to him while he loaded the car. 'Breakfast will be ready soon.' she said disappointed that his stay had been so short, but then he had brought her father and Ette down to the cottage, and they would be staying.

Edward smiled brightly at her, pleased that they were able to have some time alone. He wanted to stay, to be with her. 'When you return to London, we will have a party. We will have a ball – but not like the one at Chequers!'

They laughed at the memory as they stood holding each other.

Strawberry came to the door of the cottage to call them to breakfast. Lia and Edward walked up the path unhurriedly, laughing and chatting together.

Strawberry's breakfast was a grand affair, which they consumed in no time at all. When everyone had finished, she returned to the kitchen and, in the swish of a kitchen cloth, the dishes were washed and the kitchen left neat and tidy. Then she and Glas gave everyone a goodbye hug and started on their journey home. Lia watched them from the cottage gate as they disappeared upon the horizon in the direction of London. Edward came out soon afterward to say goodbye. Lia waved until the car was out of sight. Turning to go back inside, she was met by Ormus, who was closing the front door behind him.

'Come along, Lia; we are going out for a while.' Ormus lifted his cloak around her shoulders as if to fly, but this time his action was only to comfort her. Lia was now deeply in love with Edward, and Ormus knew she would be feeling lonely without him. They walked along the cliff-tops, the white foam of the ocean swelling and crashing onto the rocks below.

'Do you remember the name of the Mer you met in the caves below us, Lia?' Ormus asked.

Lia looked up at Ormus, her eyes nervous and questioning, 'Yes, it was Catfish, or at least it sounded like it.' Lia, having answered his question, pushed it aside. 'Ormus, I must ask you what is to become of Ette and her family when the changes come. After what I have learned, I am concerned for them. Ette, unlike father, is not aware of what is happening, although she is unwittingly part of it.' Lia felt a quickening in her stomach telling her she would not like the answer.

Ormus looked up at the sheer blueness of the sky and the white furls of cloud blustering along at enormous speed.

'Ette and her family will return with your father to Saturn. There is no easy way to tell you that, Lia. But you will have Edward by your side and will have a family of your own in time to ease your heartache and loss.

Lia stood motionless; she did not understand. She did not want to understand. Saturn! How could her father – they – return there without her?

Ormus listened to her thoughts and answered, 'For mankind, here upon Earth, there is only one believable form of life, which is physical. Believe me, Lia, out there in the universe there are many races that mankind is not capable of seeing or hearing or having any comprehension of in the form in which they exist – and they are right beneath mankind's nose, so to speak. And, yes, what you intuitively feel is right. Ette cannot be part of the migration and must die in order to change. When your father leaves the Earth, he will return home with his grandchild to Saturn. Your sister and her husband will journey on to the other-worlds to further their learning before being reunited with your father on Saturn. But you are distressed and need time to think. We can talk more of this later, if you wish.' Ormus gave Lia a comforting hug. 'Today was not the day I would have wished you to know this, Lia, but circumstance often makes the choice for us.' Ormus turned back towards the cottage, leaving her to think on what he had told her.

Lia felt as though a shroud had replaced the warmth of Ormus's cloak. Her family's death was no longer a premonition. What comfort ignorance was, what bliss as opposed to the confirmation of one's instinct. Lia began to cry as the truth raged through her mind. The beautiful memory of just a few hours past had been swept away by the circumstance of life. Lia turned back towards the cottage and her family.

Most days, Lia would climb down to the cave early in the morning and be back by the time Ette and her family were ready to enjoy the day with her. Lia was now used to the Mers presence, and Millie and Max would bring others to teach her about their world. René spent most of his time working with Ormus on his manuscripts, entering the final words that would become an important part of the teachings in the new world. The pain she had felt knowing she was to be separated from her family, especially Ette, her twin, had become tolerable. She accepted that, however painful, the time left with them was to be happily cherished.

One morning Ormus accompanied Lia to the cave below the cottage, his intention being to return Lia to the City of Memories and leave her with Catfish, the Keeper of Souls. Catfish lived below the oceans, in the meadow of many flowers, where his home was a shelter constructed of trees from the tidal forests, trees that had ended their life cycles and could be of use in other ways. Most days Lia would take her lessons in the sparse but comfortable shelter and, on warmer days, Raphiel and Ormus would join them outside to instruct her. They explained to her the interaction of plant and animal life and that the life of a tree was very important to mankind. Mankind depended on the forests to release oxygen into the atmosphere, whereas the trees absorbed carbon dioxide to exist, thus completing a cycle of the Earth's ecosystem. Catfish explained the diverse cycles of the planet in detail, and Lia began to understand why the forests were so precious. Man had destroyed the

Earth's rainforests over a very short period of time, promoting his own disaster by felling them. Often during these periods of instruction, Lia found it difficult to understand her kind's behaviour. Mankind was intelligent, bright, and capable. His ability to engineer nature's wealth of resources and to build great cities and monuments was amazing; yet, he seemed unable to recognise the peril that his actions were bringing nearer to him each day. One morning, Lia and Catfish sat looking out towards the tidal forest.

Catfish said, 'Lia, look beyond the first meadow to the one that spreads itself below the mountain to the east.'

From where they sat Lia could see the meadow clearly, as the forest was sparse where a volcanic mountain rose up from the landscape. Catfish began to tell her about the water meadow in the east where the spirits of all new babies, whatever their kind, were born to Earth.

'They are brought here to begin their journey into physical life. Here they decide whether to continue on to a life with their chosen parents and family, or remain in the other-worlds until another life experience manifests.'

'What do you mean "choose"?' Lia queried.

Catfish answered, 'The spirit-soul does not enter the unborn infant until the time of birth, when it passes into Earthly existence; until then, the spirit can choose to terminate his or her coming. The spirit of the mother never hosts the spirit of the infant; each must remain separate while experiencing physical life. Each spirit-soul has its own unique summation of energy. Until the time of birth, the unborn child is merely a replication of the mother and father's physical matter – human genetic material programmed with the ancestry of both families. The child can feel and move as it grows, but his or her unique fragment of spirit-soul does not enter the infant until the first breath . . .' Catfish paused. '. . . Lia, can you see the gate separating the two meadows? Look above it.'

Lia did as Catfish asked and focused her eyes above the gate. A purple haze that covered the meadow began to lift, and she could see an expanse of blossoming 'infant energy' of various cultures and colours. Each one revealed its future form in the hazy atmosphere of the meadow. In the background, the unnatural light from the outpouring volcanic magma tinged the fluid atmosphere with the gold's and reds of an Earthly sunset. These gossamer beings were the spirits waiting to be born, to manifest life within a physical infancy.

Drawn from the dreamtime to the edge of the meadow were many expectant females. Some were holding hands with partners. These couples waited eagerly for their new infant, their combined energy field radiating a golden eminence of togetherness. Other couples stood apart, their separated energies emitting the coldness of denial that was uninviting to the spirit of the blossoming child.

It was the latter group that Catfish continued to speak of. 'These unborn children will make their journey to Earth knowing that it will be difficult for them. They are not wanted. However, they wish to help these souls: parents who are lost within their Earthly cycle of existence and needing to bestow love but unable to do so. The unwelcome spirits born to these parents will eventually group with others like themselves to find love. The infants who are welcomed into a life of happiness and love will not find their passage on Earth so hard while in infant form.'

Lia thought of her father and the love he had bestowed on her and Ette. She realised they had been very lucky.

Catfish went on to explain that at this time there were many souls being born under difficult circumstances, but that many more were coming to families that wanted them. He continued, 'This is also true of the herds, the animals in bondage, which are used for protein farming and are treated so inhumanely. They also do not welcome their young but wish themselves to die, and they welcome the diseases that are forcing man to slaughter them.'

Lia began to cry tears of anguish and alarm, 'But I don't understand – why are they coming, if they are not wanted?' Lia's thoughts turned to the abuse of the young, old, and vulnerable, which made daily headlines. 'Why, if they have this knowledge, do they decide to come to Earth?'

Without answering her question, Catfish bade her look above the gate. 'Tell me, what do you see, Lia?'

A hologram appeared suspended over the gate to the meadow. Lia dried her eyes.

'The hologram you are looking at is the gateway from the spirit world. When a spirit-soul joins with the flesh of a newborn infant, it loses all conscious memory of any previous existence. Only while in the dreamtime is the spirit-soul able to access this information, which mankind finds almost impossible to remember and interpret. If he could, his dreams would tell him the purpose for which he was born. Go to the meadow, Lia. Pass through the gate and listen. I will allow you back when you have heard all you need to hear, for I am the Keeper, the Keeper of Souls. I watch over those who return to and from the physical world. It is my responsibility to see that they make the transition at the exact moment that their destiny requires it. Go now, and I will return you here when the time is exactly right.'

Lia made her way across the first meadow and climbed upon the gate. Within the hologram above her, a spirit child appeared, with long red hair that curled thickly around her smiling face. Red-headed Rosalie was yet to be born to her Earth parents; she would be a child of the future when man had made his first step towards the sixth world. She was a child who would be born to endure much but with the guidance of those around her who offered immense love. When that time came, Lia would be her maternal grandmother and would call her Reds.

The Initiators had asked Catfish to arrange the meeting between Lia and her future granddaughter, Rosalie. Lia climbed over the gate into the meadow and waited for her to appear. The child in the hologram appeared in the meadow. Lia and Rosalie stood facing each other, both overwhelmed by the strong bond of love that was to be between them. Lia stirred within for the child she had yet to hold, the mother of the spirit child Rosalie. Both were unknown to Lia, and yet already she loved them. No words could pass between them, as all future events were yet to come.

Before Lia returned from her journey beyond the gate she witnessed hers and Ette's birth, and understood the lessons she had committed her spirit-soul to experience among mankind.

Catfish held out the familiar cup of golden liquid and invited her to drink: 'Lia, drink up. Then we will journey to the Halls of Learning to discover a little more of mankind's future ...'

Ormus had asked the masters if they would receive her again, since Catfish had taught her what she needed to know. They had agreed. Lia was ascending the tree of life, surmounting the steps of knowledge one by one. Each step was not to be passed until experienced – another lesson that mankind had forgotten.

Chapter 30

'What of all this, Lia?'

Lia constantly questioned what she believed she had not grasped of the teachings. Each day she disciplined herself to accept the future, when, in fact, she knew that acceptance without understanding was never achievable. Had she misunderstood some information, or had she not reached a point when the information could be made available to her? The questions continued to go round in her head without answer. Lia thought of Einstein. The major part of his work had been completed in his early life, after which he seemed unable to go further. Was it because the universe was not ready to give up the answers he so fervently worked for? Mankind was bypassing the ways of nature for science and creating change without the foresight of understanding. Lia realised that it was this sightlessness that had incurred many of the dangers mankind now faced. The gaps in his knowledge of the Earth's nature were beginning to show, and another of mankind's great civilisations was about to disappear into an abyss of devastation. The lost ten strands of knowledge that had been bestowed upon mankind by the wise ones held the secrets that would have guided the Earth nations in the ways of Hafnium, God of Fire.

As Lia sat beside Catfish in the Halls of Learning, the masters appeared one by one upon the podium to speak.

One spoke of the ancient karmic diseases that were returning to Earth as part of the solution to rid the Earth of mankind. Another spoke of the children who suffered emotional and physical abuse. These children were so full of anger that they retaliated by spreading terror among the young and old alike. 'Like their parents, they will find the redress needed to right this wrong – albeit grievous and painful. The disappearance of their teachers is only the beginning. The scales of justice must balance and right the wrong that is manifest upon Earth.' The Master stepped down.

A dense black cloud appeared above the open roof of the forum and slowly devoured the light. Within the blackness, Lia could hear every bad thought that was manifest upon the Earth. She could taste the evil in the shroud that blotted out the light. Mankind's obstinacy, ingratitude, and violence had spread like a disease within his mind, body, and spirit, turning his soul to ugliness.

The darkness gave way to a clear blue sky. But Lia still felt the evil about her. Beneath the bright blue sky there now floated mile upon mile of grossly bloated bankers, ministers, judges, and barristers. They smiled brightly as their swollen, air-filled bodies sailed serenely by. Lia watched them as they passed her, their smiling faces singing in a united chorus of one voice. They sang out to mankind below them, promising to provide them with all they desired. Mankind could pay tomorrow!

Another master appeared, who said, 'There are many among mankind who are good and responsible people, but behind the words of these parasites there is nothing more than theft with a smile. They steal mankind's future – without conscience or logic.'

The scene above them faded and the forum became silent. Soon the fate of man would be moving on again. Lia held her breath. She was paralysed with fear: fear from the knowledge that was now hers, and fear of what mankind had chosen for himself and other species. Lia was jolted back into wakefulness, her body signalling that she had stopped breathing. She fumbled to her feet, crying uncontrollably at the knowledge she had been burdened with.

Catfish spoke to her in a voice that was soft and soothing. 'Lia, go to sleep. Heal your body and soul.'

'I want to see Ormus,' Lia sobbed. 'I don't want to go back to sleep until he has spoken to me. Why hasn't he come? He always returns when I am frightened.'

Catfish could not answer her question. Ormus was unwell again.

Catfish held a cup to Lia's lips and insisted that she drink. 'Come, Lia; let me see you put your cloak of protection on to stop your dreaming. I will help you.'

'I need answers if I am to be at peace,' she answered.

'And you will have them. I promise. But, for now, go to sleep.' Catfish drew a cloak of healing around her and returned her to the cottage. Lia had learned enough of the future for now.

When Lia awoke, Ormus was sitting in the chair opposite her.

'You have slept most of the afternoon, Lia. How do you feel now?'

Lia realised that she felt more at peace than she had done for a long time. It was as if her last experience had exhausted her fear. 'I feel fine, thank you,' she replied carefully, wondering what was coming next.

Ormus stood up and walked towards the window, 'What of all of this, Lia?'

Lia stiffened. 'I don't know – perhaps you will tell me,' she replied curtly.

Ormus felt the rift that Lia's knowledge of her family's death had caused between them. She no longer trusted him now that she knew her family would be gone at the outcome.

'Lia, there is one thing that you must understand as well as accept. The transformation to another life form beyond physical death is a wonderful experience. Mankind's biggest mistake is his trying to avoid it.'

'You cannot blame mankind,' Lia said. 'Death is painful and isolating, which I have seen upon my father's face most of my lifetime. And if it is true that we live on, what is the point of us coming here to learn of such hardship?' Lia felt angry and waited to dispute his reply.

'It was not meant to be this way. That is why it must come to an end. The spirit has been lost within the physical form, rather than the spirit being handicapped by it. The reason that Hafnium created the Earth experiment is this. The matter from which the Earth and 'all' life upon it is created comes from the planets and the most eminent stars in Universe Four. They were at one time dormant in Hafnium's being, a thought process that he manifested into matter from an expression of thought – first light. Before that time, those planets and stars were no more than black holes, zero energy of the binary world in another macro universe, and, from this Hafnium created Universe Four. Not all universes have spirit trapped in physical matter; what they do have is gargantuan black holes – imploded stars with their darker side intact that contain knowledge which has served its purpose, and, will eventually return to the one which equates to zero energy, having been forgotten by Hafnium. In Universe Nine, there are imploded stars as big as Universe Four and they are balanced by the radiance of the Raytec spirals which are similar to stars, and the one world, Holocene.

Each creation must have a duality; Hafnium wanted some of the stars to show only brilliance in Universe Four, so he created the Earth and many more planets to take their darker side. The animal life from which man evolved was a by-product of this darker side and the reason that the stars remain so brilliant. The eternal light of your soul is universal science and not, as mankind believes a religious conviction. When mankind leaves Universe Four, having evolved to a higher vibration, the twelve zodiacal constellations will take back their dark side, and, in doing so, they will be consumed within themselves to become black holes again – they will cease to exist. Hafnium will forget them until he is ready to create again. Universe Four is an experimental galaxy or perhaps a laboratory for scientific creation would be a truer analogy. Truly, you are not in your real environment, Lia.'

Ormus was tired. He wanted to be back home as the 'one being' he and Lia represented in their world, which was made harder by the fact that Lia would remain on Earth for some time after his departure. At worst, she might never return to their world, Holocene. This he knew he must accept.

Lia now understood how mankind had come into existence. He had been created from the stars in Universe Four. The brilliance of mankind was a gift from the twelve stars of the zodiac. How had something so bright, so brilliant in substance, given life to something so heavily laden in darkness?

'Ormus took Lia's hand and visualised the universal chequerboard, in order for them to see the game in progress. He knew that as bad as things appeared to Lia, Hafnium's knight was still protecting his vulnerable king, while the queen, the female energy, was making headway alongside Lia in the challenge for mankind's future. 'You see, Lia, there is always balance between good and bad circumstance.'

During the weeks that followed, Ormus and René familiarised Lia with the homes of the twelve star tribes that lay out in the galaxy alongside the planets. The newly acquired knowledge made Lia feel that she belonged there, and her feeling of emptiness gradually disappeared. She also knew she would soon be on her own and having to make decisions for herself, but the acceptance of transformation gave her a feeling of wholeness, of hope. Nothing lost, nothing gained – only altering, shifting, and changing.

Chapter 31

The Future: A New Direction

Lia turned to Ormus, who was sitting quietly in the corner, to ask him about the star-shaped entrance gate to the City of Memories. It was then she realised that he was 'out'. Running to the window, she caught his youthful spirit flying towards the horizon. The rays of orange that streaked across the evening sky had turned his flowing hair into golden embers, his winged childlike figure moving swiftly beneath the glow of the setting sun. 'He has little time left here, and soon I will be moving on alone. It's forward or nothing.' Lia murmured the words as she settled down by the fire to await his return. Snuggling down into the soft tartan rug, she marvelled at its warmth which made her feel drowsy. The embers of the open fire flickered, the sparks darting here and there, the colours of red, orange, and yellow flowing over and through one another like synchronised dancers. Lia became mesmerised by the sound and warmth of the peaceful quietness it created, which, after a while, released her from the physical world into the dreamtime ...

Lia stepped into the future to see Ette driving at speed down a tree-lined narrow lane and then the impact of two cars colliding head-on in slow motion. Lia's mind became one with her sister, and she felt Ette's body lift on impact. Ette's child, husband, and father disappeared from her sight as blackness clouded her vision. Lia could see all four spirit bodies, her father holding his grandchild, and Ette and Andre separated, standing alone. Andre, unable to see Ette, was calling out for her, a look of surprise registered across his bleeding face. Within seconds, they had passed through the blackness of death to awareness within the ghost of their physical forms, all four now looking at their lifeless bodies within the wreckage of the crushed vehicle. Ette could hear Lia calling her and felt she was being drawn back into her body. Raphiel appeared before Lia and began to pull her away from Ette, extending the line between them until it was no longer visible. 'It's broken,' were Ette's last words to her.

Lia stumbled on through her dream until Raphiel returned to speak to her.

'Come with me, Lia. I have come into the dreamtime to help you accept this future event. I have a future time to show you that will make your heart lighter. You are stronger now and are beginning to accept transformation as a natural occurrence. Let us move on, shall we?'

Lia found herself within the City of Memories, where she stood watching a young couple walking together with their two young sons. As they passed by, they stopped to speak to her.

'Have you been here long, in the City of Memories?' Lia asked, as they stood and chatted.

'Why yes, all of our lives,' answered the elder of the boys, brightly.

The father smiled, 'This is our son, Haydes. He doesn't wait to be asked twice. And this is my wife, Mariana, and I am Deron Dubar-Major.'

'My name is Kiron,' said the younger one. 'Do you live here? I haven't seen you before in the City.'

'Yes,' Lia answered candidly, knowing this to be true.

'May I ask why you made the journey here?' Lia asked the boy's mother.

Mariana answered, 'We came to live here as young children when the Earth's surface would no longer sustain healthy life.'

'And how is life sustained here?' Lia inquired.

Mariana looked puzzled at Lia's question, Lia having said she lived among them, but she explained, 'Those of us that live here in the world below the oceans create our own homes. Our home and surroundings are created entirely from our thoughts, and the city fluctuates in size to accommodate the thoughts of those who live here. Apart from our food, our thoughts materialise our every need. As a bubble contains its own space, so our thoughts become our world. When we move on, it is in our thoughts that we can change our habitat and dress per se. The nature of our new world changes as our consciousness evolves. We do not need to produce material products; everything we need is provided by nature, as is our food, which the Mers help us to grow and harvest. We have homes that harmonise with our needs and are restful to our minds. Life is simple, natural, and we are happy.' Mariana added, 'Our way of life here is preparation for when we evolve to a non-physical existence in other-worlds, and universes, after our human existence is ended.'

Lia thanked Mariana, and, turning to Deron, she asked, 'Do you remember your journey here as a child?'

Deron looked deeply into her eyes and Lia felt he recognised her as someone from his past and perhaps the present.

'I do not. I was a small child when I came here with my parents,' he answered, 'There are many who do remember, though. They came to the city from different parts of the world and in various ways. The recent earthquakes upon the surface have made those who remember the past speak of the extreme weather conditions leading up to the final migration and of the super tsunami that quelled the fires of the holocaust. Of course, the migration was completed by then. We, the one tribe of man, are a contented people, and our way of living is simple and natural.'

Lia's attention was drawn to the two boys, who were playing. She could not see what they were playing with, only that they were throwing something back and forth to one another. Lia asked the younger one what it was they were playing with.

'The orb of light,' he answered. 'Those who truly understand love are always surrounded by its presence.'

Lia was amazed by the child's answer and asked his mother what he meant by 'truly understanding love.'

Mariana replied, 'In this world, we are our own healers and mentors from the time we enter adulthood. During childhood, we are educated to understand a philosophy of love that accepts all situations with compassion and grace. We understand that you cannot possess another soul and that all souls must be free to love any and all. We understand that the primordial physical body, with its desire for control, tries to deny this, a lesson that mankind has found hard to conquer. The globe of light is an energy force of good that protects our world from evil and will eventually balance the darkness surrounding the Earth's surface, allowing us to return there.

'Energy body,' Lia murmured, thinking *light body* and remembering Ormus's example.

'Yes,' replied Mariana, 'the fields of energy that vibrate within man, animal, plant, and fish. Each day, as the sun and moon rise over the oceans, we are slipped into one of the three hundred and sixty degrees of planetary energy that creates our experiences within life. By activating our subtle energy body, the planetary forces enable us to create and share our experiences with those of similar energy. Our lives are shaped by the numerical equation of our date and time of birth, as a photo captures a moment of still life. Those numbers follow us through our lives, giving us the experiences that will challenge us and help us achieve our destiny, right up to the moment of our deaths. If you look back on your life, you will see that the same numbers recur constantly. We are taught numerology and astrology to learn about such matters, in order to understand ourselves.'

The vision faded, and Lia was left standing with Raphiel upon the universal chequerboard.

'You see, Lia, the future opens up, as the past closes behind you.'

Chiron appeared, 'If mankind was to look closely at the ways of nature, he would see the truth of life and how it was intended to be. When man cultivated emotions of the two extremes, good and bad, he began his descent into oblivion. Moreover, leaders of religious faiths who direct mankind to believe they speak for Hafnium, the creator of Universe Four, have taken them further from the truth, and men no longer listen to their inner voices, or to be precise the voice of their soul, for the inner voice of the ego has always much to say.'

Lia watched as the energy of the players moved back and forth across the board. Man's darker emotions willed Aspheseuos's knight to win, while man's desire to champion Hafnium's knight struggled to bring light to the world again.

'You see, Lia, the challenge is for man to listen to his own conscience and decide for himself. Only then will he learn wisdom and compassion for himself and others. He will find the courage to face evil, allowing the lion within to roar. He will come to know every facet of human and spiritual consciousness, and his soul will evolve. Although the light is less at this time, its power is strong, because the universe is focused upon mankind's struggle with evil. Remember, the universe's scales are balanced; otherwise, nothing could exist. Upon the Earth there is a game of evil being played out, while below the oceans tolerance and compassion abounds – is it not so?' Chiron faded from view.

Lia smiled wistfully, 'I have left much behind, Raphiel, and I know that what is broken can rarely be mended, that nothing remains static. Things always move forward, always need change.'

Ormus appeared beside them. 'That is right, my dear. I am not the person you know, as to those who knew me when I first arrived upon Earth – I am not the person I was fifteen hundred years ago, for, if I had remained so, I would have ceased to exist, as would you, had you not continued to grow in body, mind, and spirit. Come with me, Lia.' Ormus held his hand out and Lia took hold of it . . .

Lia awoke to find Ormus leaning over her. Uncurling from within the cosiness of her blanket, she stood up. The light from the window reflected upon Ormus's body, and she thought how frail he looked. The twinkle in his eyes that had always shone from his craggy old face was gone, never to return. The mould was broken.

'Some refreshment would be welcome, my dear,' said Ormus. He sat down to wait while she prepared them tea.

Lia paused, remembering her question of the gate, 'Ormus, tell me about the gate to the City of Memories. It is two triangular shapes that, when closed, become a six-pointed star.

'That is so,' he answered, 'and each gate contains six concealed triangles that hold the sum of zero energy. Let me explain how they work. The City of Memories is a fluctuating circle of three hundred and sixty degrees of subliminal crystal energy that houses every thought, every idea that the one tribe of man creates. Those formations of subconscious energy are of the same energy that operates the city gates. The power source of three hundred and sixty degrees of energy is the same throughout the city, and, indeed, Universe Four. When the binary pyramid exists in pure energy form, it allows all signals to move through it, transmitting high-frequency light currents that interconnect with the other-worlds, thereby providing instant communication between all points of origin. The quartz crystal that conducts the energy from within the gates is a most versatile broad-spectrum element of the mineral kingdom. The geometric resonant attraction between the quartz and the pyramidal form creates a condition of combined intensification; the void of energy created becomes a crater of inert wholeness in which creation can begin anew, and the space between this and all other universes can be accessed.'

'And the universes that can be accessed, Ormus: where are they?'

Universe Four is the building block of earth, water, fire, and air. The energy of nine divides and multiplies between nine universes, all of which expand out from the globe of healing energy and all of which have a circumference of thirty-six, however many times the number is squared. The youngest is Universe One and the oldest, Universe Nine. Each one is an expansion of the last, like the ripples on a pond, and all are connected by zero energy, the universe's motorways.'

'I think I understand,' Lia answered. 'But the first world would be the oldest, surely, and therefore be called Universe One.

Balance, Lia. Remember, opposites and all that is contained within: the reverse of what is familiar to you – Universe Nine is manifest from 'all' knowledge contained within the universes, one to eight, and retains the multi-universal Akashic records, and, as I have said, the vast amount of knowledge that will be forgotten by Hafnium and returned to the Globe of Living Energy, is held within the Black Holes. The Holocene race is beginning to realise that there is a whole new mathematical equation unknown to us, beyond Universe Nine, which we have yet to learn about, should another universe exist or be created before we return to the *one*.

What is your world like, in Universe Nine?'

Ormus did not answer but sat in the chair with his eyes closed and his tea untouched.

Chapter 32

Checkmate: Ormus's Passing

Lia had been sitting in the garden when Raphiel appeared. The challenges were over for Ormus, and she must go at once.

'We must travel to the Heavenly Mountain, Lia. Ormus awaits you, as the time of his leaving approaches.'

Lia knew instinctively what he meant, and did not question him. Raphiel took Lia's hand to guide her to the mountain . . .

'Banished from this world . . . Oh, I know it's not like that; I know that – but that's what it feels like.' Ormus spoke quietly, his eyes closed. He knew that Lia was there and he was pleased that her challenges had been met. Lia took his hand, and he began to talk again. 'But change arrives in one form or another, when it does, for a reason, I suppose, and maybe it's the way of fate, destiny's way of sorting things out for us. Pythagoras was right; we all have to stay within the square, within the four components of the life force here on Earth, and to try to break free is to become non-existent. I have pushed beyond what is safe many times. Now I have lost . . . destiny! We have, they say, free will, and we choose to do what we do, and, to a certain extent, I suppose that's true. Do I have free will to go, or not to go? Not total free will, because my free will – my total free will – would be to stay and fight with you. However, I am tired, and my physical body longs to be at rest. So, how free is free will?' Ormus mumbled on, not wanting to face his final challenge on Earth: physical death – and to depart without her. 'There are an awful lot of factors to take into consideration with free will, and those very factors that help you to decide what to decide, freely, willingly, are in fact pushed and coerced, persuaded, shoved, squeezed in such a fashion that I tend to think it is no longer free will.'

Lia listened, realising for the first time that Ormus was as fragile as he was strong. She was now firmly of the belief that one's chosen destiny was to be accomplished by daring to face the challenge to achieve it. *But then ... how would she be when her time came to pass through to the other-worlds?* Lia pushed the thought to the back of her mind and turned her attention back to Ormus.

' ... And life's experience and personal emotions, involvements ... well, destiny does all the colouring. Destiny actually decides which way your free will allows you to take your rationale, your thought patterns, or to decipher somebody else's thought patterns, somebody else's actions. And then, how you will react to somebody else's needs and somebody else caring for you. These are all factors in moulding your free will – in fact, destiny's will.'

Lia answered softly, 'But surely, Ormus, it is still our choice, how we let others influence us?'

Ormus ignored the now-wiser Lia, who was arguing a point upon which he was stubbornly set.

'Destiny decides what will happen and what won't happen. Destiny has decided how long things will last, how long they won't last. Destiny has decided how I will act, how I won't act, and destiny controls ...' Ormus paused, his voice becoming weaker. 'I used to think that destiny controlled the result. But destiny's not content with that ... destiny's not content with that ... to control the end result. Destiny has got its own way of meddling and interfering, so that, in fact, it has got control ninety-nine percent of the time. Moreover, it has control ninety-nine per cent of the time because it knows the result and knows the path it's going to lead you on to get that result. Free will! Actually, free will is a joke, isn't it?'

Lia lifted Ormus's head, her eyes meeting his; she was beginning to accept that his time had come to pass. 'Free will is always ours, Ormus – however difficult, however insurmountable a situation appears. It is our emotional and irrational conditioning that blinds us to logic, holding us in an imaginary prison of our own making. Do you not remember telling me so?'

Ormus gazed through her as if she were not there. 'We have the ability to use our thought processes and intuitiveness to direct us. And, having looked at the pros and cons, we then make decisions – but, more often than not, those logical pros and cons are shrouded by past experiences that are familiar to us, both good and bad. Sometimes you know what your destiny is!' Ormus continued in a whisper, as if unaware of Lia's words. 'One . . . one's thought processes could actually envisage that knowing the end would make getting there that much easier. But it's like a jigsaw puzzle: you've got one piece in the middle, and you've got four on the corners, and you've got a trillion other pieces that you share with many other souls doing the same puzzle . . . and destiny has control of every one of the pieces. Victims! I say *victims*, because the more I look at it with this rationale, the more I see we are victims.'

Lia's heart felt heavy; she had never heard him speak this way. He was now cynical and tired, fading away. His voice was like a sound on the wind; less and less could she hear him. Lia bent over his fragile body and tried to comfort him, realising this was not the Ormus she knew.

Ormus continued, 'We sometimes arrogantly feel that we control our own destiny. We arrogantly feel and think that we are doing things with free will by choice. It's a laugh, isn't it, doing things by choice? And what has destiny done to make us think we've done it by choice?' Ormus raised his voice beyond a whisper, 'It manoeuvres, it cajoles, it blackmails, it pushes, it shoves, it misleads, it manipulates, it gets its way, and I'm beginning to believe, perhaps, perhaps we are powerless in its game . . .' Ormus lay still for a moment, his defiance exhausting him. 'It appears to give no credence to actual feelings, to actual personalities, and an individual's make-up. Destiny will have its way with its property by hook or by crook . . . I suppose with that thought process, perhaps the ideal answer would be to lie back and let it happen. But then, if we lie back and let it happen, do nothing to find our own way, do nothing to at least think we are finding our own way, what would we be – robots, perhaps?'

Ormus continued talking of his inner turmoil, while Lia's thoughts drifted to the person with whom she had shared her adventure to enlightenment. Lia wondered sadly if this was the way that all souls left the Earth.

Raphiel, hearing her thoughts, entered into them to comfort her. Ormus was releasing the pain and sorrow of this Earthly lifetime before his death. It was a life that had spanned fifteen hundred years and been filled with embittered experiences – a lifetime that Lia knew little of.

Suddenly aware of Raphiel's thoughts, Ormus retorted breathlessly, 'And none are given the right keys to the right drawers to get the right information for the right situation. It's one hell of a game, and the dice are loaded. We just can't win.' Ormus laughed weakly. 'We just can't win.'

Lia spoke gently to him, 'But we do have the answers, Ormus. Remember, we only have to search for them. And we can search by ourselves or accompanied by the most wonderful people, as I did with you.' Lia had become aware of the Mer spirits' presence. She could feel the coolness of their energy and smell the sea air around her. Turning, she acknowledged them, and they whispered her name.

'Lia, we have come to say goodbye to our dear friend Ormus.'

Ormus was dying, his physical presence on Earth nearing the end, after which he would continue life in another world. Lia turned back to Ormus. He was unaware that they had come to see him in his last moments upon Earth.

Ormus continued his voice even weaker than before, 'Destiny controls all. So, who or what is destiny? Is it Hafnium, the master strategist, the master chess player of Universe Four? Or is destiny working independently of him? Or is Aspheseuos, in fact, destiny? Who or what is destiny? And if we don't like the path destiny is leading us on, is there anything, anything that we can do to change course? I don't know any more. I don't know . . . if ever I did know. I lived my Earthly life as best I knew to help mankind. Was I playing my predestined role in life? Of course I was.' Ormus laughed again. 'It was doing what was right in my opinion. What was needed in my opinion, even though sometimes it led me astray.'

Lia countered, 'You did the best you could at the time, with the free will that you were given, the end result being of your own making.' Lia ended her statement benignly, not wanting to remonstrate with Ormus, who had taught her so wisely.

'Yes,' said Ormus comfortably. 'I've done the best with the knowledge that I had and ... and that is acceptable.' His face crinkled into a smile.

Many had gathered to be with Ormus as he began his journey to a life without physical pain and illness. There were those present who wanted to say goodbye and those who were waiting to greet him in his new life; they had come collectively to support his transition. They listened in silent wonder to this master who would soon be with the Holocene race again. For Ormus, his transition was not surety that his future would be on Holocene. He had made mistakes, and being a wise one did not give him certainty of a future until the transition of death had taken place.

The scene upon the Heavenly Mountain was spectacular. The sun was rising, just as it had been when Lia and Ormus flew from the mountain at the beginning of the challenges. Lia remembered how her heart had soared as they flew high above the Earth, the beautiful memory now tinged with grief. The twelve Initiators and the masters, the fairies and the elves, man, bird and beast – they all came to listen to Ormus's last mortal words.

'I don't mean to be cynical, Lia, nor do I understand how I came to this way of thinking. Death is a frightening challenge to face, a veil behind which no soul knows what lies.' Ormus sighed, 'I will miss you, Lia, my dear. I will miss you terribly, and all my dear friends here on Earth: sad destiny, sad destimy.' Ormus smiled, 'I cannot pronounce the wretched word now. Ormus let out another long sigh. 'Sad destiny ... Off I go, alone, leaving you and Raphiel to battle on. It would have been wonderful to stay and fight the battles to come, but you are right; every turn I made was bringing me to this, my end, and each step was of my making. I am ready to go now to open my wings and fly. To enjoy being freer than the birds that soar at a whim on the breeze and the rising heat of the summer winds ... and the falling rain ... falling through the clouds to the other-worlds. Bye, Lia ...' his voice drifted into silence as the world around him began to disappear and he began his return to the cosmos.

Ormus felt the draw of his spirit leaving his body. Lia knelt beside him, crying softly. This was Ormus's time of physical death, and no one or no thing should intervene. Ormus moved and shifted slightly, as if to ease his body from the stress of death. His eyes remained looking straight up into hers, her face slowly fading from his vision to be replaced by the lights of the tunnel of transformation. Suddenly, Lia panicked at the intense loneliness she felt, and, placing her hands upon his forehead, she drew his energy back. The projected energy burned within the palm of her hand, willing the healing rays to enter. Ormus felt an abrupt pull on the celestial cord that held his physical body to his spirit-soul. Once more Ormus looked into Lia's eyes as his heart took a beat.

'Lia, let go.' The command from Hafnium was absolute. 'How many times have you watched men wrenched back to a horrendous existence by those who think life must continue for no other reason than to exist physically? How much pain and suffering has been caused to the soul because of the ignorance of mankind? Let go, and rejoice in Ormus's freedom from that shadow of a human cloak he has carried for centuries. Ormus's freedom is his reward, Lia. And when he is situated once again in his role as Choice Absolute to the Holocene race, he will rejoice at his favour with me. Do not be afraid to let go, Lia. Only when you find the courage to let go will you become liberated from fear.'

In the following silence, Lia became aware that she had released her hold on Ormus. Her hands were now holding his, as he lay at rest. For a long time she sat with the body of her dear companion who was now in another dimension. Later on, she realised, when her loss had dissipated there would be no distance between their worlds. Lia covered Ormus's body, not wanting him to get cold. The setting sun showered its glowing colours of red, orange, and gold upon the heavenly mountain. Ormus had had his day to die. Lia pondered on when she had first come to the mountain at sunset and in the morning departed on the rising sun; it had been a time of new beginnings for her. On Ormus's day of transition, the parallel had been reversed.

Crying softly Lia cradled Ormus, rocking him gently back and forth, more for her own comfort than for his. Gradually the sun faded and all became still beneath the twilight. All those who had come to be with Ormus at his death had departed; only Lia and Raphiel remained.

Raphiel rose from his resting place and came to sit beside Lia. 'My dear, it is time to leave. Ormus will be well taken care of. You will see him again after he has rested and healed from his long Earthly life.' Raphiel took Lia gently by the shoulders and her hands slid away from Ormus's body.

Lia stood up and looked out from the mountain top. 'Goodbye,' she whispered. In the months to come she would understand why her friend, her protector, was no longer needed. Lia felt at peace, as though she had come through the biggest challenge of all. She faced Raphiel, 'I am happy for him, happy that he is resting at peace.'

'That is good, Lia. You have truly come to understand that death and rebirth are an inevitable process of life's continuing cycle, and that is wisdom indeed, my dear.' Raphiel waited for Lia to compose herself; her anguish and sorrow at the loss of her mentor were so painfully visible.

Lia knew that Ormus would return to this world in some form; he was needed here. But, for now, he would return to the world of the Holocenes.

'You have done well in the challenges, Lia, and I am certain you will continue to do so throughout your lifetime. Fear, you now realise, is an illusion created by evil and can be overcome by testing its power and causing it to melt away. You will always have the wisdom Ormus taught you. Use it as your shield and armour against all negative forces.'

'Thank you, Raphiel. I will always remember Ormus and try to reach him in my dreams.'

'My dear child, do not fret so.' Raphiel could not go on while feeling the emotion and loss that Lia was enduring. Raphiel would now bring to Lia's guidance a gentler approach, replacing Ormus's austerity that was no longer needed now that she was able to decide on matters for herself. Raphiel coughed nervously; he was uncomfortable with such strong emotion and wondered if a time among the masters might be beneficial to him.

A voice cut in to his thoughts, 'Raphiel, my friend. Do not be concerned by your earthbound emotions. You will return for a time of rest as soon as your assignment is completed.'

'Keep my thoughts to myself,' Raphiel muttered. 'That's one archangel I can do without.'

'Pardon, Raphiel – what did you say?' Lia, having heard the conversation, looked at Raphiel in surprise.

'Sorry, my dear, but you cannot think around here without someone listening in. Here upon the Heavenly Mountain, there is nothing that escapes the notice of the Initiators. They cannot have slapdash emotional behaviour up here. Everyone working with the Earthly challenge needs to be constantly searching for the truth, in case Hafnium changes the plan. We must always be at our most spiritually aware, which means that we must not let lesser emotions blind us to reality.'

Lia glanced beyond him to see Ette calling her, drawing her back to their life together. The mountain was disappearing, and Raphiel was fading into the haze …

Lia awoke at the Hotel Renoir feeling completely at peace. Her gaze travelled to the mirror on the wall, from which hung some white heather, the tiny white flowers so vibrant and pure, like the memory of her dream. Suddenly a lump came to her throat, and the tears ran down her cheeks as she remembered. She now fully understood the recklessness of mankind and realised the world was dying about her.

A silvery iridescence of Glas' human form appeared before Lia. Glas was already many light years away from Earth and no longer in the physical body that Lia knew him as. 'I am returning to Holocene with Ormus, Lia.'

Lia looked at the silvery figure but did not answer.

'I have come to reassure you, Lia. Though the Earth must first come to darkness, and you have no choice but to be part of it, eventually it must return to Hafnium's will and light will be restored to the Earth.' Glashadou moved closer, his form fluttering like the beating of butterfly wings. Lia watched in awe as his silhouette changed to reveal his true Holocene form.

'The leaders of the Earth make ready to struggle for supremacy again. They call to one another by name; they boast of all they will do, but, of course, it is all words of little truth. They have no real power, for they are under the influence that governs the world at this time – a supremacy that grows bigger and more powerful with each rising sun. The world's leaders are being drawn into this darkness one by one. Soon all nations will join Aspheseuos. Yet, as I have said, there will be intervention. Aspheseuos consumes light and love, the energy of harmony and balance, as a plague of ground ants destroys vegetation. His followers are iniquitous and loyal to only one, Aspheseuos, the angel of darkness.

These people are unable to see the pain and suffering that their beliefs bring forth. They follow a figurehead, conscious only of the power and wealth behind it. Only when a unified belief in what is truly spiritual arises from within mankind, dissolving their differences, will there be peace and genuine thanks for their existence.'

Lia lay listening to the lyrical tone of Glashadou's voice; it was clear and pure in the stillness.

'Lia, I do not wish to shadow your return to your family, but you must know of these things in order to prepare yourself. And remember, Raphiel will always be at hand to help you.'

Lia thanked Glashadou before drifting back to sleep.

Chapter 33

Paris: Life Continues

When Lia awoke, she felt cold and strained. Tears lay salty on her cheeks. From nearby she could hear her sister, Ette talking on her mobile phone to their father. Ette was laughing. She sounded so happy. She had moved on from the tragedy in France, and their coming to London for a break was working for her. Lia felt thirsty; she wanted to go outside and sit in the garden to breathe the morning air. It was then she realised that she was sitting in the garden. Getting up, she walked towards her sister and placed a hand upon her shoulder.

Ette's chattering ceased as she looked up at Lia, 'It's about time, sleepyhead. It's nearly time for lunch.'

Lia remained silent for a moment, trying to recall her dream; the nightmare of losing her family and their home in France suddenly made her feel overwhelmed with grief, and then it was gone. *It had been a dream.* 'I'm going to become a writer, Ette.' She said lightly, 'I'm going to write of all the wrongs in our world, and I'm going to write them in story form so that children can understand them and voice their thoughts. Then, when the time is right, they may have a say in their future.'

Ette looked up quizzically and smiled, 'Okay, Lia; fine. If that's what you want to do.' Ette went back to her conversation.

Lia left Ette in the garden and mounted the steps to the breakfast room. Passing through the terrace doors into the cool interior, she made her way to the main dining room, where the waiters were busy preparing for lunch. She crossed the room towards the French windows, asking a waiter for a glass of Perrier water, and went outside to sit on the balcony overlooking the garden. Lia closed her eyes against the brightness of the sun to enjoy the warmth that was softened by the coolness of a fresh breeze. 'How perfect,' she murmured.

'Isn't it,' Edward answered.

Lia had been unaware of Edward, who had fetched her water. Having slipped silently through the French doors, he now stood watching her. How his feelings had changed for her in the last few months. He now saw a woman whom he had grown to love much more than his childhood friend.

'Such deep thoughts, Lia,' he added.

Aware of Edward's presence, Lia opened her eyes. She immediately felt embarrassed, conscious of her dishevelled appearance and her tear-stained face.

'Where were you?' asked Edward, smiling at her.

Her thoughts drifted back to her dream. *Was it a dream?* Lia smiled back at him. 'I wonder ... would you believe me if I told you?'

'I would believe what you told me, Lia,' he said seriously, 'because I believe in you.' Edward sat down next to her. 'Lia, my father has asked me to go to Paris for a few days to visit friends and to observe how they manage their hotel. Perhaps when I return I will be able to introduce some changes here at Renoir's. I think my father would like me to take on more responsibility for managing the hotel ... and I was wondering if you would like to come with me.' Edward smiled at her. 'You would be well looked after by my friends during the day, and we could see the sights of Paris by night. You would make me very happy if you were to say yes. And, will you marry me?' he finished seriously.

Lia felt the peacefulness she had experienced earlier. 'Yes, and yes, I will,' she said, 'I would like that very much.' Lia began to giggle, her dream now forgotten.

Seeing Lia's sadness fade away, Edward began to laugh with her.

René could hear them laughing as he walked in the garden below the balcony. René knew the truth of his daughter's dream. In time, Château Dubar would be gone, and they would never return. But his life's work would be safe in Cornwall, and it was a comfort to know that within three years Lia and Edward would be married with a child. It was sad, he thought, that beyond that future event life would never be the same for any of them. Ette called to her father from the garden, her son clinging to her bosom as she bounced across the lawn with her usual vitality.

'Why are you hidden away there, Father?'

'Lia, Father's spying on you,' Ette shouted towards the balcony.

Lia and Edward popped their heads over the balustrade.

'René, Sir,' Edward called, 'I have asked your daughter to marry me and she has agreed. I hope we have your blessing.'

René listened with resigned pleasure to the proposed marriage made a trillion light years from Earth. Lia would be safe with Edward, and her children would become part of the one tribe of man.

Edward's father, Ralph, appeared and walked towards the balcony.

'All is not lost – the challenges have gone well,' René murmured softly to the person approaching him.

'So they have,' Raphiel replied.

Other Titles by Barbara Dean

Rattalia's Birthday Stories

Rattalia Rat
and
Musette Mouse

ISBN Hardback 978-0-9572470-4-8
ISBN Paperback 978-0-9572470-5-5

The Progeny of Angels

Zrsiofour, King of the Mers
Book 2

ISBN Hardback 978-0-9572470-1-7
ISBN Paperback 978-0-9572470-0-0

The Progeny of Angels

ZRSIOFOUR, KING of the MERS

Book 2

The tsunami that ends mankind's fifth civilisation will travel across the globe, taking all in its wake. There will be those who are swept along on the buoyancy of its joyful surge; there will be those who cough and splutter, clinging to hope as they desperately struggle to stay alive; and there will be those that lie beneath its mighty strength, stilled and lifeless within its power.

The one tribe of man: may they be reawakened to the vision of their destiny to experience all there is to know.

Prologue

Throughout the world at the beginning of the twenty-first century, billions of people were becoming ill with a pathogenic illness that attacked the respiratory system. The disease gradually softened the ten anterior ribs and enlarged the capacity of the lungs. The change in the afflicted made breathing difficult and produced the same symptoms as chronic asthma. The illness was blamed on global warming and the consequent rise of atmospheric pollution, and, the diseases carried by infected insects. Worldwide, medical research institutions struggled to find a cure for yet another life-threatening disease. In mankind's modern history, nothing of this nature was known to medical science.

The reactivation of ten molecules of deoxyribonucleic acid, DNA, had stimulated an unknown physical condition in man that was awakening the genetic code inherent in the first organisms to exist within the Earth's oceans, genes that had lain dormant in man from the beginning of time. Many people had already died, their bodies unable to endure the transmutation, but for those who survived, it was to be their deliverance. These people were called the lightworkers – healers, philosophers: those that believed in the coming of a new age upon Earth, an age that was to begin after the destructive forces that were soon to be released upon the world. Within the laboured chest cavity of mankind, ten supple aquatic spines were growing, behind the redundant anterior thoracic ribs, to increase the lungs' capacity for inspiration. The new lung buds that were forming, which were mistaken for cancerous growths, were capable of filtering oxygen from water when necessary. Mankind was taking a step backward to their period of amphibiousness.

The lightworkers were preparing to adapt to a future life in the oceanic world of the Mers. They believed the prophesy of future events that their dreams brought them: a global holocaust and a journey to a world below the oceans, where they would begin a new life. Many moved away from the cities to live in coastal areas, believing this to be where the migration would take place. Those that remained inland took work that required diving skills, or skills in water sports, in order to acclimatise their changing bodies to long periods under water. Across the globe, the resettlement of thousands of families was seen as a good thing, a boost for the countries' economies, as house prices spiralled due to the demand for change.

A new way of life had opened up in Lia's country of origin, England, where major changes were taking place. Many British scientists and engineers living abroad returned home to work on two British science projects: the Mars space travel project and a major farming development that they hoped would boost England's food supply for the burgeoning masses. The return of the scientists had been seen as a natural development, rather than a sign of serious shortages in the food chain. Most were disillusioned with working abroad, and, with a new government calling upon their skills, they had returned home.

Under these influences, Britain had divorced itself from Europe, which by then had become a self-elected sovereignty. With the government deciding to go it alone, Britain stood unaided, divorced from Europe, to do battle for her trading ground.

While these changes were causing unease among the British population, below the oceans another decision was causing misgivings among the oceanic people, the Mers. The Mers were to receive among them a nation of people towards whom they had deep misgivings. It was a matter of mistrust, concerning mankind's lack of respect for all things living, which the Mer race had seen much evidence of in the ocean world above them.

Under the Pacific Ocean, deep beneath the Mariana Trenches, rose the gateway to the Mer world. Nearby, upon a vast plateau, stood the City of Memories, a city three hundred and sixty miles in diameter that had been lost to mankind in a time of his misrule. On the surrounding flatlands, acres of pyramid-shaped buildings stood inverted upon their apexes. These multi-level pyramidal greenhouses, made of quartz crystal, were producing the food needed to support the lightworkers, the one tribe of man. The multi-level rows of vegetation thrived in abundance, the colours, shape, and textures created to encourage the human appetite. The vegetation was anchored in beds of crystal particles, which formed thousands of conical poles spiralling upward to the top of each inverted pyramid, while the point of each pyramid was anchored deep below the ocean bed. The buildings rose eerily from the seabed, their square, flat tops echoing the watery reflections of a high-rise metropolis beneath flood waters.

The design had been copied from one in progress on land worldwide, the CROP project. The CROP project's aim was to return millions of acres of agricultural land, on all continents, back to forestry, in order to reinstate the planet's natural climate. Future records would show that the radical changes within food production had come too late to stabilise the surface of the planet. The plan, however, had worked admirably below the oceans, where the Mers were using pyramidal farming to support the humans who were entering their world.

The one tribe of man would have to embrace hardship from all sides to survive the changes in their way of living. They would need an unwavering faith in a future beyond the watery sanctuary that was to be their home for forty-five years. Changes to their diet would mean the absence of wheat, oats, and similar grains that would not survive the future growing conditions below the Earth or upon land after the holocaust. The one tribe of man would not be allowed to kill the ocean dwellers for a source of protein food. They were to live in peace among the Mers – a race of half-man and half-fish – and all ocean dwellers within the world's oceans.

The main source of protein for the one tribe of man would be latvie, a vegetable-based food eaten by the Mers. Latvie was harvested from the tree roots of the vast ocean forests; it was a cone-shaped source of protein that had the taste and texture of red meat.

A few years before the holocaust, the weather patterns worldwide became uniformly tropical, as the ice masses of the North and South Poles thawed significantly. The result was heavy rainfalls that continued for weeks on end, regardless of the season. After that, severe gales would follow, combined with periods of extreme heat. By this nature, the oceans became warmer, and the new species of vegetation that would sustain the one tribe of man flourished. The acres of inverted pyramids contained a humid atmospheric condition, which was kept constant by the volcanic magma that continually poured onto the ocean floor from the surrounding volcanic ridges.

The weather changes were catastrophic for all species on land, and many appeared lost to the Earth forever. As heavy rain poured from the heavens year after year, to be followed by extreme heat, the world's food crops dwindled and the Earth's forests began to rot, making atmospheric conditions worse. The crops failed on most continents at the same time, causing another hardship to overwhelm mankind.

Next to assail mankind was a plague of insects, similar to woodworm but able to survive in any climate. They began to breed rapidly on all continents. The microscopic insects invaded all inert wood, including the building timber used in towns and cities across all continents. Under these conditions, the world's civilisations began to deteriorate rapidly.

These were not the only problems that troubled mankind's daily life. Governments worldwide continued to suppress the public with fast-track legislation that fuelled the growing instability, especially among the young. Throughout the world morality had become tribal, with aggression towards outsiders malevolent and ever increasing. Territorial fighting and fatal wounding were an everyday occurrence. In England, a social war was raging out of control, as violent mobs turned on frightened law-abiding communities to kill and steal from them in order to survive. For the first time in decades, neighbours stood by each other against rebellious mobs of all ages that smashed their way into homes to steal and maim. Street lookouts were posted to raise the alarm, and everyone – men, women and children – came out to protect a home under attack. England had become a nation of small communities that did not welcome strangers. Racism and resentment vanished, as good neighbours and trusted friends were accepted, regardless of colour or creed.

The news most days included the Middle East war. Iran, with the help of her ally, Russia, had overthrown the democratic government in Iraq, forcing the long-standing British and American forces out. The British government publicly avoided the gravity of the situation, as they prepared to put into action their covert plan, code name ESCAPE.

Beneath all major cities and surrounding open land, secret underground sites were ready, sites which had been built to withstand an atomic war. Places were surreptitiously allocated to those identified to survive: the influential, high-ranking, and those most needed for the survival of mankind. Access to these zones was simply, but cleverly, concealed beneath the sprawling concrete jungles of stations, walkways, large shopping malls, underground car parks, and airports – anywhere the government had allowed large areas of land to be covered, areas where the presence of people with large amounts of shopping or holiday luggage would be usual.

Within the national network of public walkways were sign-coded corridors that could be entered by any person recognised by their DNA imaging.

The corridors' strangely subdued lighting did not attract passers-by but, in fact, deterred them from approaching. Because of this, those entering the corridors could disappear undetected, which would enable any evacuation to proceed like clockwork. The nation's public had no idea that the places built for their recreation had such a sinister secondary purpose. Those of the human race who were to be secretly evacuated beneath the unseeing public eye were the privileged few that would survive, while ninety percent of the world's population was to perish.

The wealthiest and most influential had gathered for decades beneath the banner of 'world humanity', while, in truth, they were brought together to discuss the plan for a minority of mankind to survive World War Three. Meanwhile, the world's public and lesser statesmen believed they were discussing the guiding principles for world food production, peace, and the survival of mankind in entirety. Beneath the surface of every continent lay a network of tunnels that led to the main sites, underground cities able to support five thousand people and maintain their survival for fifty years.

The dream within a dream: The dreamer is trying to persuade himself that something unsavoury is only a dream. What would otherwise seem all too real and meaningful is devalued, reduced to a fantasy, and need not be reckoned with. This is a way of dismissing what the mind is trying to communicate, or perhaps the other way round: the mind may know only too well that the one way to get the individual to recognise facts is by making them appear harmless.

Author, Tom Chetwynd: Dictionary of Dreams: 1972

www.ingramcontent.com/pod-product-compliance
Lightning Source LLC
Chambersburg PA
CBHW030426310726
48979CB00009B/1630/J

* 9 7 8 0 9 5 7 2 4 7 0 6 2 *